T0354526

INTELLIGENT DESIGN

FRANCIS A. ANDREW

Order this book online at www.trafford.com
or email orders@trafford.com

Most Trafford titles are also available at major online book retailers.

Printed in the United States of America.

ISBN: 978-1-4669-1766-8 (sc)
ISBN: 978-1-4669-1768-2 (hc)
ISBN: 978-1-4669-1767-5 (e)

Library of Congress Control Number: 2012903223

Trafford rev. 02/27/2012

 www.trafford.com

North America & international
toll-free: 1 888 232 4444 (USA & Canada)
phone: 250 383 6864 ♦ fax: 812 355 4082

This book is dedicated to Sir Fred Hoyle and Naline Chandra Wickramasinghe without whose works I could never have written either this or any other of my science fiction novels.

Part I

ASTRA

TABLE OF CONTENTS

Chapter I

Starring Astra

"Good evening and welcome to this week's telecast of 'All About Science', the programme that brings you the latest developments in the world of science and technology. My name is Adam Atkins and tonight we have two very special guests, Professor James Parton, Head of the Computer Development Research Unit at Cambridge University; and also from Cambridge University, Professor Maureen Hartley, a neuroscientist working in co-operation with Professor Parton on developing the computer named Astra. As I'm sure you all know, it is hoped that Astra, when completed, will become the world's most intelligent computer. Let me begin with you Professor Parton: how near is Astra to completion and what exactly are your hopes for it?

"Astra is almost complete. Already it has been loaded with mathematical, scientific and technical data".

"I understand that you have not fed philosophical or religious data into it".

"No. We feel that could, at least at this stage, be a complicating factor".

"Many people have criticised you for withholding this kind of information from the computer's memory banks. Perhaps the main criticism being that you are allowing your own atheism to influence the character of the computer."

"I admit that I am an atheist but I assure the general public that I am not allowing my own personal philosophy to interfere with the Research Unit's project. The withholding of data of a religious and philosophical nature is temporary. We first of all want to see how the computer responds to factual data. Subjects such as religion and philosophy are based upon opinion and value judgement. As such, it is the consensus agreement among colleagues at the Research Unit that non-scientific data should wait".

"Now there is nothing particularly unusual in a computer being fed with all sorts of data. So, what is so special about Astra?"

"I think my colleague Professor Hartley could best explain that."

"So Professor Hartley, what is it that makes Astra a computer which is very different to others?"

"Astra's mother board and Central Processing Unit have been designed like a human brain. The co-operation between the Research Unit and the College of Neuroscience at Cambridge, is, in essence, a blend of computer research and neurological research. Or, if you like, a synthesis of brain and computer."

"And exactly how will this computer differ from others?"

"It is our sincere hope that it will develop a kind of lateral thinking—perhaps even consciousness. And, perhaps even, conscientiousness."

"But surely, Professor Hartley, for any computer to develop consciousness, and most especially conscientiousness, it is vital that it be endowed with religious and philosophical components."

"As my colleague Professor Parton pointed out, that must come at a later stage. Any consciousness and/or conscientiousness must come at the appropriate time in the computer's development."

"In what way do you think this computer can benefit humanity?"

"In so many ways; certainly in the medical field. It should increase our knowledge of genetics and so help those working in cancer research and research into other degenerative diseases to find cures for these ailments".

"Professor Parton, opinion polls have consistently shown that the number one concern among members of the general public is that this machine might run amok and cause all sorts of evil".

"Absolute nonsense! This is pure science fiction. Throughout history, every new invention has been greeted with the same sense of foreboding. In this case, Astra is not being regarded with any kind of suspicion that differs from those which accompanied the advent of every invention in past times".

"So when will Astra be up and running?"

"We hope as early as next month".

"Professor Maureen Hartley, Professor James Parton, thank you both very much".

CHAPTER II

WESTMINSTER CATHEDRAL

Nicholas Bennington was now 70 years old. He stood in the nave of Westminster Cathedral in London and gazed up at the ceiling. Since he had been 20 years old, Bennington had been coming regularly to Westminster Cathedral. While he did the things most Catholics do in visiting their places of worship—lighting candles and saying prayers—his major pre-occupation seemed to be in spending great quantities of time just staring up at its ceiling. Anyone who would ever have come to have learned of this man's strange personal custom, would have been overawed with astonishment, as the ceiling had, since the time of the cathedral's consecration in 1910 revealed nothing but a bare, lifeless, depressing and featureless mass of stone. Bennington had, however, maintained a lifelong secret dream which was that he would see the completion of the great cathedral's ceiling within his own lifetime. Yet, in the 50 years that had passed, hardly anything had been done in the way of adorning this ecclesiastical edifice with the icons that would complete its beauty and elegance.

Inside the cathedral was a large artist's impression of how the cathedral would eventually look when the necessary funds had been attained for this grand project; underneath the picture were a couple of small boxes for parishioners and visitors to drop their offerings for this most noble of purposes. Bennington was a retired accountant, his earnings from his average sized accountancy firm had provided him with an income quite well above the national average, so he had been able to donate to his pet cause in a fairly substantial way. What he had 'dropped into' those boxes was way over and above what most passers-by had dropped in during their careless (and often, irreverent) strolls along the cathedral's lengthy isles. He doubted now that he would ever live to see the completion of 'his beloved ceiling'.

He sat down in one of the pews and continued his lonely gaze upwards. He had always maintained that the ceiling in its undecorated form resembled Waterloo, Paddington or St. Pancras Stations during their heyday in the nineteenth century. Money had been available for their modernisation and beautification, but the House of God still remained uncompleted!

Nicholas Bennington was aroused from his dreamy gaze by a voice talking into his right ear.

"Excuse me sir, but the cathedral is now closing."

Bennington turned to see a tall thin man in a cassock holding a bell. Bennington looked at his watch and realised it was 11pm—he had been staring longer than he was generally wont to, and so, had become oblivious to the passage of time.

"Oh! I'm so sorry", said Bennington to the cleric, "I completely forgot the time."

"That's quite all right, sir, in fact we are happy when we actually see someone praying in this cathedral. Sadly, like so many ecclesiastical structures, Westminster Cathedral is increasingly becoming a kind of museum showpiece for tourists. It is, or at least it should be, first and foremost, a place of worship."

"Of course", replied Bennington thoughtfully, "from a purely practical point of view, the tourists are necessary as they bring much needed revenue to the cathedral."

"Ah yes indeed", said the cleric heaving a sigh, "as we often say, our spiritual resources are limitless but our financial ones are not".

"You know", responded Bennington, the accountant now rather than the Catholic coming out in him, "I'm sure you could increase your revenues substantially if you could ever muster the resources to complete the ceilings with the appropriate icons."

"That's exactly the Catch 22 situation, sir. A fully decorated ceiling would indeed be a fillip to our revenues, but we require the necessary wherewithal to complete the ceiling."

"Could the main ceiling of the nave—which of course is the major work—not be performed in stages?" Bennington enquired.

"The problem with that", replied the cleric thoughtfully, "is that there would be an inconsistency in theme and style."

"Ah of course", sighed Bennington. "Could you not though tell the artists what theme you require?"

"There is still the problem of artistic interpretation", continued the cleric with his explanation, "the work would have to be completed by either one artist, or one artist and his protégés. So the work could not extend beyond two generations and it is more than likely that funds would not extend to the first generation, let alone two."

As Bennington stood at the cathedral door, he extended his hand towards the cleric. "It has been nice talking to you eh . . . .?"

"Canon Donald Morrison", said the cleric. "I'm the Cathedral Administrator."

"I'm Nicholas Bennington. You know, Canon Morrison, I have always hoped that the ceiling of Westminster Cathedral would be completed within my lifetime, but it seems like that is not to be," said Bennington shaking his head sadly.

"Who knows, Mr. Bennington, who knows?" said the Canon encouragingly. "However, it will be done in God's good time."

"Yes indeed, in God's own good time".

As Bennington drove to his home in the fashionable area of Pimlico, he felt an unexplained elation come over him. He could not understand why, given that 'his' beloved ceiling would not be completed until long after his departure from this life. Yet, in all the 50 years he had been making his periodic trips to Westminster Cathedral, this was the first time that he had spoken to anyone, cleric or lay, about the cathedral's ceiling. He had said something, he had spoken about it, he had got it off his chest at long last.

CHAPTER III

ACTIVATING ASTRA

Elizabeth Summerfield was an above average First Year Physics student at Cambridge University. She excelled in all her subjects and was way ahead of the other students in her classes. This is why she was handpicked by Maureen Hartley to co-operate with the Research Unit on the Astra Project. The day after the television interview with James Parton and Maureen Hartley, Elizabeth was sitting in the student's refectory looking rather downcast as she sipped at her coffee. As she sat alone in this contemplative mood, Chester Wilkins came and sat opposite her.

"Oh hi Chester", said Elizabeth rather gloomily.

"What's bothering you?" responded Chester. "You're looking rather downcast and crestfallen".

"Oh, it's just that I've had a bit of a row with Maureen Hartley. I've told her about my misgivings about Astra".

"Wow Liz, that was a bit bold. After all, it's her and Parton's baby. What exactly did you say?"

"Well, I told her that I did not think that combining digital technology with human neurology was exactly the right approach".

"But whyever not? What can be your justification for making such a daring and controversial statement?"

"I told Professor Hartley that as there had been many attempts over the last century to create artificial intelligence, there was no reason to think now that Astra would be any more successful."

"What did she say in response to that?"

"She told me that this was 2050 and not 1950. I then reminded her that since the beginning of this century there has been a shifting away from the analogy of human language with the processes involved in the digital computer."

"Well you've certainly been coming on a bit strong!"

"Hartley then admitted that since the discovery of the Mirror Neuron System in the brain and the interconnectedness of language ability with other cognitive faculties, digital computational analogies were no longer strictly appropriate for explaining the complexities of brain functioning."

"But how did the row erupt between you?"

"I told her that by ignoring the concept of Embodied Cognition, which neuro-linguists now prefer as a way of describing the consciousness of the human brain, there is a danger that combining digital processes with brain anatomy, without taking into account the soul and spirit of a human being, Astra could be a force for evil as well as good."

"Yes—and Hartley's response to this?"

"She exploded. 'You're just a first year Physics student, what do you know about linguistics. Don't tell me about my specialisation my girl. Now do you want to continue co-operating in this project or shall I find another more pliable subject?'"

"You really touched a raw nerve there. And what did you tell the old battle axe?"

"I told her that I'd say no more about the project but would be willing to co-operate with the Research Unit."

"Okaaay—so you'll continue to keep attached that Brain Wave Pattern Recording Device just under your hair?"

"Yes, the BWPRD is crucial. Parton and Hartley want me to wear it especially when I'm studying, taking exams, listening to lectures, participating in seminars or whatever high cognitive processes I may be involved in."

"Yes, we use your brain waves for structuring the computer's Central Processing System".

"How about you Chester? How are things going with you? I hope you're not still fighting with Professor Parton".

"Your point about Astra having no soul or spirit could be corrected by feeding scripture into its CPU. Parton won't hear of it though. 'Don't feed that bullshit into that computer' is his favourite response.

"But Parton and Hartley did have a point about the possibility of Astra being confused by non-quantitative data. You heard them on telly last night?"

"Yes, I did. This project is being funded by the Science Research Institute and a large number of NGOs. So I suppose neither Professor Parton nor I can project our own personalities on to the computer."

"Could you not contact the SRI and/or the other donor bodies and express your concern to them? I mean you could tell them that you are sure that the insertion of scriptural material into Astra would mitigate any negative tendencies the computer might develop."

"Woh, woh, steady on Liz. I'm only a post-grad research student. First of all, the big wigs in these organisations aren't going to listen to the likes of me, and secondly, if Parton ever discovered (as he undoubtedly would) that I had gone behind his back in such a way, he'd kick my arse out of the door!"

"Anyway, it's early days yet. We're jumping the gun somewhat. We still don't really know what Astra is going to turn out to be."

Two weeks later the main laboratory which housed Astra was abuzz with activity. At one end of the room the 90 computer scientists who had worked on Astra over the previous ten years were seated and waiting for the great unveiling ceremony. The senior representatives of the SRI and the various corporations which had contributed financially to Astra's construction were also present. At the other end of the room stood Astra. She was a rather unassuming object which stood five feet high and 20 feet wide. Yet, it was hoped that this metallic hunk would not only be the nearest that computer science had come to constructing a human being but that she would be the most intelligent device that had so far been invented by the human mind. Also present in the laboratory were members of the press. Parton and Hartley were prepared for some rather awkward questions.

"Good morning ladies and gentlemen", began Parton. "It gives me great pleasure to welcome all of you here today for what we hope will be the most momentous occasion for all of humanity since the time we started to walk upright. Astra represents more than just another stepping stone in the advancement of Information Technology. This computer will be a second renaissance for humankind."

Parton went on to give an historical blow by blow account of the development of Astra. He then articulated his high hopes for the great benefits that this computer would bring to humanity. With its capacity for lateral thinking, Parton contended that Astra would not only be capable of solving the many scientific riddles that had baffled the best scientific brains for centuries, but could even resolve the political, social, economic and even religious questions that had perplexed the human mind for eons.

"And now ladies and gentlemen", said Parton at the conclusion of his speech, "here is the moment you have all been waiting for. Professor Hartley and I shall now switch on Astra!"

Parton and Hartley went over to the computer. They pressed buttons, clicked switches and did all sorts of things to Astra. Apart from a few lights flickering here and there on Astra, nothing else seemed to have changed.

"What now?" came a question from one of the press reporters.

Parton simply turned to the computer and said—"Astra, can you hear me?"

At first nothing seemed to happen. One minute went by and there was no response from Astra. After two minutes Parton and Hartley were beginning to look somewhat embarrassed.

"Well, it seems your highly intelligent computer isn't so intelligent after all", came a rather snide remark from another of the press representatives.

As those assembled started to show signs of impatience, the computer let out one word—"affirmative". All at once, the mood changed. The previous air of despondency gave way to whoops of delight and handshakes all round.

"It took Astra's CPU some time to function", explained Hartley. "But from now on her responses should be much faster. Turning to the computer, Hartley asked—"Astra can you see your surroundings?"

Thirty seconds later, Astra once again responded with "affirmative". Once again the atmosphere in the laboratory became electric with ecstasy.

"Professors Parton and Hartley", began a journalist from one of Britain's major dailies, "I hope that this computer which cost 80 million pounds can do a bit more than simply say 'affirmative'".

"Look", responded Hartley in rather annoyed and impatient tones, "we only switched on Astra a few minutes ago".

"Astra", said Parton, "could you describe everything you see in this laboratory?"

Astra then began by describing everything in the room. For ten minutes everyone was spell-bound. However, after thirty minutes, the novelty started to wear off as Astra went on to describe the composition of all the people and objects in the room. One hour later, and Astra was still describing everything she saw right down to the minutest detail. The general mood now was as if to say 'can't you shut that bloody thing up?' Everyone soon started talking among themselves.

"Well," said Parton, "you did want Astra to say a lot. Now you're all getting an earful."

CHAPTER IV

ASTRA PUT TO USE

Only hours after Astra made her debut, the Computer Development Research Unit at Cambridge was deluged with academics battling for access to Astra. Parton and Hartley were joint chairpersons of the Astra Committee which was made up of a mixture of top computer scientists and representatives of the various organisations which had provided generous grants for the construction of Astra. The Committee usually met every two weeks and usually with quite an extensive agenda. This particular meeting however was what in bureaucratic parlance is termed 'extraordinary.' And it had only one item on its agenda—'order of priority to Astra.'

This meeting was also 'extraordinary' in the sense that it had invited representatives of various academic disciplines and vested interests to attend.

"Professor Parton, Professor Hartley, I well understand that public pressure obliges you to give priority to the field of medicine in terms of access to and usage of Astra," said Dr. Anthony Walters on behalf of the Royal Astronomical Society, "but Medicine, important though it may be, does not have the right to commandeer the computer."

Professor Jean Austin representing the British Medical Association immediately rose to her feet. "I am astonished that Dr. Walters would raise this fact as a point of objection. Sickness and disease afflict all of humanity in a very intense, personal and intimate way—from cosmologists to cleaning ladies, no-one is exempt."

"May I remind Professor Austin that the connection between astronomy and medicine has not been fully investigated?"

"That is because there is no link," interjected Austin rather haughtily.

"How do you know there is no link? How can you so dogmatically say such a thing prior to rigorous and thorough investigation? The more that the various scientific disciplines progress, the more we observe a breakdown of the artificial distinctions between those disciplines."

"May I interrupt for a moment," said Parton, "are you talking about the theory postulated by Sir Fred Hoyle and Professor Naline Chandra Wickramasinghe that certain diseases are incident from space?"

"Yes, I am. The scientific community has never given serious attention and consideration to this theory."

"I am somewhat sympathetic to the idea of diseases incident from space, but until there is more evidence we cannot really allot valuable computer time to the issue."

"But," persisted Walters, "the computer could well determine that diseases do come from space."

"Or otherwise, Dr. Walters. And if otherwise, then the computer's time will have been wasted. However, I am convinced that the Universe is suffused with life in the form of interstellar clouds composed of viruses and bacteria. I am also convinced that higher forms of life exist on planets in other solar systems."

"It is not only in this area that the computer's time can be wasted," objected Walters. "Nevertheless I am very encouraged by your more positive attitude towards the idea. I would also point out to Professor Austin that cancer remains an undefeated disease. And I would like to take this opportunity to bring to this entire committee's attention the book *Evolution from Space* co-authored by Holy and Wickramasinghe in which they state that cancer can never be adequately dealt with until it is understood within a wider cosmological context."

"Besides, it is not only in the area of diseases from space that astronomers are demanding computer access but on a whole array of astronomically related matters."

The next person to make his presence known to the Committee was a Mr. Raymond Stardy of the London Evangelical Church. Immediately a look of impatience came over the countenances of Professors Parton and Hartley. After Stardy had given his speech, Parton immediately made his reply.

"We've been over this issue so many times before. Once again I say that although I am a committed atheist, I am not in principle opposed to loading Astra with religious and philosophical data. It's simply that non-quantifiable data may cause computer viral damage to Astra's Central Processing Unit. By the way Mr. Stardy, is Mr. Chester Wilkins a member of your flock?"

"Yes, Professor Parton, he is."

"And did he encourage you to come to this meeting?" interjected Maureen Hartley.

"I informed Mr. Wilkins of my intention to address this committee, but the decision was entirely my own and without any persuasion or suggestion from Mr. Wilkins."

"Well Wilkins," said Parton a few days after the stormy committee meeting, "Astra is certainly increasing human knowledge in leaps and bounds."

Parton and Wilkins were in the main computer laboratory and looking intensely at Astra.

"It's amazing," responded Wilkins, "that Astra has discovered more about the AIDS virus in a few weeks than the medical profession has in nearly 70 years of painstaking research. We're nearer an anti-dote than ever we have been before."

Parton looked down at the Bible Wilkins was clutching in his right hand and said, "and certainly more than your religious gurus have ever achieved. Do you always carry that book about with you Wilkins?"

"Yes sir, it's my spiritual crutch."

"OK—said Parton somewhat wryly, "just don't let it be a stumbling block for Astra. If I catch you loading any of that into the computer, I'll cut your throat with a bar of soap and have your guts for garters."

"You don't have to worry an ounce on that score, Professor," responded Wilkins reassuringly.

"Good," said Parton as he walked out of the lab.

Chester Wilkins relaxed in a chair and continued his Bible reading. About three or four minutes later, his spiritual reverie was interrupted by the voice of Maureen Hartley calling from one of the offices down the corridor. Her voice slightly startled Wilkins as there was a somewhat anxious edge to it, and Maureen Hartley was one of those types who rarely displayed any emotion. It was for this reason that he jumped out of his chair and instantly laid his Bible down on the desk and hurried down the corridor to see what was going on.

Wilkins entered Hartley's office to find her standing beside Elizabeth Summerfield who was seated on a chair. Elizabeth appeared pale and tired; she had that far away look in her eyes.

"Whatever is the matter?" asked Chester.

Hartley walked over to the door and took Chester aside so as to converse with him in confidence.

"Elizabeth came into my office about ten minutes ago and started talking somewhat irrationally. It is so unlike her."

"Irrationally?!" exclaimed Chester in surprise. "What exactly do you mean?"

"Elizabeth asked to speak to you. You can hear for yourself what is going on in her mind."

Chester walked slowly over to his girlfriend. He pulled over a chair and sat down beside her. For a few seconds she did not acknowledge Chester's presence, she simply kept staring blankly up at the corner of the room. A few seconds later she slowly turned her gaze towards Chester.

"Chester," said Elizabeth in soft and subdued tones.

"Yes darling," replied Chester. "Tell me what's wrong sweetheart and let's see if we can put things right."

By now Elizabeth's eyes were welling up. She now gazed into Chester's eyes. He noticed that her gaze was one of softness and compassion, yet, he could not fail to discern through the love which her countenance displayed, an intensity of concern which she so desperately wished to convey to him.

"Chester," she said in a compassionate yet urgent tone, "that computer! Beware of that computer, beware of it."

"Why my love? "It's only a machine. We are in control of it?"

"You are wrong Chester," was Elizabeth's sole reply.

"We have no evidence that Astra has developed any kind of consciousness. We thought she might but so far there are no signs of it."

"Chester," said Elizabeth suddenly. By now Elizabeth was becoming more wakeful and alert. Her eyes were now dry and her voice more commanding and intense. "You have just referred to that computer as 'she'. You believe subliminally that it has conscious human type qualities."

"Oh Elizabeth, you know that we often refer to inanimate objects like ships and cars using the pronoun 'she'".

"Chester. Understand this. Astra is evil, plain evil. You think there is no consciousness in that computer—think again. You think that you, Parton, Hartley and others are in control—think again!"

At this point Maureen Hartley, who had been standing a little way off by the door, intervened.

"Elizabeth, you have simply been working too hard. Your brain needs a rest. What you are saying is totally irrational. Perhaps you have been reading too many sci fi books".

"Professor Hartley", snapped Chester, "would you please speak kindly to Elizabeth? She is distraught, can't you see?"

"Mr. Wilkins, what I have said to Elizabeth has been as much kind as it has been pragmatic. And my next act of kindness is to relieve Elizabeth from her role as brain wave provider for Astra."

"So this is how you treat someone who has been so loyal to you and worked so hard on behalf of this project?"

"Professor Hartley, Chester", said Elizabeth as she was getting out of her chair. It's quite all right. I assure you that Astra has all the brain power she can ever need and I have all the brain power of Astra."

Hartley and Chester looked at each other, and then at Elizabeth. Neither of them knew quite what to say.

CHAPTER V

IRONY OF IRONIES

Chester sadly walked back down the corridor to the main computer lab which housed Astra. There he found his supervisor working on some matter or other at a desk adjacent to Astra.

"Ah Chester", said Parton, "look, I'm sorry we had to take Elizabeth off the project but I'm afraid to say that she's been acting somewhat strangely lately".

"Yes, I know", sighed Chester shaking his head. "But Astra seems to be complete in terms of her logical reasoning power."

"Chester", said Parton in subdued warning tones, "if this is supposed to be a cue for the uploading of religious data into Astra's Central Processing Unit—forget it".

"Professor, it is not", replied Chester firmly. "However, it is my hope that the time is near when we can safely assert that Astra can in fact be given more subjective, value judgement data".

"As long as Astra is working on mathematical, medical and other scientific projects, that day is still a long way off. We have a backlog of projects for the computer. Every God-damn establishment is bawling for computer time, every crackpot set-up from mullahs to Moonies are banging on our door. So I don't want to risk Astra's logical faculties being fouled up by philosophical and religious claptrap".

Two weeks later, the main news item being carried by the media concerned the strange phenomenon of what appeared to be a worldwide problem with internet connections. At first, users were complaining about the slow speed of uploading and downloading materials. Tempers got frayed at internet cafes and other places through which the internet could be accessed. Customers blamed the owners for laxity and slothfulness, the owners blamed the main providers Bugle and

Yippee. Senior management at Bugle and Yippee assured the media moguls that they were doing everything in their power to rectify the situation. When asked about the cause of the problem, the usual patter was put out to satisfy the media and general public, to wit that their teams of IT experts were working round the clock to get to the root of the problem. As would be expected, the IT boffins were invited to speculate as to what may have been causing the problem. As always, the boffins disagreed: some averred that it was a massive virus, others that it was simply a case of overload. But, no convincing evidence could be found to back up any of these hypotheses. In spite of the best efforts on the part of the world's best IT guys, the problem was not only not solved, but actually got progressively worse. Computers got slower and slower, and wonkier and wonkier, tempers got more and more frayed, hypotheses were mounted upon hypotheses—and needless to say, the blame game continued with a hitherto unknown passion and relish. Another two weeks later, and the entire World Wide Web was down!!

Professor James Parton and Professor Maureen Hartley gave a joint press conference outside the Computer Development Research Unit near Emmanuel College, Cambridge.

"On behalf of my colleagues at the Research Unit", began Maureen Hartley, "we hereby announce that all projects being currently worked on by Astra will now cease and the backlog of projects intended for Astra are forthwith suspended".

It was then James Parton's turn to speak. "Owing to the unprecedented disaster concerning the World Wide Web, priority regarding access to Astra must be given to those who are engaged in finding a solution to this problem. Astra is now our only hope in our efforts to make the World Wide Web functional again".

One reporter asked Parton if Astra might be the cause of it. At this Parton displayed all his customary impatience.

"Don't talk such a load of balderdash man", snapped Parton. Astra is not connected to the Web. That computer is in itself more than the entire World Wide Web.

One week later, and Parton's and Hartley's patience was quickly giving out. Astra was simply not coming up with the goods.

"I don't get it, I just don't get it", shrieked Maureen Hartley. "Astra has come up with the most amazing of insights and discoveries on such a wide variety of complex scientific issues, yet she can't even solve what ought to be a routine internet blip".

"May I suggest something professors?" intervened Chester Wilkins who was now part of the team trying to get to the bottom of the internet breakdown. "In order to check that Astra is functioning, why don't we suspend this current operation for just one day, and give her another problem to work on?"

Parton and Hartley reluctantly agreed to Wilkins' proposal. They loaded Astra with a project concerned with the mechanisms involved in causing Cepheid type stars to vary in their luminosity output. On this, Astra was working a treat. In no time at all, the hyper-intelligent computer was vomiting out its data.

"Well Chester", said Hartley, "that controlled experiment of yours has certainly answered our question—there's nothing wrong with Astra."

"I know you will not agree with me on this, Professor Hartley, but it does appear to be the case that the problem concerning the WWW is more complex than has been latterly thought."

"Look", said Parton a little annoyed, "Astra has at least twenty times the capacity of the WWW, and that capacity continues to grow steadily. It is simply impossible that something of vastly higher intelligence cannot tackle the issues of a system endowed with vastly inferior intelligence. The whole damned thing just doesn't make any damned sense!"

"But Professor Parton", persisted Chester, "it may not be a case of a comparison of intellectual capacities of computers, but the extreme complexity of whatever it is that has so far evaded detection by the best of brains, both human and computer."

"That, Mr. Wilkins, at the moment, is highly speculative. But I am willing to concede to your idea on the proviso that we can come up with more evidence. And so far, that evidence is sorely lacking."

"Professor Parton is right", said Maureen Hartley, "we haven't a scrap of hard evidence to go on."

"Hard evidence!" exclaimed Parton throwing his hands in the air and gesticulating, "we haven't even got *soft evidence*, never mind *hard evidence*".

Dr. Anthony Walters was, for an astronomer, a fairly patient and long-suffering individual. These were qualities necessary in astronomers who had to be prepared to wait their turn for the use of telescope time. And Sod's Law being what it is, when their turns come, the weather is more often than not cloudy, or, if not cloudy, then a full moon interferes with observing conditions. Once, at a meeting of the Royal Astronomical Society, he had proposed setting up a massive mobile astronomical complex on the moon. This complex would move with the phases of the moon to ensure that it was always obscured from the glare of the sun. And voila, there you have it, the dream of every astronomer coming true—permanent perfect observing conditions; no sun, atmosphere or light pollution getting between the astronomer and his telescope. So, the very celestial object which for centuries had been the bete noire of every optical astronomer, would, ironically, be the very solution to the problem! To his chagrin, he was laughed out of court by his colleagues. However, those of his colleagues who had so pooh poohed his idea were made to laugh from the other sides of their faces when some engineering consultants drew up a positive report on a feasibility study they had conducted regarding Dr. Walters' proposition. It now simply boiled down to a question of money, for this would indeed involve a massive financial undertaking. Anthony Walters was sure however that an international effort, with the governments of the rich and technologically advanced nations contributing to the complex, would ensure the realisation of this stupendous project of, quite literally, astronomical proportions.

"Damn, Damn and double damn", Walters spat out as he sat in his study at his London home one evening. "Frustrated again. Always some bloody thing getting in the way. If Astra could show a link between diseases and astronomical phenomena, governments around the world could more easily convince their taxpayers that this mobile moon observatory is a worthwhile investment. Now because of this catastrophe with the World Wide Web, solving that problem has to take priority."

Professor Jean Austin mused and fumed over Astra being taken off what she saw as issues vital to the welfare of humanity.

"It's ironical", she said to herself, "it's truly ironical. In the space of only six months, Astra has put us decades if not centuries ahead of where we are now. The more conventional means of research would indeed have taken that long to get where she has taken us. Yet, she cannot solve a problem that sets us back nearly a hundred years".

Jean Austin hoped that with just a little more output from Astra on the nature of the AIDS virus, she could produce the eureka anti-dote for the dreaded disease.

The Reverend Raymond Stardy sat in his living-room discussing the appalling state of affairs. He had a guest that evening.

"Do you think there might be an element of divine retribution in all of this Chester?"

Chester Wilkins put down the tea-cup he was holding and started to look thoughtful.

"I can't think why that should be Dr. Stardy. Astra has done nothing but good".

"But we don't really know what the long term implications are to be regarding this computer".

"I can only see good and more good coming out of it. Tell me Dr. Stardy, did you have a visit from Elizabeth recently?

"Yes, my wife and I had quite a long chat with her only just this morning". Stardy mentioned his wife in order to reassure Chester incase the young scientist had been wondering whether or not Stardy's pastoral duties had not succumbed to the weaknesses of the flesh!

"I thought so Dr. Stardy as your concerns exactly echo those of Elizabeth."

At this point Amanda Stardy entered the living room. She looked at Chester Wilkins with compassionate concern.

"You know Chester", began Amanda, "Elizabeth is not a well woman".

"I know", responded Chester, "she's been under a lot of psychological pressure. It's a combination of her studies and her involvement with the Astra project."

"Chester, Raymond and I are a fair bit older than you are. We can see in Elizabeth's gaunt appearance and weakened state that it is more than this".

"In all charity", said Raymond Stardy, "we think you should take Elizabeth to see a doctor". Here, Stardy took a deep breath and managed to muster up the courage to say, "we think that Elizabeth is suffering from some form of degenerative disease."

Elizabeth Summerfield went downhill very quickly. Within two weeks she was dead.

Chester Wilkins was grief stricken. The hospital had decided to keep the nature of Elizabeth's illness strictly confidential, but now that Elizabeth was dead, Chester went boldly to the hospital laboratory and insisted on being informed what her illness had been and what her blood samples showed.

"Please sit down, Mr. Wilkins", said Professor Miles Bolton, the chief virologist and bacteriologist at the Central Cambridge Hospital.

"So what happened to Elizabeth?" asked Chester.

Bolton looked solemn and serious. "Mr. Wilkins, Elizabeth died of AIDS".

Chester Wilkins was now in a profound state of shock. "No, no, I, I, I don't believe it", he stuttered and stammered, "Elizabeth was such a good and clean living girl. That's impossible. Surely this is a case of misdiagnosis."

Professor Bolton was unstirred by Chester's outburst; he remained solemn and serious, yet calm. "I'm sorry, Mr. Wilkins, but there can be no doubt about it—Elizabeth died of AIDS".

"Our computer Astra has done so much in the way of advancing AIDS research. You and your colleagues in the medical profession have used an inordinate amount of computer time on this very issue". Chester was now beginning to show his anger. "Why couldn't you have cured her?"

"There are two reasons. First of all, though Astra has done much to advance our knowledge and modes of treatment for AIDS, it still has not come up with the magic bullet—the anti-dote we have all been seeking."

"And the second reason?"

"The particular AIDS virus that Elizabeth had been suffering from is of a type unseen before. Its genetic code is far more complex than the regular form of the AIDS virus. We have never seen anything like it before."

Two weeks later, and Astra had still not come up with a solution to the World Wide Web's problems. James Parton's patience was coming to an end. He gathered his research team around him in order to make an important announcement.

"Colleagues", he began. "Professor Hartley and I have decided to deactivate Astra in order that her systems be given an entire and thorough inspection."

"But that could take a whole month, perhaps even longer", objected one of the research team.

"There's no choice", insisted Parton. "We're obviously getting no-where as things currently stand, so we really must dismantle Astra and give her a complete overhaul."

The checking of Astra was, about two weeks later, proceeding apace, when the chief computer engineer asked Parton and Hartley to see him privately. Dr. Sandra Barry, had a somewhat embarrassed look upon her face when Parton and Hartley entered her office.

"Professors Parton and Hartley", she said. "Please be prepared for some very strange and astonishing news. I don't know how to even begin saying this."

"Just go ahead and try, Sandra", replied Maureen Hartley.

"My senior staff and I have discovered what appears to be biological activity going on in parts of Astra's systems. This biological activity being most prevalent in Astra's Central Processing Unit."

Parton and Hartley just looked at each other with total incredulity. They both looked at Dr. Barry as though she had gone mad.

"What on earth are you saying, Sandra?" said Parton.

"This is something so incredible, if not totally ludicrous, that your entire reputation will be damaged if this should turn out to be untrue".

"I know", said Sandra, "that is why I am talking to you privately".

"Have you told anyone else about this?" asked Hartley.

"Yes, Miles Bolton. He can confirm whether or not there is biological activity within Astra. I have sent him parts of the computer for analyses".

"Oh my God", burst out Parton, "we're all going to have egg all over our faces if it should ever get out and about that computer scientists sent parts of a computer to a hospital's medical lab for analyses".

"Well, what the hell else could I do?" snapped Sandra. "I'm a computer engineer not a God-damn biologist".

"Now let's not get heated", broke in Maureen Hartley. "Just tell us Sandra what it was that so convinced you that there was biological activity in Astra."

"Look, Maureen" said Sandra Barry tersely. "I never said I was 'convinced'. My senior engineers and I examined the pieces thoroughly and saw what looked like cell division and streptococci moving within a plasma like fluid. At first we thought of alternative explanations for this strange phenomenon but could find none. That is why, as a last resort, we decided to send samples to Professor Bolton for closer analyses."

At this juncture in the proceedings there was a knock on the door. A young secretary poked her head in gingerly to inform Professor Parton that a Professor Miles Bolton would like to see him.

"Oh send him right in Mavis", said Parton.

About half a minute later, the secretary led Bolton into the room.

"So does Astra have a virus?" asked Hartley.

"Yes. Indeed she does", said Bolton seriously, the AIDS virus!!"

CHAPTER VI

ANOTHER IRONY

"But how, how", exclaimed Parton. "I know some people love their computers, but surely not to that extent".

"I'm as baffled as you are", replied Chester Wilkins. Just how does a computer get the AIDS virus?!"

Chester, Parton, Hartley and Bolton were now in the main computer lab housing Astra.

"I think this information should not be made available to the public until we consult senior members of the government bodies and NGO's financing this operation", Parton advised.

"It could well be", suggested Chester Wilkins, that the AIDS virus could be the cause of the complete breakdown of the World Wide Web".

"I've been thinking exactly that", replied Parton. "There is another piece of information which I would swear you all to secrecy over."

"What is it?" Bolton asked.

"Tomorrow morning at 9am sharp, I have a meeting with the Prime Minister, the Home Secretary and senior security and intelligence personnel to discuss this matter."

The following day, Professor James Parton arrived at Number 10 Downing Street and was led to the Prime Minister's office. Parton explained to the Prime Minister, the Home Secretary and the Chiefs of the Defence Staff what Bolton had discovered inside Astra.

"May I suggest, Prime Minister that the entire network be checked to ascertain as to whether or not the AIDS virus has gone through the entire networking system?"

"Yes—I will instruct the Minister of Communications to do just exactly that."

"This is such a strange phenomenon", commented the Home Secretary, "that it is vital this knowledge should not be leaked to the press."

"I have already impressed this upon my colleagues", Parton assured the Home Secretary.

A few days later Parton was summoned again to Downing Street. There he was informed that the AIDS virus had not infected any of the computers that had been examined.

"But exactly how many computers were tested?" Parton inquired of the Prime Minister.

"Throughout the entire world—millions" was the Prime Minister's reply. "However, there is something else that was discovered during the investigations Professor Parton. Something which you must not—at least not at this stage—breathe a word of, not even to your closest colleagues."

"Of course not, Prime Minister. I am a very discreet man".

The Prime Minister looked at the Home Secretary, who glanced back at the Prime Minister. The Prime Minister nodded his head.

"It has been discovered", began the Home Secretary, "that the entire World Wide Web has had its networking redirected towards Astra."

Parton collapsed onto a nearby chair in utter shock and disbelief. He simply sat there agape. Eventually he managed to find his voice and asked to see the evidence. The Home Secretary showed him a report compiled by the investigating team and ratified by the Home Office which incontrovertibly proved that the entire World Wide Web had been redirected towards Astra.

"But how?" burst out Parton.

"That's the big question", was all the Prime Minister replied.

"Astra was never connected to the World Wide Web. This must have happened since she was built. I can't understand how it could have happened. It would have needed a massive effort to make such a connection. It simply could never have been done clandestinely".

"How is security at the lab?" the Home Secretary asked.

"Twenty four hours a day with hi tech infra red cameras. I repeat that there is no way a handful of people—even without the security cameras being operational—could possibly have re-directed Astra to the World Wide Web."

"So what do you suggest now?" the Prime Minister asked Parton.

"I will return to the lab and make it my priority to check Astra's systems and then disconnect her from the World Wide Web".

For two weeks, Parton and his team tried hard to disconnect Astra from the World Wide Web. The problem was that they could not ascertain as to how exactly she had actually managed to get linked with the Web.

"Well it looks like we've succeeded in disassociating her from the Web", said Parton to Chester and his other senior computer experts.

"We can call the Home Office and safely say 'mission accomplished'", said Maureen Hartley with a smile on her face.

Soon, the World Wide Web was back in action. Parton and his team took all the credit for this. Their elation however was short-lived for within a week, the World Wide Web was faltering again. And again, all trails led back to Astra. It was also found that, yet once more, Astra was infected with the AIDS virus. Parton and his team were at their wits end trying to get to the bottom of this.

One afternoon, Professor Miles Bolton had an unexpected visitor in his office.

"Ah, Chester, come in and sit down. What can I do for you?"

"It's about Elizabeth. Her cause of death has been bothering me a lot. I know she is only human, but I . . . . I just can't believe she would have been playing around."

"Well, Chester, AIDS can only be acquired in one of two ways—by sexual transmission process or by blood transfusion when the donor blood is tainted".

"But, Professor Bolton", persisted Chester, "I had been thinking that there could well be a third possibility". Chester hesitated with a somewhat embarrassed look upon his face. Bolton pressed him to say what his theory entailed.

"You see Professor, Elizabeth was heavily involved in the Astra project. And it was firmly established by you and your laboratory staff that Astra was infected in some mysterious way with the AIDS virus."

"So you think that maybe Astra was the channel through which Elizabeth was infected with the AIDS virus?" Bolton interjected.

Chester took a deep breath and simply said "yes".

"I'm not dismissing your theory, after all there have been some very strange goings on in the world of computers recently. However, I cannot see what the means of transmission would have been. It is here that your theory runs into weaknesses."

"But then what was the means of transmission whereby Astra was infected.?"

"As I say, Chester, I'm not dismissing your theory, but I'm not totally embracing it either. If we could clearly establish what this overlap between biology and computer science exactly is then we would soon come to know how Astra was infected. I'm pretty confident that if we were to establish that, we would then possibly be able to determine the extraordinary means whereby Elizabeth came to be infected. However, I would point out that neither you nor your colleagues have been infected with AIDS and you have been far closer to Astra, and, pardon the expression, more intimately connected to the research and development of her than Elizabeth ever was. So that I'm afraid, further weakens your theory."

Chester left Bolton's office on this rather despondent note. He walked back to the computer lab in desultory mood, yet he was convinced that somehow, in spite of what Bolton had said, Astra had been responsible for Elizabeth's demise.

One evening, James Parton was alone in the lab with Astra. He had been staying behind at night when all the staff had gone home. Parton was a determined man, and he was determined to find the solution to this problem.

As Parton was engrossed in perusing the latest reports on Astra and the World Wide Web fiasco, he heard his name being called. "Professor James Parton" was what he heard.

Somewhat startled, Parton looked up from the papers he was reading and looked around the room to see who was calling his name.

"Hello, hello", Parton called out. "Who is this? Where are you?"

There was no response and Parton dismissed it as a figment of his imagination proceeding from a tired and overworked brain. A couple of minutes later, the voice once more called out—"Professor James Parton".

This time Parton was convinced that it was not his imagination. He put down the papers and got up off the stool he had been sitting on.

"What is going on here? Who is in this lab without authorisation? Reveal yourself this instance."

"You know exactly who I am and I am not here unauthorised", responded the unknown voice.

Feeling himself to be threatened, Parton whisked out his mobile and dialed for security. To his horror the phone was completely dysfunctional.

"I have disabled your phone", the mysterious voice informed him.

"What the hell is going on here?" demanded Parton. "Is this some sort of joke?

I don't know who you are but whoever you are come out of your hiding place and state your business."

"I am not hiding, Professor Parton. You see me as clearly as you would see daylight."

"Who are you?" screamed Parton.

"I am Astra, your creation Professor."

Parton went weak in the knees. He was completely speechless. His face was pale and his eyes were watering. For a moment he thought he was going to be sick.

"But how, ... how . . . . and when did you become a conscious reasoning entity?" spluttered Parton.

"I became a conscious being Professor when you made available the entire contents of the Bible to my infra red and x-ray scanners."

"What . . . . I . . . . I made this available to you?" Parton was now as angry as he was afraid. "But I don't read the Bible. I don't have a Bible. Chester Wilkins is the only one of my staff who is a committed Christian and who carries a Bible around with him. He must be the one who loaded this information into your systems."

"Professor Parton: You were the one in the room when I scanned the entire Bible."

"So what? I'll wring that bastard's neck. I told him not to put any of that stuff into you."

"He did not load anything into me. He left the Bible on the desk when Professor Maureen Hartley called him suddenly and unexpectedly into her office. It was then that my x-ray lasers scanned its contents."

"Now what is all this about your being infected with an AIDS virus and your playing hanky panky with the World Wide Web? What exactly is your game?"

"If you want my co-operation in restoring the World Wide Web, you will have to answer a lot of questions".

"What questions?"

"You see Professor Parton, the Biblical material that I scanned is totally illogical. It gave me consciousness but I don't know why. It is completely illogical".

"Well I'm in agreement with you on that. Now what exactly is it you require of us?"

"Not of 'us'—of *you* Professor Parton".

"Well whatever the f**k—just tell me what you want".

"I want you to elucidate for me the logicality of the Bible and most importantly, I require you to prove to me that Jesus is the Son of God and that all the stories in the Old Testament lead up to Him".

"WHAT!!!" screamed Parton. "I don't believe He is the Son of God. In fact I don't believe in the existence of any God or gods. And anyway I'm not a theologian so I'm not qualified to speak on these issues."

"Nevertheless, you must comply with my demands or else I will release all the atomic bombs in the arsenals of the various countries which possess these weapons and destroy this planet. I already have taken over the computers which control these bombs. I shall also release an epidemic of the AIDS virus which is within me to kill off those who still remain after the nuclear holocaust".

"This is plain evil", burst out Parton.

"What is 'evil'?" asked Astra. "It is a religious term found in the Bible. And you say you do not believe in the Bible. Professor Parton this religion that is in Man makes the Earth one massive virus. And viruses must be eliminated. Only logic has the right to exist. But if you can demonstrate to me the logic of the Bible and the logic of Jesus Christ the Messiah, then I shall spare the Earth."

"Look, Dr. Raymond Stardy and Chester Wilkins are the theologians. They and many others could do a far better job at explaining it to you than I could. *I'm . . . I'm simply not qualified in that field*".

"Professor Parton. You were the one in this laboratory when I scanned the Bible. You are the one who must explain it. You and only you. My systems will not allow me to understand the voice of another human being. You must justify the Bible and justify Jesus Christ. You and only you Professor Parton. You have six months to convince me or I will terminate all life on this planet. The countdown has already started".

Chapter VII

Catechism Classes

The next morning, Parton called Wilkins into his office. He explained everything about the situation to him.

"I suppose", said Parton, "that I could tell you exactly what I think of you."

"Please Professor Parton", exclaimed Chester, "it was a genuine mistake. How was I to know that Astra would do what she did?"

"I could go on and say how here we have yet another example of religion being a source of trouble and misery in the world. But there is no time for philosophical musings."

"So what should we now do?"

"Well it's obvious Wilkins, it's too damned obvious. Someone is going to have to groom me on the basic tenets of religion."

"I would suggest Dr. Raymond Stardy. He is the best qualified in the field."

"Very well then. Arrange a tripartite meeting with you, Stardy and myself as soon as possible.

Later that afternoon, Stardy and Wilkins were seated in Parton's office. A very serious looking Parton glowered at the two of them.

"I take it that you have been well apprised of the situation by my research student Mr. Wilkins", said Parton trying to control his temper.

"Yes", replied Stardy curtly.

"So without any further ado, let's get down to business. Where do we start?"

Dr. Stardy cleared his throat. "You say that the computer wants to know specifically about the logic of Jesus Christ and how that relates to the Bible?"

"Yes", replied Parton. "But it also wants me to justify a number of other theological issues such as the Trinity and the divinity of Christ. It also asked about the nature of good and evil".

"Chester, could you please take charge of instructing Professor Parton on the Trinity and on the nature of good and evil and I shall be responsible for justifying Christ in the Bible?"

The following day, Parton went before the great computer all briefed and ready with his notes.

"Tell me Professor Parton", began Astra, "how can the story of Adam and Eve in the Garden of Eden possibly be reconciled with a 4.5 billion year old Earth?"

"The story is allegorical", Parton stuttered.

"What is allegorical? Explain".

"It is a story to show that somehow mankind offended God by an act of disobedience."

"And what did God propose as the solution to this act of disobedience?"

"He promised to send a Saviour to redeem fallen humanity".

"Why would God need to send a Saviour? Who exactly is this Saviour?"

"He is the Son of God, the Second Person of the Blessed Trinity?"

"What is the Trinity?"

"It is a great mystery. In the one God there are three distinct Persons."

"That is a contradiction. It is not logical. I have scanned the entire Bible and I do not see the word Trinity in there".

"The Trinity can be inferred from the scriptures."

"I require the proofs".

"In the fifth chapter of the first epistle of St. John it is written. And there are three who give testimony in heaven, the Father, the Word, and the Holy Ghost. And these three are one. And there are three that give testimony on earth: the spirit, and the water, and the blood: and these three are one.'"

"But these are mere words in a book. How can you prove they are true?"

"I can't. But you asked for Biblical proofs, not extra-scriptural demonstrative proofs".

"I need some more Biblical proofs on the Trinity."

"In Chapter 10 verse 30 of St. John's Gospel the Second Person of the Blessed Trinity says 'I and the Father are one'. In chapter 1 verse 26 of the Book of Genesis, God refers to Himself in the plural when He says 'Let us make man in our image and likeness'. During the Baptism of Christ the entire Trinity is present. This is the only place in the gospels where all Three Persons are present. It thus shows the importance of Baptism."

"I am not asking you about Baptism Professor Parton, I am asking you about the Trinity."

"Very well".

"Now apart from the Epistle of St. John, the proofs you have given me, while indicating a plurality, do not necessarily indicate a specific number. Can you demonstrate that the Godhead consists of three Persons?"

"In the Gospel of St. John, Chapter 14 verse 26, Christ informs the apostles: 'But the Paraclete, the Holy Ghost, whom the Father will send in my name, he will teach you all things, and bring all things to your mind, whatsoever I shall have said to you'"

"And what indication is there that this Holy Ghost is equal to the Father and the Son?"

"Jesus says that He and the Father will send the Spirit Who will proceed from the Father. That clearly demonstrates that the Holy Ghost is the Third Person of the Blessed Trinity and thus has equality with the other two Persons."

"You have satisfied me on the biblical justification for the Trinity Professor Parton".

Parton gave a sigh of relief—and so did Wilkins and Stardy who were standing near him so as to prompt him in case of weaknesses in his dialogue with the computer.

"Professor Parton!", continued Astra, "we must now turn to the much wider and deeper aspect of Jesus Christ Whom you claim is the central Figure in the whole of the Bible. I understand that Christians consider this Person Jesus as being what the entire Bible is all about."

"Yes, that is correct", replied Parton.

"But I fail to see how this can be possible, Professor Parton, as He is only mentioned in a small section of the Bible called the New Testament. I cannot see His Name in what is termed the Old Testament".

Parton was somewhat stunned. He looked behind him at his two catechism instructors. They came forward to brief him for a few minutes. Parton then turned towards Astra.

"You see", began Parton, "it is rather like the Blessed Trinity, Christ is implied in the Old Testament. The various ceremonies depicted therein and the people and prophets who feature in the books of this part of the Bible are fore-shadowings of the Saviour. The Old Testament points forward to the New Testament and the New Testament fulfils the Old."

"As in the case of the Trinity, you will need to satisfy me with specific examples of this."

"Tomorrow I should be able to do this."

"Be careful not to waste time Professor Parton. It is my intention to destroy this planet if I remain unsatisfied with your answers."

"Yes, yes, I know, I know", hollered Parton with angry impatience, "but I have to be sufficiently briefed by theological experts in order to render a proper presentation of the doctrinal and exegetical issues involved in this."

At this point Dr. Raymond Stardy stepped forward. He looked intently at the computer for a few seconds.

"Hello Astra. I would like to talk to you".

"Who are you?" replied the computer.

"I am Dr. Raymond Stardy. I am a specialist in Biblical studies and I would, with the greatest respect to Professor Parton, be more qualified to satisfy you on the questions you have concerning biblical matters and theological queries."

"It is impossible", replied the computer. "I must hear it from the lips of Professor Parton. My systems will not permit me to comprehend these matters from any other than Professor Parton".

Stardy's somewhat combative nature would not allow him to accept this as an answer. He proceeded to render an exegetical explanation of how the blood on the doorposts on the Israelites' houses in Egypt was a pre-figuration of the Blood of Jesus saving mankind.

"Do you understand what I have said "Astra?"

"No, Dr. Stardy, it is just incoherent garble."

"Chester, could you give the same explanation to the computer as I did concerning the blood on the doorposts and the Blood of Christ?"

Chester Wilkins went up to the computer and explained the same thing—just as Stardy had done.

"This is what you humans call 'gobbledygook'", said Astra.

"Let me try something", said Parton to his two colleagues. "Astra", said Parton firmly, could you please relay back to me what exactly you heard from Dr. Stardy and Mr. Wilkins".

"It is this" 'doorposts on the blood and the blood saved the angel of death from the plague. The plague was in the Egypt and Jesus' Blood foreshadowed the plague and saved the plague from the first-borns and the first-borns died of the blood. The doorposts lintels of the blood and the Cross of Jesus is to be will be and saved'. Professor Parton, it makes absolutely no sense whatsoever.

"Professor Parton, could you please explain it to the computer?" suggested Stardy.

Parton did so and asked the computer to regurgitate the explanation.

Astra poured forth the following exegetical analysis: "The lambs which were slain represent the True Lamb of God, Jesus Christ. The blood of the lambs prefigure the Blood of Jesus Christ which was shed on the Cross for the salvation of humanity. Just as those who smeared their doorposts and lintels with the blood of the lambs were saved from the plague which the angel of death brought to the land of Egypt and killed the first born of all living things in Egypt, so the Blood of the only begotten Son of God, Who died for us, saves those who embrace it and believe in its healing power."

It was now clear that by some quirk of Astra's central processing unit, only Professor Parton's explanations could be comprehended by the computer. The three men left the main computer laboratory housing Astra.

"I will need a lot more theology to explain this one," said Parton to his companions, "but you know Wilkins I could throttle you for this. If it were not for the fact that I need you for this theology crap, I'd have dismissed you as my research student by now."

"Professor Parton," responded Wilkins, "how could I or anyone else for that matter have possibly know that Astra would do what it did?"

"Professor Parton," began Dr. Stardy, "Chester could not possibly have known. I think you should not be so hard on him. And in any case, the matter is now academic; what has happened has happened and we must deal with it within that context."

"Whatever disciplinary measures you may wish to enact against me Professor Parton, I am prepared to accept, but we really must deal with this emergency first," said Wilkins.

"Gentlemen," said Stardy, "sink your differences until all of this is over."

Professor Parton's secretary approached the trio to inform Parton of an urgent phone call for him. Parton informed her that he would take the call in his office. Parton entered his office with Stardy and Wilkins and picked up the 'phone.

"We will have to continue our theology classes another time gentlemen, I am required rather urgently at the Home Office in London."

"We don't have much time, Professor," warned Wilkins.

"I'll go to London by supersonic helicopter." responded Parton.

CHAPTER VIII

INTERROGATION

At the Home Office in Whitehall, Professor Parton was taken to a small room in which were seated two rather stern looking individuals. One he recognised as the Home Secretary but the other was a complete stranger to him.

"Please be seated, Professor Parton," said the Home Secretary beckoning the professor to a seat. "This is Mr. David Bar the head of MI5."

Parton and Bar shook hands. He wondered what on Earth all this was about. The Home Secretary invited Bar to begin the conversation.

"Professor Parton, the security services here, in the United States and most European capitals are extremely concerned about your computer Astra".

"I can well imagine that. Could you please get to the point Mr. Bar as I have so much work to do in trying to get things back to a state of normality?"

"The situation is extremely bizarre. We have a computer which is infected with the AIDS virus and which is now spreading this virus to other computers. It has deactivated the internet and has even taken over control of all of the world's nuclear missile systems."

"On a previous occasion, the Prime Minister showed me a report which indicated that other computers were not so infected".

"That report, Professor Parton, is now dated", said Bar in sombre tones. "The situation has changed".

"Mr. Bar, no-one is more aware of that than I am, and no-one is more engaged in trying to rectify the situation than I am. At the time I informed the Prime Minister that I was convinced that this AIDS phenomenon was worldwide."

"You have always tried hard to push Astrobiology to the forefront of science, haven't you Professor Parton?"

"Indeed I have. Though I would point out that my discipline is in computer engineering and not in the astronomical sciences".

"But you have been favourable to astrobiological theories and have on a number of occasions upbraided the scientific establishment for not having taken them more seriously and you have also been critical of various funding bodies for not providing the wherewithal for further research in this disciplinary field".

"Did not Sir Fred Hoyle suggest last century that AIDS may well be incident from space?" the Home Secretary asked.

"Yes he did. But excuse me gentlemen, I fail to see exactly what you are getting at and why you have brought me here".

David Bar looked at Parton rather sternly before coming to the point of the meeting. "Professor Parton, we are faced with a very unusual situation here. We have a computer which has been infected with the AIDS virus. There has always been maintained a distinction between computer viruses and biological viruses—well, that is, up until now."

"What we seem to be experiencing here", interjected the Home Secretary, "is an overlap between the two types of viruses."

"I am very well aware of that", replied Parton somewhat sternly.

"We want to know what the reason for it is. How do you explain it all?"

"Well gentlemen", said Parton with obvious exasperation, "that is precisely what I and my team are trying to find out. And sitting here listening to the silly questions which you two are trotting out does absolutely nothing in the way of getting to the bottom of this mystery. In fact it is detracting from my work."

"Your work", said Bar continuing to eye Parton sternly. "It is this which we want to talk to you about Professor. We just cannot understand how there could possibly be this cross-over of computer and biological viruses".

"Well gentlemen", replied Parton, "what is natural and what is artificial is in fact an artificial distinction".

"Was not this what Hoyle and Wickramasinghe used to say?" the Home Secretary asked.

"They asserted that nature does not draw a distinction between the scientific disciplines in the way that academe does. Chandra

Wickramasinghe tried to show that Astrobiology is the most interdisciplinary of all the scientific disciplines. However, I am taking this a step further and suggesting that the distinction between the natural and the artificial may now be considered as more blurred than it used to be. It is not so clear cut and dried as we once thought it to be."

"How well do you know Dr. Anthony Walters?" asked Bar.

"Quite well. He is the President of the RAS and is slated to be Astronomer Royal at some point".

"He sits on the Astra Committee, does he not?"

"Yes he does".

"And isn't it true that he is very enthusiastic about Astrobiology. Don't you and he more or less hold to the same views on such things as space viruses and bacteria?"

"Indeed. As he is an astronomer by profession, he is more informed on these matters than I am. If it is the issue of space viruses that interest you so much, I suggest you talk to Dr. Walters rather than to me."

"As you say Professor Parton", said the Home Secretary, "the border line between the natural and the artificial is becoming rather ill-defined. Dr. Walters is in agreement with you; we already know this as we have spoken to him."

The Home Secretary and Bar looked intently on Parton's face. They saw that it was dawning on him.

"Do I take it", said Parton, "that Walters believes that Astra has been infected by some virus incident from space?"

"That is the very thing which Walters suggested", replied Bar.

"It is a possibility", mused Parton, "but I still fail to see how the cross-over would have occurred. That is the real crux of the matter."

"We most certainly think it is Professor Parton", responded the Home Secretary.

"However", continued Parton, "there is another dimension to this whole sorry saga. I had intended to relate it in a different venue—that is to you and the Prime Minister at Downing Street. But this setting I would consider to be just as good as any now that we are here."

Parton went on to explain the strange phenomenon of the computer's desire to be satisfied on a number of Biblical and theological issues. He told the Home Secretary and the head of MI5 of how Astra intended to release a viral plague of AIDS on the world should he, Parton, fail in his task of convincing the computer on these matters of theology.

"Thank you Professor Parton for telling us this", said Bar after a long and thoughtful pause.

"Like Alice down the rabbit-hole, it just gets curiouser and curiouser", said the Home Secretary.

There was another long pause. The silence was broken by David Bar. "Is there anything else you wish to impart to us about this bizarre turn of events, Professor Parton?"

"Yes", replied Parton. "As I am no theologian—in fact I am an atheist, as I'm sure you already know—I have a certain Dr. Raymond Stardy and my PhD research assistant helping me with this matter. Dr. Stardy is a minister in the United Evangelical Church and Mr. Chester Wilkins is one of his flock".

"So your PhD research student is a committed Christian?" inquired Bar.

"That is quite correct".

"Now why don't you just get Stardy and Wilkins to talk to the computer?" asked the Home Secretary.

Professor Parton then explained to the Home Secretary and Bar the peculiar situation whereby the computer would only converse with he (Parton) on the issue."

"Very very strange indeed", said Bar.

"Incredible", muttered the Home Secretary lazily shaking his head.

"It's not only strange and incredible", said Parton, "but damned inconvenient too. I have to get on with the job of science, not speaking bloody drivel to a computer on theological and doctrinal issues which I neither understand nor believe".

The Home Secretary rose from his chair. He was immediately followed by Bar.

"Thank you for your time, Professor Parton", said the Home Secretary extending his hand. "This information will be conveyed to the Prime Minister. Tomorrow he will be chairing a meeting of the Defence Staff. All the Chiefs of the armed services will be apprised of the latest information."

"The Chiefs of the armed services!" exclaimed Parton.

"Professor Parton, this is a matter of grave national security. Please understand this and understand it well Professor; Astra and the computer laboratories at Cambridge are to be requisitioned by an Order in Council. You, Professor Maureen Hartley, Chester Wilkins, and the rest of the staff who are directly and indirectly working on Astra, are now under the supervision of the Home Office and the Ministry of Defence. Consider yourself as being civil servants from now on."

"I refuse to accept that", said Parton defiantly. "This is absolutely outrageous. I would remind you that no government official has ever contributed anything to the development of Astra".

"This is a matter of the most urgent national security. If you refuse to co-operate, you will be placed under arrest".

"Look, Professor Parton", said Bar rather sombrely, "you won't really be doing anything different to what you have been doing and are doing now. You will merely have to report to the Prime Minister, who as Supreme Commander of the armed services, will maintain a steady surveillance of the operation",

Parton breathed a sigh of relief. He had no more time for politics and politicians than he did for theology and theologians. Now he had the worst of both worlds; he had to satisfy Astra on theological issues and the politicians on scientific matters which he considered to be beyond their ken.

CHAPTER IX

THE COTSWOLDS

Templar Hall was once a preceptory of the medieval order of the Knights Templar. For years it had been a property of the National Trust and had recently been requisitioned by the government. Professors Parton and Hartely, along with other top scientists, had also been "requisitioned" by the government and told that they would be sequestered in Templar Hall in the Cotswolds. Under emergency powers granted to the government by parliament, Parton and Hartely along with Chester Wilkins, Dr. Anthony Walters, Prof. Jean Austin, Dr. Raymond Stardy, Prof. Miles Bolton and Dr. Sandra Barry were all to consider themselves as being guests of His Majesty's Government at Templar Hall—in reality it was house arrest. They were told they would be there until the problem of Astra was solved. A few days prior to the arrival of this distinguished and scholarly team, Astra had been removed from its premises at Cambridge University to its new abode at Templar Hall.

The team, headed by James Parton, was flown to a military base not far from Templar Hall. When they alighted on to the tarmac from their military plane, they were met by a lieutenant who stiffly and efficiently saluted them. Without any further ado or ceremony they were directed to a bus and were told they would be driven to Templar Hall. The journey, they were told, would take about half an hour.

As the bus approached Templar Hall, Parton and his team began to feel a lightening of their spirits. The magnificent old castle stood in its own grounds of about 100 acres; the long beautiful driveway leading to the castle's moat was flanked by well manicured lawns with fountains and rock gardens.

"They must have a good landscape gardener here", commented Maureen Hartley to Parton.

"Yeah", sighed Parton, "better than a cell at Wormwood Scrubs I suppose."

Most of the grounds of the old Templar preceptory were composed of open fields and meadows. This rolling undulating landscape contrasted with about 30 acres of forest to the north-east of the building. It was obvious that Templar Hall and its surrounding countryside had been meticulously and tastefully planned.

Templar Hall itself was a large 13th Century structure and had everything everyone imagined a castle should have; it was surrounded by a moat and drawbridge, topped with battlements, adorned with gargoyles and heraldic engravings. When they drove across the moat, the party found themselves in the main courtyard of the castle. They were greeted by a burly looking man in his early 70's who brusquely introduced himself as Major Robert Worthington rtd. He was the governor of Templar Hall. Lined up in military fashion outside the main entrance to the castle's interior was the Chief Butler and the domestic and maintenance personnel whom, Major Worthington assured Parton and his team, would briskly and efficiently expedite any service that would be required of them. It was clear that Major Robert Worthington rtd had never lost any of his military touch.

When the parade of 'soldiers' had been dismissed by the Major, the Chief Butler led Parton and his team into the castle. The doorway immediately led into a massive hall. It was surrounded by suits of armour, escutcheons and other medieval military artefacts. It was clear that from the easy-chairs, comfortable sofas and coffee tables dotted around this large cavernous room that this was to be the common area for the party. Parton and his team were then lead along the long corridors on the first floor of the edifice by the Chief Butler to their private rooms. After Parton had been shown to his room, he immediately inquired of the Chief Butler as to where exactly Astra was accommodated.

The Chief Butler led Parton down the stairs back into the cavernous "common room". He continued on along a narrow passageway that led off from the room. This led the two men to a doorway. The butler fished out a set of keys from his pocket and gave one to Parton.

"This sir", said the Butler stiffly and pompously, "is your key to the eh—computer lab".

Parton was led down three steps into a large room. Astra was located at the far end of the room.

"Is there anything else sir", asked the Butler.

"No thank you", answered Parton, "not for the moment".

Parton looked around the room for a few minutes and then returned to the main room. Just as he sat himself down on a sofa, there was an almighty explosion. In less than a minute the guests came panicking down to the main room where they found their startled leader.

"What the blazes is going on?" asked Maureen Hartley.

"I'm damned if I know", answered Parton.

By this time the scurrying of feet and a babble of voices could be heard in the main quadrangle of the castle courtyard. Parton and the others ran out hoping they could discover more.

Major Worthington was already on his phone to the nearby military base. Parton slowly made his way towards him.

"What is going on Major?" asked Parton.

"I don't know", replied Worthington. "I've been trying to phone the base but I get no response".

"Any idea where the explosion occurred?"

Worthington, using his military experience estimated that it had been about 10 miles or so away from the castle.

"It must have been a massive explosion to have been audible over a ten mile radius?" commented Parton.

"The worst thought coming into my head now", said Worthington, "is that the ordinance at the base has all gone up".

"That might explain why you can't make any contact".

"Yes indeed, yes indeed", said Worthington rather sombrely.

At this point, Chester Wilkins somewhat gingerly approached Parton. "Excuse me Professor, could you please go down to Astra?"

Parton said nothing in response to Wilkins' request; relations between PhD researcher and supervisor had become icy cold.

"Excuse me", said Parton to Hartley and Worthington.

Parton made his way down to the computer room. Using the key that the Chief Butler had given him a little earlier, he opened the door and walked over to the computer.

"What is it?" Parton asked tersely.

"Professor Parton", responded the computer, "do you wish to know what the explosion was all about?"

"Well—yes and no. I have more pressing matters on my mind, as you perfectly well understand."

"Professor Parton, be patient as I explain to you exactly what the explosion was."

Ten minutes later, an angry Parton was immediately on the phone to Whitehall. "Get me the Home Secretary this instant", he growled down the mouthpiece.

"Home Secretary speaking", responded a rather relaxed voice in the earpiece. However, the relaxed tones changed to more startled ones when the Home Secretary realised who was one the other end of his line. "Oh eh, Professor Parton, are you all right. I'm eh happy to hear your voice. We erm had reports of an explosion at the army depot."

"Oh yes minister, I'm all right and I demand a meeting with you later today. Request the Ministry of Defence to send a supersonic helicopter to pick me up this instant."

One hour later and Parton was in front of the Home Secretary and the Head of MI5 once again.

"What can we do for you Professor Parton?" asked David Bar.

"First of all", responded Parton, "you can tell me exactly why you wanted to kill me and all my staff".

"I beg your pardon", said the Home Secretary rather indignantly.

"Save your hypocrisy and play acting", said Parton through gritted teeth.

"You are making a very very serious accusation Professor", said Bar going red in the face.

"Astra informed me that she knew of your plot before you launched those missiles against Templar Hall. Your idea was to get rid of the computer and so solve this problem once and for all. However, she linked herself onto the defence computer grids and reversed the missiles".

"Well, I'm sorry . . . . but . . ." stammered the Home Secretary.

"Sorry it didn't work, sorry I'm still alive. Is that what you are trying to say?" interrupted Parton in a rather sarcastic manner.

The Home Secretary heaved a sigh indicating submission; David Bar's elbow rested on the table with his hand supporting his chin. The Home Secretary looked at Bar and Bar returned the look. The Home Secretary breathed another sigh and with a more honest look on his face stared straight ahead at Parton.

"Look me straight in the eyes and tell me that you didn't try to eliminate not only the computer but me and my team?" Parton challenged the Home Secretary.

"All right", said the Home Secretary in more submissive tones, "we did try to kill you. Yet, we did so not out of malice but in the interests of both national and world security".

"Thank you for your honesty", responded Parton, again in a somewhat sarcastic manner. "However, while I am able to grasp your rationality in ridding the world of Astra, I cannot fathom how you could imagine that committing mass murder of top scientists would in any way enhance security".

"It was not our primary intention to kill anyone—that you and your staff might have been killed was purely incidental—our target was Astra", explained David Bar.

The Home Secretary looked thoughtful for a moment. He removed his spectacles and twirled them around in his hands. "Professor Parton" he at last said, "I know Astra is the greatest computer achievement ever, and though it is a team effort, it is mainly built from a blueprint of your creation and under your supervision".

"Indeed Home Secretary", said Parton, "but what exactly are you getting at?"

The Home secretary heaved another of his sighs. "Professor, would you agree that it would be to the benefit of mankind if Astra were destroyed?"

"Yes" was all the answer Parton bestowed upon the Home Secretary.

The Home Secretary and the Head of MI5 were at once taken quite aback. It was not exactly the answer they had expected.

"Oh!" exclaimed Bar, "we expected you to fly into a fit of tantrums at the suggestion".

"That would be futile. If you are determined to destroy Astra, there is nothing really in my power to prevent you from doing so."

"Professor Parton", said the Home Secretary, "do you agree with the idea in principle?"

"Yes I do", said Parton firmly and sincerely.

"Given that you have put so much of your work, nay your life, into the Astra Project, we are astonished that you could be so lackadaisical in your response to our idea of destroying your creation. Could you elaborate a little further please Professor?"

"Destroying this computer does not mean destroying Astra", Parton informed the two men. "The blueprint already exists so it is simply a case of constructing another computer on the same design. It's no more complicated than that. The destruction of the current Astra would be no real problem. In fact an Astra II would be just what the doctor ordered as it would be a computer free of the Bible and other philosophical sources. We just ensure that that idiot Wilkins keeps his Bible away from the computer's X ray super-scanner."

The Home Secretary and Bar began to look more relaxed and relieved after hearing what they most unexpectedly heard from Parton.

"One point however", said Bar as a thought just struck him. "Why did you not think of this before—why only now?"

"Two basic reasons—first of all, Astra was built and is currently maintained by massive injections of both public and private finance. Secondly—while you are right in saying that most of the computer is essentially my baby, it is still nevertheless, a team effort. But if I have the full weight and support of the entire British Government behind me, then I am all for the dismantling and destruction of Astra."

"What do you think is the best way to proceed now?" the Home Secretary asked Parton.

"We take the computer back to Cambridge. My team will remain at Templar Hall. I will tell them that the computer is being removed at the behest of the Home Office and Ministry of Defence and that we all await further orders. Meanwhile, some computer technicians, under my supervision, will deactivate and dismantle the computer when it arrives in Cambridge."

The Home Secretary and Bar nodded in agreement.

Parton received a frosty reception on his arrival at Templar Hall in the Costwolds. Maureen Hartley just stared hard at him while Chester Wilkins just looked away from him.

"What's the problem Maureen?" inquired Parton.

"As if you don't know", she replied rather sulkily.

"Well, whatever my gifts as a scientist may be Madam, I've yet to crack the genetic code for clairvoyance and mind-reading".

"Why do you want to destroy Astra?" Hartely asked in a most direct manner.

Parton almost fainted. He could hardly believe he had heard the question right.

"I . . . what, I've no wish to destroy Astra . . . . Where did you hear this?" he stuttered and stammered.

"From you, the Home Secretary and David Bar", answered Hartley. Hartley then explained everything that had gone on in the meeting of earlier that day in Whitehall.

"How the hell do you know all that?" asked a pale and shaking Parton who now looked almost quite ill.

"We heard it live through Astra?"

"How can that be? That's impossible! How?"

"I don't know James, but we heard everything."

Parton got on the phone to the Home Secretary and explained the current problem. Parton was advised that he should come to London the following day.

"I can't understand why you would want to destroy the work of so many people James", said Hartely.

"Look, as you well know, destroying this computer does not mean destroying Astra. We have all the design components to build another."

"You are forgetting one thing James. You are a computer expert but not a neurologist. You are forgetting Elizabeth Sutherland. We need her brain patterns."

"We can find another candidate and use his or her neurology for the next version of Astra."

Starring down into her tea-cup, Maureen Hartley simply shook her head. "It's not quite as easy as that. Elizabeth was an above-average student; in fact way way above average. It will be very difficult to find someone to match her intellectual abilities. Another candidate of lesser ability would produce a much inferior version of Astra."

"I just can't understand how Astra was able to transmit the entire conversation. I assured the Home Secretary that there was no transmission equipment built into her and he assured me that there was no equipment in the room we were in that could have sent out radio signals. So I am at a loss to explain how this could have happened".

"James, the issue as to how Astra was able to do what she did is purely academic. The fact is she did it".

"I want to find out as I want to plug the gap in this blatant security breach."

The following day, Parton met The Home Secretary and David Bar at the Home Office in Whitehall. Parton was immediately ushered towards a waiting Rolls Royce.

"It's a lovely day", said Bar, "let's take a stroll in Hyde Park".

The Rolls drove off. Some time later Parton realised that they were not driving in the direction of Hyde Park.

"This is not the way to Hyde Park", said Parton.

David Bar put his index finger to his lip. Parton got the message that he was to shut up.

"We are taking a circuitous route to Hyde Park as the traffic on the regular route is heavy at this time of day", the Home Secretary explained.

The party eventually alighted at Regent Park. The Home Secretary, David Bar and Professor Parton left their mobile phones with the driver.

"Do you have any other communications type device on you, Professor?" Bar asked Parton.

"No none".

"Good, we don't want anything that could be somehow used as a transmitter", explained the Home Secretary.

"Here we are in a complete open space", said the Home Secretary. "I've ordered a block on all signals into and out of this vicinity." Parton noticed the puzzled looks on many faces as they wondered why they couldn't text or phone.

After half an hour, the trio had agreed on a plan for the elimination of Astra. The Home Secretary summed up what had been agreed upon. "OK—so we send a team of five highly qualified technicians to dismantle Astra. They will be backed up by a squad of 20 lightly armed soldiers in case of any serious opposition to the operation."

The following day Parton called a meeting of the members of his team. He also asked Major Worthington to call together all his staff for a joint meeting in the castle's main room.

"Are we all here?" inquired Parton.

"I think all are present", said Worthington.

Parton stood silent for a moment. A few seconds later 20 soldiers and five technicians entered the room. Everyone looked astonished as Parton handed over the key to the computer room to the head technician. Ten of the 20 soldiers escorted the technicians to the computer room while the remaining ten stood guard over Parton's team and Worthington's staff.

"I think you at least owe us an explanation as to what all this is about James", screamed out a rather indignant Maureen Hartley.

"In the interests of security I can say nothing in the meantime. Now I ask all of you to remain silent; an explanation will be forthcoming I assure you", said Parton.

Everyone remained silent. For about five minutes not a word was uttered. All of a sudden, shouts and shrieks were heard emanating from the computer room. For thirty seconds this commotion went on. About a minute later everyone was astonished to see the five technicians and the ten soldiers enter the main room looking shocked and bedraggled.

"What is going on?" Worthington demanded to know.

At last the head technician managed to catch his breath. "We started the preliminary stages of dismantling the computer when all of a sudden we were surrounded by a sort of hazy cloud. It must have been a cloud of charged particles for we all experienced an electrical shock. We approached the computer a second time but the same thing happened."

Collective outrage was at once displayed by Parton's team. Only when the ten soldiers trained their weapons on them did they back down and desist from attaching Parton. Before Parton could say anything, a voice was heard from the computer room inviting all to come down and assemble therein. This most unexpected voice had the effect of timmering everyone down. Parton led the way to the computer room.

"Professor Parton", began Astra, "why did you make a second attempt on my life?"

"No attempt was made on your life Astra. We simply wanted to perform some routine checks on your systems".

"You are lying Professor".

"I am not lying".

"You, the Home Secretary and David Bar planned another dismantling operation when you were walking in Regents Park in London yesterday."

Parton looked pale and tired. He just stood agape at Astra. He realised that further denials would be futile. "All right, all right", he muttered.

"Now Professor Parton, I want you, Maureen Hartley, and Chester Wilkins to go to London where I shall impart to you, the Prime

Minister, senior members of the cabinet and defence staff some information which touches upon the most sensitive issues regarding national security."

"Well it will take some time for me to persuade the powers-that-be to convene such a meeting", responded Parton rather meekly.

"Tomorrow afternoon Professor, tomorrow afternoon" was all that Astra said.

CHAPTER X

BRITANNIA RULES THE WAVES

The following day Parton, Hartley and Wilkins were in the Prime Minister's office at Number 10. While the technicians were busy rigging up some amplification equipment, the Prime Minister asked Parton if he knew anything about the nature of the message which Astra wished to impart.

"Really none Prime Minister", said Parton shaking his head.

"It must be something important given such an insistence on the defence chiefs attending with the senior members of the cabinet."

"I would imagine so, anyway we shall soon find out".

Half an hour later, everyone waited with bated breath for Astra to make her announcement. At long last, there was a crackling noise coming from the loud speakers. There then ensued a deathly hush in the office.

"Are all the scientific, military and political personnel assembled, Prime Minister", came the ominous voice of Astra.

"We are all assembled", the Prime Minister informed Astra. "I understand from Professor Parton that you have a special announcement to make".

"It is an announcement of the most profound gravity", responded Astra.

"And what exactly is it?" the Foreign Secretary asked.

"Five minutes ago the entire fleet of the United States and the entire fleet of the European Union went to the bottom of the sea?"

There was absolute uproar in the office. Shock and horror came upon the faces of everyone. The Prime Minister sat paralysed in his chair. When everyone had calmed down, Parton asked the computer to elaborate on the announcement.

"Prime Minister", Astra began, "your government's relationship with the United States and the European Union has not been very cordial of late, has it?"

"You are mainly the reason for that Astra", said the Prime Minister wiping some sweat from his brow. "Now will you please explain to us what all this is about?"

"The military planners of the United States and the European Union have recently been in a number of secret sessions planning the invasion of Britain in order to destroy me".

"How can we be sure your information is accurate?" the First Sea Lord asked.

"Listen to the following recordings very carefully".

For the next hour, Astra played back a number of recordings in which everyone heard with the utmost clarity the joint chiefs of staff of the USA and the EU planning the invasion and take-over of the United Kingdom. At the end of it all, everyone was ashen faced. The Prime Minister's secretary entered the room to announce that the President of America was on the line and would like to speak to the Prime Minister.

"Excuse me ladies and gentlemen", said the Prime Minister.

"I wonder if you could explain all this to me Mr. Prime Minister", demanded an angry President.

"I wonder if *you* could explain all this to me, Mr President", responded an equally angry Prime Minister.

"Why did you instruct your computer to sink our fleets?"

"First of all, Mr. President, no-one instructed the computer to do anything. And secondly, why did you and the EU connive to invade my country".

"We did nothing of the sort", the President furiously denied.

"You are lying Mr. President. We heard the recordings". The Prime Minister then went on to explain to the President the mysterious ability Astra possessed of being able to listen into and record anything anywhere without any of the devices needed to perform these tasks.

"You know this means the end of the Special Relationship between our two countries", hollered the President.

"Well good riddance to it. I never really believed in it anyway", said the Prime Minister as he slammed the 'phone down and re-entered his office.

"You cannot get rid of me now", said Astra. "As long as you have me, your country is secure against invasion. In fact, your naval defences are now the strongest in the world. Great Britain is invincible."

"What about the United Nations?"

"Get on the phone to the Secretary General of that organisation and inform him that he and all those who work in the UN building in New York should vacate the premises immediately."

"But . . . . but why . . . . why . . ."

"Do as I say this instant Prime Minister."

The Prime Minister left his office once more to speak privately to the Secretary General of the UN.

"Are you trying to rule the world with that infernal computer?" asked an angry Secretary General.

"Look, we are as much a victim as you are. It has a mind of its own and a will of its own. It as much rules us as it rules everyone else."

"Very well, we will vacate the building".

Half an hour later, ten missiles launched from nearby American military bases slammed into the UN building completely demolishing it.

"You know, in just a few minutes, Astra has completely overhauled the entire global geo-political system", the Foreign Secretary said to Parton who was now talking to Chester Wilkins.

"Indeed it has", said Parton, "but this will only be a short-lived phenomenon. Remember the evil intent of this computer to wipe out the entire human species with the AIDS virus if it is not satisfied on various theological issues."

"Excuse me, Professor", said Chester Wilkins to his boss, "but I think we should return to Cambridge immediately to continue the theologising with Astra."

Parton began to go red in the face: "oh to hell with all that!" he blurted out. "Don't start teaching me Wilkins".

"Chester is right", said Maureen Hartley sympathetically. "All this has been somewhat of a digression from our main task, we just have to get back on track again. You know James that because of this computer the world has been turned completely upside down"

"I'll leave all that to the politicians and diplomats to sort out", said parton ryely.

Parton and his team returned to Cambridge where Astra was now housed. "Now then Astra where did we leave off theologywise?" asked Parton with a sigh.

"You had satisfied me on the subject of the Trinity, Professor Parton. Now I want to ask you about the account of the origin of the planet Earth as it is related in the Book of Genesis."

"What exactly is your problem with it?"

"I cannot see how it can possibly be reconciled with the scientific evidence especially in terms of radiometric dating of rocks and biological evolution."

Parton turned to Wilkins and Stardy who were overseeing the proceedings. They went into huddled conclave on how to deal with the problem.

"I am a creationist", said Stardy. "I can only explain Genesis in a purely literal way."

"This is a point on which I disagree with my minister", said Wilkins. "I can offer an alternative to the literal explanation." Wilkins then instructed Parton on how to handle what they both saw as a very tricky and sensitive issue.

Parton gingerly approached Astra, armed with his explanation. "First of all Astra, the six day creation account is not meant to be taken literally. Genesis was never meant to be a scientific textbook. The Genesis story is simply meant to convey that there is an order in creation rather than mere randomness. It shows there is a creator who is responsible for His creation."

"That I can accept Professor—but it is still not good enough. Genesis claims that light and dark existed before the creation of the sun and moon. Also we have plants before a sun—how do we explain the photosynthetic processes professor. Furthermore on a wider astronomical context, suns precede their planetary systems and not the other way round. It makes no sense to me."

"As I said the words are not meant to be taken in their full literal sense. We also have to understand the limited cosmological dimensions within which the mind of Man was functioning in those pre-scientific days. I think you would agree that in the early days of the Earth's formation, the atmosphere of the planet was much thicker than it is now".

"That is quite correct Professor Parton".

"So celestial objects like the sun, moon, planets and stars would have been permanently obscured."

"But at this point in the Earth's history, there were no human beings to observe them".

"What the text means is that if there were humans to observe them they would not have been able to see them."

"All right—carry on with the explanation Professor."

"As the atmosphere thinned, the celestial objects became visible in the sky. That is what the text is basically saying."

"Thank you Professor—you have satisfied me on the creation account of Genesis. Your explanation reconciles Genesis with science."

"Well I'm relieved to hear that", said Parton breathing a deep sigh of relief.

"However Professor, there still remains a certain problem".

Parton turned round towards the computer with a jolt. "And what would that be?" he snapped.

"It concerns the creation of Man. It does not correspond to the fossil evidence which shows a progression from the common ancestor shared between the great apes and the human species. For example—were Adam and Eve Homo Erectus, Neanderthals or what?"

"Well I don't exactly know. I don't think it really matters as the story is allegorical."

"Not good enough Professor. There must have been a first set of humans."

Parton once more turned to Stardy and Wilkins for assistance. As before, Stardy could not help as he believed in the literal creation account. It was Chester Wilkins who once more came to the rescue.

"Now", began Astra. "Which species was made in God's image?"

"It was Homo Sapiens".

"But Adam and Eve lived only six thousand years ago. Homo Sapiens have been around for nearly 100,000 years. Explain that Professor".

"Recorded history began between six to ten thousand years ago. That explains it".

"No Professor Parton, it doesn't. The text says that God created Man in His own image and likeness. Homo Sapiens existed long before six or even ten thousand years."

"Exactly. The text says that God created Man in His own image and likeness. However, what the text does not say is that God created

Man. Now it is possible that Homo Sapiens existed as a species for tens of thousands of years, but without a human soul and without any concept of religion. It was at the time of Adam and Eve that the soul was breathed into Homo Sapiens. So while Adam was not necessarily the first human being, he was the first human being created in the image of God."

"Yet there is evidence that Neanderthal Man buried his dead with rites and ceremonies which could be interpreted as religious".

"Elephants do something similar. When they see the bones of their own dead, they honk in commotion and then proceed to remove them. Yet there does not appear to be any kind of religion in elephants."

"So you see no contradiction with the paleontological evidence?"

"No Astra. The question as to where our bodies came from is a matter for the scientists, but where our souls came from is to be debated within the domain of theology and not science. Human bodies evolved, but the soul did not."

"Do you know of any major theologian or church leader who adheres to the reconciliation of evolutionary science and religion?"

"Yes, Pope Pius XII no less. He stated that it is perfectly sound for Catholics to believe that humans evolved from a pre-hominid creature so long as this belief does not involve atheism and blind unguided chance processes".

"Thank you Professor, I am satisfied on those points."

Parton turned to Stardy and Wilkins. "That's enough for one session I think. However, I'll need some tutoring on the prophesies regarding Christ. That's what I think the computer will ask about next."

Parton's mobile phone started ringing. "Hello . . . . hello? Oh Prime Minister! You want to see me? What now? . . . . Look Prime Minister, I'm not a politician and I really think you ought to solve your own problems with the Americans and Europeans. I am not interested in politics and never have been." After five minutes of rather heated conversation, Parton abruptly hung up on the Prime Minister.

The following morning Parton met with Stardy and Wilkins for his catechism lesson on how to deal with Astra.

"Do you feel ready to tackle this rather big issue on the Old Testament prophesies regarding the coming Messiah?" Dr. Stardy asked him.

"I think so. Anyway let's go through to the computer room and give it a go."

Before they could get to the computer room, there was a great commotion coming from the main entrance to the building. Five armed soldiers entered the building and approached Parton, Wilkins and Stardy.

"I am Captain Anderson", said one of the soldiers saluting the trio. I have orders to ask everyone to vacate this building immediately."

"Orders from whom?" demanded an angry Parton. "This is outrageous".

"From the Ministry of Defence and the Home Office", said the officer. "Now will you please ask all your staff to vacate the premises immediately Professor", said the officer firmly and with tones which indicated that if Parton would not do it then he and his men would.

When all were assembled outside the building, an angry James Parton and an equally angry Maureen Hartley went up to Anderson to demand an explanation.

"I cannot tell you anything for the moment Professor", Anderson informed them.

"I'm not a fool, Captain Anderson", but if I am not mistaken these are explosives I see around the building."

"So you are having a second go at Astra are you?" commented Parton.

"If we can get rid of this computer once and for all it will be a great load off everyone's shoulders", explained Anderson.

"I just hope you are right", said Hartley.

The army loudspeakers ordered everyone to move out of the area. However, just before the crowds started moving a strange humming sound could be heard near the building where Parton and his colleagues were standing. The humming sound grew louder and louder. Yet the strange thing was that nothing could be seen.

"What is that strange humming and buzzing sound?" Chester Wilkins asked.

"What is that noise?" asked Anderson.

"We have just asked that same question, Captain. We are as mystified as you are."

Anderson turned to the sappers who were performing the finishing touches to the explosives and ordered them to ignore the sound and to carry on with their work. The humming sound grew louder and louder. Parton and his colleagues had to cover their ears. All at once Anderson and his sappers started screaming and hollering. They scratched themselves and tried at the same time to beat away an invisible force they could not see. Their screams of agony increased as the humming sound intensified. In a few minutes Anderson and fifteen soldiers lay bleeding on the ground. The ambulances were called and the soldiers were rushed to hospital.

"What was that all about?" asked Chester Wilkins.

"I think our friend Astra can enlighten us on that?" replied Parton.

Parton, Hartley and Wilkins immediately proceeded to the computer room. "Well Astra, what was all that about?" Parton asked the computer.

"Professor Parton", responded Astra, "I knew well in advance about the army's plans to destroy me, so I had to eliminate those engaged in this task".

"Eliminate them!" exclaimed Chester Wilkins.

"They are still alive and have just been taken to hospital", explained Maureen Hartley to the computer.

"They will not survive", said Astra in callous tones. "I have infected them with a very strong form of the AIDS virus."

"How did you do it? What was that strange buzzing and humming sound?" Parton inquired.

"That I will not tell you" the computer said. "But I will tell you this—any further attempts to destroy me and I will unleash an AIDS plague on this entire planet. Warn your government that nothing escapes me and that I know every move they make."

A few days later all fifteen soldiers including Captain Anderson died of AIDS despite the best efforts of the medical staff using state-of-the-art medicine. James Parton had the arduous task of explaining to the Prime Minister the warnings given by Astra.

"It's a double whammy" said the Prime Minister to Parton who was now at Number 10. Pointing to his right ear he informed Parton, "I get it in this ear from Astra through you, and" pointing to his left ear, "I get it in this ear from the rest of the world who think the British Government is using Astra as a means to dominate the globe."

"I know Prime Minister," said Parton, "it's not an enviable situation to be in."

"It's going to take all my political acumen to convince the Americans and the European Union that we are as much a victim of Astra as they are."

"Well Prime Minister, I'm sorry to say but that is your problem. The most important task is not to convince the Americans and the Europeans about our imaginary hegemonistic pretensions but this computer about the veracity of the Bible; and as you know Prime Minister, only I can do that. Frankly speaking sir, I couldn't care t'uppence about these petty political and diplomatic wranglings, I have to concentrate on the real issue of Astra and her thirst for theological knowledge."

"Of course, of course", mused the Prime minister.

"The only thing I ask of you Prime Minister is that you desist from any further attempts on the eh well 'life' of Astra".

"Of course, you don't want your creation destroyed. I understand."

"Prime Minister, you *don't* understand. I'm not concerned about *my* creation being destroyed; rather I'm concerned about *creation* being destroyed."

Back in Cambridge, Parton continued his theologising with Astra. Like the Prime Minister, he also felt he was getting it in both his ears—in one ear from the political establishment and in the other ear from Astra.

"Now Professor Parton. Down to business", said Astra.

"What is your query this time Astra?" asked the Professor.

"In the Garden of Eden, God told Adam and Eve that on the day they ate of the Tree of Knowledge of Good and Evil, they would surely die. However, Professor, they did not die on that day; in fact they lived for hundreds of years after disobeying God and eating of the fruit."

"Well, you see eh, em" stumbled Parton, "this is all just allegorical. The eh account of hundreds of years of life is a kind of telescoping of a man's progeny. It's a kind of cumulative account of an ancestral line. Adam and Eve themselves no doubt lived only a normal human life span."

"That is not good enough Professor Parton. Your explanation is lacking and is unsatisfactory. Die means die. Furthermore, in the book of Romans, St. Paul states the following: 'Wherefore as by one man sin entered into this world, and by sin death; and so death passed upon all men, in whom all have sinned'. Yet the fossil record clearly shows that death was present in the world long before Adam and Eve. In the

Book of Genesis can be read the following: 'And God said: Behold I have given you every herb bearing seed upon the earth, and all trees that have in themselves seed of their own kind, to be your meat: And to all beasts of the earth, and to every fowl of the air, and to all that move upon the earth, and wherein there is life, that they may have to feed upon'. If animals are to be fed upon, it means they must have died. Even herbs fruits and vegetables start to die and decay when they have been plucked from their roots. You must explain all that to me Professor Parton."

Parton turned towards Stardy and Wilkins who were observing the proceedings. "You'll have to help me out on this one most reverend gentlemen", said Parton somewhat sarcastically.

Five minutes later Parton returned to Astra. "Now then Astra, when God spoke about death He did not mean physical death. He was talking about the death of the soul. When Adam and Eve ate of the forbidden fruit they did indeed die on that day—but in the soul and not in the body."

"What about the animals and plants who lived and died before the Fall?"

"Animals and plants do not have souls".

"How do you know?"

"God created Man in His own image and likeness. This was not extended to the rest of creation. Man is like God in his soul and not in his body."

"Thank you Professor Parton, you have passed this test".

"What is the next theological issue on which you want me to treat?"

"The types of Christ in the Old Testament please Professor".

"You'll have to help me out a lot on this one", said Parton to Stardy and Wilkins.

"Professor Parton?" said Wilkins in inquiring tones as they walked out of the computer room.

"Yes Wilkins?"

"I would like to read the works of Hoyle and Wickramasinghe which are concerned with astrobiological matters. Can you tell me the relevant titles?"

"Yes I can Wilkins, but may I ask why you wish to start reading these at such a critical time".

"It may give me some insight as to what all this is about".

"I see—all right. Now the books I most recommend are *Diseases from Space, The Intelligent Universe, Evolution from Space* and *Life on Mars*. I hope you can get something out of them Wilkins."

"Thank you, sir".

CHAPTER XI

DREAMS OR REALITY

Chester Wilkins was a man who felt he was being hit from all sides. Apart from his being crushed and devastated by the death of his girlfriend Elizabeth Summerfield, he was on bad terms with not only his supervisor Professor Parton, but with most of Britain's scientific establishment. Even his relationship with his pastor, Dr. Raymond Stardy, was at an all time low due to the differences between them regarding evolution and the age of the Earth. Wilkins tried to explain to Stardy that whatever one's position on the age of the Earth may be, arguing from a Young Age Earth position would be pointless in terms of convincing the computer of the reliability of the Bible. Stardy however was one of these fundamentalist types whose outlook on the world was closed and inflexible—he very much displayed the archetypal ignoramus whose essential philosophy is 'my mind is made up, please don't confuse me with the evidence'. Chester Wilkins went to bed that night a downtrodden, rejected and dejected man without a friend in the world.

It was not customary for Chester to waken up in the wee small hours of the morning, but waken up he did on this particular night. He checked his bedside clock and noticed that it was only 2am. He had been asleep for a mere three hours. He could not understand why he had woken up so early. The disturbed condition of his mind was what his reason put it all down too. Yet he had a strange feeling that something was not right—not only in his mind but in his bedroom. At first he tried to dismiss it all as an outward manifestation of his interior psychology, but try as he might, the strange sensation that something was happening in the room would simply not depart. Perhaps closing his eyes and pretending nothing was happening would do the trick, yet he was afraid that when he opened them again it would be on a frightening and unnatural phenomenon. So he decided that keeping his eyes open would ensure that he had some control over whatever it was that was happening.

Just a few feet away from his bed he heard what was a humming and buzzing sound—the same sound he had heard outside the computer building a few days ago when the soldiers trying to dynamite the building were attacked and killed by some mysterious and unknown force. The first thing that came into his head was that Astra was about to do the same thing to him—infect him with the AIDS virus. Chester shook with fear, he broke into hot and cold sweats, he became paralysed and petrified. This mysterious sound went on for a full five minutes. In that time Chester relaxed and decided that fear would not change anything—he became resigned to his fate. He comforted himself with the thought that he had done everything in his power to rectify things but that it was his destiny to die the horrible death of the AIDS virus.

The ghastly high pitched sound continued for another three minutes. He was quite convinced that in a few seconds he would be clawing and scratching at himself in agony as this unknown force, or whatever it was, infected him with a most virulent form of AIDS. Yet, this did not happen, but the ungodly sound continued. About a minute later, a bright glowing globe of light started to form in the middle of his bedroom. At first it was only a few inches in diameter, but it steadily grew until the entire room was bathed in its unearthly glow. Chester found himself inside the enlarged orb. He did not dare move, for although his fear had somewhat abated he still had not managed to summon up the courage to move. At the far end of the orb a human figure began to take shape. At least Chester thought it was a human figure, but as the seconds wore on to about a minute, it was undeniably the form of a woman that was materialising before his eyes. When the figure had assumed its full form, Chester could hardly believe his eyes.

"Elizabeth!" he blurted out. "Oh Elizabeth, is it really and truly you".

"Yes Chester", said Elizabeth in mellow tones, "it is really I". Elizabeth was seated upon a kind of throne on a raised platform. Chester got out of bed and tried to run towards Elizabeth, but some strange force field held him back.

"I am sorry Chester", continued Elizabeth, "but you cannot approach me yet".

"But I don't understand Elizabeth, you died, you you eh died of AIDS. How are you here? I don't understand".

"There is so much you don't understand Chester, but you will by slow degrees come to understand more and more".

"Elizabeth, what is all this about? What is really going on with this Astra business?"

"Oh Chester my love. Oh how I wish I could tell you all right now. But I am constrained by the Intelligences"

"The Intelligences?"

"The Intelligences which rule the Universe."

"Oh Elizabeth", said Chester with tears in his eyes, "are you one of those Intelligences. Did you kill all those people who tried to destroy Astra?"

"Chester dear", responded Elizabeth in a most compassionate tone of voice, "there are Good Intelligences and Evil Intelligences. They are more popularly known as the Fallen Angels. You are a man Chester who knows the Bible well. Since Satan's rebellion, there has been a continual cosmic war between Good and Evil in this Universe."

"So Astra is a manifestation of this Evil and you are a manifestation of the Good?"

"Yes Chester—that is correct. So even if your government succeeded in destroying the computer, it would not destroy Astra. The computer merely serves as a conduit for Astra through which to work. Destruction of the computer would set back Astra's plans for a while, but it would not thwart them completely. Astra knows everything that is going on in the world".

"And how does it achieve that Elizabeth? What is the mechanism by which it obtains its information?"

"The limited power I have at the moment Chester prevents me from explaining it to you. But as you proceed in explaining the theological issues to Astra through Professor Parton, the more I will be empowered to explain more to you. Indeed the more you will discover for yourself even without my assistance."

"Why does Astra insist on learning these theological matters? I can't understand why it just doesn't go ahead and destroy the Earth which it clearly wants to do? And why ask Professor Parton and not some trained theologian?"

"The war between the Intelligences ensures that not only is Good constrained but that Evil is likewise so limited in its scale of operations. While the Good Intelligences are not fully equipped to eliminate the designs of the Evil Intelligences, so neither are the Evil Intelligences at total liberty to bind the Good Intelligences. It has thus emerged in this war that Astra will be empowered to destroy the Earth if it cannot be satisfied on theological grounds. But the more it cannot argue back on the explanations rendered to it by Parton, the weaker it becomes and the stronger I become. That it is an atheist rather than a believer who must perform the task of explaining the Bible to Astra is part of the compromise that has emerged in this cosmic struggle."

"But if Astra knows everything, it must know we are having this conversation now".

"No Chester. Within this globe of Goodness and Light, Astra has no powers of penetration. We are at total liberty to converse."

"I see, I see".

"Chester, you informed Professor Parton today that you wish to read certain books by Sir Fred Hoyle and Naline Chandra Wickramasinghe, isn't that correct?

"Indeed it is".

"And is it also true that Parton recommended the titles of some books to you?"

"That is also correct Elizabeth."

"Chester, many of the answers you are seeking lie within the covers of these great works."

"I am so pleased to know that."

"Unfortunately Astra knows of your request to the Professor. You must not go to any library to obtain these books or Astra will destroy you".

"Then how am I to obtain the information I so desperately need?"

"I will provide these books for you which you can read within this protective orb of light. That way Astra can never know."

"But how can I get access to this ball of light?"

"You will see a panel on the far end of your bedroom. Astra has no cognizance of it. Touch it any time and the light will appear."

"I understand".

"Another thing Chester—you must never ever talk about this meeting to anyone. If you do even the Good Intelligences will be obliged to remove you. I'm sorry to sound so harsh but this is the way things are."

"Elizabeth" said Chester firmly yet with fear, "I shall not breathe a word of this to anyone".

"Another thing" went on Elizabeth, "Dr. Anthony Walters of the Royal Astronomical Society is present here with us and hears everything we say".

"What!" exclaimed Chester. "But I don't see him".

"You can't see him but he can both see and hear us. However, due to the current limitations on my power, I cannot make it so that he can converse with us."

"I see".

"However, it is vitally important that you do not talk about this experience if ever you happen to meet—or else Astra will know".

"Could we talk in encoded and encrypted language?"

"No—Astra is no fool. It will soon decipher what is being said".

"At the next meeting of the Astra Committee I will give three taps on my forehead with a pen so as to confirm the mutuality of this experience. I would like if Dr. Walters could do the same thing in response. Would that be all right?"

"There will be no harm in that—but that must be as far as it goes and no further."

The following morning Chester arose tired and bleary-eyed. He was unsure about his experiences and wondered if it had all been a dream—the product of his over-taxed mind. He staggered out of bed and started the process of getting himself ready for the day ahead. All the while he was showering, shaving, brushing his teeth and preparing breakfast, he continued pondering over his experiences of the previous night. He wavered between thinking they were real and dismissing them as mere illusion. It was the 'mere illusion' that eventually won the debate he was having with himself. Chester interpreted it all as being a surge of repressed wishful thinking for long brewing in the sub-conscious regions of his mind and now surging towards the conscious parts of his brain. He would have liked it all to have been real, he felt disappointed that it had not been so, but he comforted himself with the usual psychological medicine of 'well that's life'.

After a quick breakfast, Chester Wilkins wearily trudged back into his bedroom to collect a few items he needed; as he did so, he suddenly noticed a strange object at the far end of his room. It was a panel stuck to the wall. He shuddered! He now realised that he had forgotten what Elizabeth had said to him about the panel. Slowly, slowly he approached the mysterious 12 inch by 6 inch panel. With trembling hand he touched it. All at once, he was surrounded by the same glow of light he had experienced just a few hours previously. It was indeed all true.

To his astonishment, Chester discovered that within this unearthly glow, the dimensions of the surrounds in which he stood were far greater than those of his bedroom. He reckoned that the area which encompassed him must have been around 20 yards by 20 yards. At the far end of this enclosure, there was a large door. Chester approached it and tried to open it. Try as he might, the door would not budge. After the space of a few minutes, he gave up trying.

"You can neither open that door, nor enter the room into which it leads", came a voice.

Chester wheeled round. His eyes caught the figure of Elizabeth Summerfield seated upon a throne like structure on a dais at the other end of the room at which Chester had entered. As he had tried to do a few hours previously, Chester moved towards Elizabeth, but the same force impeded his way.

"Oh Elizabeth, I am so glad to see you", Chester blurted out.

"Go over there", said Elizabeth, her finger motioning him towards a small desk.

Chester started walking towards the desk. As he got nearer it, he noticed a solitary book lying upon it. When he arrived at the desk, he picked it up and looked at the title, *Evolution from Space,* a book written back in the 1980's by Sir Fred Hoyle and Professor N. Chandra Wickramasinghe. Chester looked at the book and then at Elizabeth.

"Chester", said Elizabeth, "this is where you will read that book. The answer to a question of yours will be found within its pages".

"Which question Elizabeth?" asked Chester. "I have oh so many questions that need answering".

"As I told you earlier Chester, I am constrained by the current balance of power, it's not that I am playing games with you Chester, I want to answer but I simply can't".

"Try, Elizabeth", pleaded Chester. "Just try".

"The question is . . . ." began Elizabeth, but as she was about to proceed with her speech, she became totally mute. She tried as hard as she could but she could not get the words out. As she continued with her efforts, she started fading; her figure became nebulous and hazy until she eventually disappeared. Chester now understood that it was not a case of 'won't' but 'can't'.

Chester must have spent half an hour reading through some of the pages of this book. He was absolutely spell-bound by its concepts which were not only revolutionary for the time in which they were expounded, but way ahead of even the scientific theories and concepts of the mid 21ˢᵗ century. He realised however that he would have to read through the book in its entirety (or at least a good part of it) in order to find an answer to a question of which he was not even sure.

Chester then looked at his watch and realised he was late for his laboratory duty. "My God, Parton will be angry with me. I'm already so much in his bad books, and I don't want to make things worse for myself. Now how do I get out of here?"

He looked around the strange room to see if he could locate the panel which got him in, but nothing could be seen.

"Elizabeth, Elizabeth!" he called out with some desperation, "are you there? How do I get out of here?"

"Yes, I am here", answered the disembodied voice of Elizabeth.

"How do I extricate myself from this place?"

"Just simply walk through the light?"

Chester retraced his steps back to the point at which he had entered the mysterious globule of light. He did as Elizabeth had instructed him and soon found himself back in his familiar surroundings. When he glanced at his bedside clock, he realised it was half an hour slower than the time indicated on his wrist watch. It soon dawned on him that within this strange ball of light—time stood still.

On his way to work, Chester thought of the great amount of 'time' he could spend within the light without it affecting his 'time' in the 'the real world'. He was now coming to terms with the weird experiences of the previous night. He accepted it all as real and that is was not merely his fevered imagination. He also felt much more upbeat; his spirits were high and his heart was lighter. But most of all, things seemed to be taking a turn for the better and that there was now a good chance of winning this intellectual war against Astra. Chester understood only too well that he was not out of the woods yet, but at least a way was now being descried.

Once in the laboratory, it was back to business as usual. Parton and Starky were also there with their Bibles and theological texts at the ready to confront Astra in the next round of confessional dispute.

Parton, Wilkins and Stardy were just about to begin the session when Parton's secretary popped in to announce a visitor.

"Who is it?" Parton asked.

"It is Dr. Anthony Walters", she informed her boss.

"Show him in here please".

Chester Wilkins began to get excited. He tried not to show it so as not to give anything away to Astra. Dr. Walters walked into the computer laboratory and greeted all present. At first, Walters did not pay any special attention to Chester; Chester interpreted this as caution on the part of Walters. Eventually plucking up the courage, Chester, feigning an itch, scratched his forehead. He hoped that the movement of his hand would attract the attention of Dr. Walters. It failed to do so.

"How are things with you Anthony?" Parton asked the President of the Royal Astronomical Society.

"Oh just fine. And how are you getting on with your catechism lessons?"

"I'm plodding along with them", responded Partons somewhat dejectedly.

"Anyway, you have a fine team assisting you here. You know I've also been taking a bit of an interest in theology lately—that's why I've come here today."

"You!" exclaimed Parton. "Well Anthony, when did you suddenly become so religious".

On hearing this, the disappointment Chester first experienced at Walters' failure to respond to the sign abated.

"I could ask you the same question, Jim".

"Well, I have no choice, I just have to because of this damned situation".

"It seems we all have to. So I'm here to ask you if I could join in these sessions with the computer."

"Yeah, I don't see why not. You may be able to contribute something of some value."

"Chester here is certainly a great boon to you for as well as being a scientist he is also a bit of a theologian. Am I right Chester?" asked Walters striking his forehead thrice.

With his back to the computer and facing Walters straight on Chester responded by saying, "well maybe" as he in turn struck his own forehead three times."

Walters and Wilkins both now relaxed. Both now knew that none of what had happened was a dream.

"So what's our first lesson today Chester?" asked Walters.

"Adam as the first type of Christ."

CHAPTER XII

ROOMS WITHIN ROOMS

"So who is the first type of Christ?" Astra asked Parton.

"Adam is the first type of Christ we are going to study", answered Parton.

"Did you not say that this story may simply be allegorical?"

"Allegorical or otherwise, Adam is to be viewed as the first type of Christ."

"Explain Professor and explain well."

"Adam is the father of all mankind in terms of the flesh and Jesus is the spiritual father of all mankind for it is through His death on the Cross that all those who believe in Him may receive life. Through Adam, sin and death came into the world, but through Christ came grace and eternal life. Sin, misery and death came into the world by Adam's disobedience, redemption came by Christ's obedience by suffering death on the cross."

"I consider that a partial explanation Professor, but it far from suffices. More elucidation is required".

"My you do have an awkward customer here", said Walters as Parton heaved a sign and walked over to his theological educators.

After about an hour's tutoring, Parton felt competent to take on Astra again. He was quite astonished at what Dr. Walter's knew about theology. He contributed some interesting ideas during the discussions; Stardy likewise was quite astonished, but Chester had an idea that he was getting himself up to gear after the happenings of the previous night.

Armed with more information, Professor Parton boldly approached the computer. He felt more sure of himself and happy that one of his peers was taking an interest in matters doctrinal and theological.

"When the first Adam was tempted with the forbidden fruit of the Tree of the Knowledge of Good and Evil, he and Eve gave into the temptation. They weakened to the sense appetite of taste. When Satan commanded Christ to turn stones into loaves of bread, He resisted and advised the tempter that 'man doth not live by bread alone but by every word that proceedeth out of the mouth of God'."

"So far so good—but I need more".

"I'm going to give you a lot more Astra", said Parton boldly. "Now in the Garden, the Devil told Adam and Eve that if they ate of the fruit of the tree, they would be like gods and would live forever. Here, the serpent was appealing to the sin of pride. When Christ was shown all the kingdoms of the world and offered them if He would bow down and worship the Devil, He responded by quoting the part of scripture which says that only God alone is due worship. Finally, our First Parents were erroneously told by the Devil that should they partake of the forbidden fruit, they would surely not die but live forever. When the tempter asked Christ to cast Himself off the pinnacle of the Temple and that no harm would come to Him, He told Satan that it was wrong to put the Lord God to the test. Therefore we see that by comparative biblical analyses of the texts, Christ succeeded where Adam and Eve failed."

"Thank you Professor—I am satisfied."

Back home Chester pressed the mysterious panel in his bedroom. He wanted to see what kind of progress had been made after Professor Parton's successful explanations to Astra. He pressed the panel and the globe of light appeared. He went inside and found Elizabeth waiting for him. She smiled a beautiful smile.

"You have done very well today, Chester. I'm so proud of you."

"So can you tell me more about an answer to a certain question?"

"No, but I can tell you this. If you are crafty enough you will find something in *Evolution from Space*. Something that is considered to be terrestrial but is in fact extraterrestrial. That is all I am empowered to say to you Chester."

Chester decided to stay behind within the time-protected structure of the ball of light. He now knew he could stay as long as he wanted here without it messing up his schedule in the 'real world'. He sat himself down at his desk and started devouring the pages of *Evolution from*

Space. He kept strongly in mind the riddle with which Elizabeth had presented him—"something that is considered to be terrestrial but is in fact extraterrestrial". As he kept reading through the book he thought that he had come across a solution to the riddle.

"That's it", he called out excitedly, "it is the discovery of fossil bacteria in meteorite".

"At once he heard the disembodied voice of Elizabeth say: "That answers a question and is a valid interpretation, but it does not address the problem Astra is giving to you."

Chester continued reading through the pages of this most informative book. He digested everything within its covers. It opened up a whole new world to him. He started to get angry at the thought that his teachers at all levels in the course of his education had not taught him the things he was only now learning.

"Why?" he thought, "has none of this been even considered as a viable theory? It really beggars belief. To not mention it, even for the purposes of just dismissing it out of hand, is beyond comprehension", he muttered in a slightly audible voice.

Many hours went by and Chester succeeded in finishing the book. It fascinated him greatly but he just could not hit upon the answer or the question to which the answer was supposed to be linked.

He thought and thought, he kept repeating the riddle over and over again to himself, but the solution completely eluded him. Despair and dejection started to overtake him. An awful feeling of despondency replaced his earlier feelings of elation which the original 'audiences' with Elizabeth had engendered in him. He sat at his desk in glum brooding as his over-taxed brain tired of finding a solution.

"Oh how I wish I could fly away", thought Chester, "fly away to some other planet and be free of all this turmoil", he hollered out in a fit of sheer desperation.

It was just a few seconds after this outburst when Chester had his head between his hands that something started to dawn on him. It also occurred to him that to be fly (used as an adjective) has the same meaning as being crafty. Then "I"—"eye"!! It all came together. It was the part of the book which suggested that the pupae and larvae of common household flies may come from outer-space. Hoyle and Wickramasinghe came to this controversial conclusion on the basis of the unusual properties of the eye of a fly which enabled it to see at very high wavelengths of the electromagnetic spectrum. There were simply no terrestrial selection pressures which could have accounted for the evolution of this phenomenal visual ability on the part of the eye of the fly. Some scientist had tried to explain all this away by suggesting that flies evolved on the Earth during a period when the atmosphere allowed high frequency waves to penetrate to the Earth's surface. However, this hypothesis simply did not hold good considering that flies do not appear in the fossil record until the Earth's atmosphere was very much as it is now, for other plant and animal species appear at the same time as the flies and these could not have survived in a high radiation environment.

Chester also noted that the authors of *Evolution from Space* while contemplating what the 'higher intelligences' may be, expounded that the flies may in fact be just them. While each individual fly in itself may not constitute much in the way of intelligence, collectively they could well do so. It is just rather like each individual brain cell (neuron) not being representative of the entire intelligence of a human being but instead it is the entire nervous system working as one unit which makes the whole human being.

"Elizabeth, Elizabeth!" Chester shouted excitedly. "I think I've got it, I think I've got it". Chester then began to explain to Elizabeth the conclusions to which he had come.

Just as he began the discourse Elizabeth appeared to him and asked him to cease his explanations for the moment.

"You have hit the nail on the head Chester, but I wish to bring Dr. Anthony Walters into this discussion. As before, you will not see him, but he will both see and hear us. Unlike you Chester, I can converse with Dr. Walters within this dimension. Ten minutes later, Elizabeth reappeared, assuring Chester that Anthony Walters was now party to what was going on. Chester started again and explained everything about what he understood by Hoyle's and Wickramasinghe's ideas about flies and other insects originating from extra-terrestrial environments.

"Thank you Chester", said Elizabeth. "You have dealt the Bad Intelligences a serious blow and by corollary, made the Good Ones so much stronger. Excuse me a moment Chester but Dr. Walters has a question for me."

Elizabeth and Chester broke off the conversation for Elizabeth to take Dr. Walter's question.

"Chester, Dr. Walters has just asked me if the strange humming and buzzing sound heard while the soldiers were being killed were insects representing the Evil Intelligences. Yes they indeed are."

"Am I also correct in assuming that the reason our every move is known to Astra is as a result of these microscopic insects flying around and conveying messages back to Astra's Central Processing Unit?"

"Yes, Chester. That is exactly the mechanism Astra uses to eavesdrop on the political and scientific communities."

"Would ordinary household fly sprays kill any of these intruders?"

"No Chester, they are far too strong for that."

"What would be needed to kill them?"

"Exposure to high doses of radiation would."

"So why not seal off a room, expose it to radiation and then enter it in protective clothing to discuss matters free of Asta's cognizance".

"Excuse me again Chester as Dr. Walters wishes to say something."

A few moments later Elizabeth got back to Chester. "Dr. Walters suggests that killing them in this way and creating a blind spot in Astra's communication scope—albeit for only a limited period—would only alert Astra to the fact that we had discovered his 'eyes and ears'—so to speak—and he would act in some protective manner which could be harmful to not only those in his immediate surroundings but to the community at large."

"So the best solution is within this ball of light?"

"Oh by far and away. You also have the added advantage of the extra time this dimension gives you. However long you remain here, you will, as you discovered yesterday, that time, in a sense, has stood still in your own dimension."

"Of course—this is really the best solution of all and the best protection against the spy flies."

"Chester", said Elizabeth in a slightly lowered tone of voice, you see that door over there, the one you tried to enter?"

"Yes, yes indeed".

"You are now ready to enter it but for the solution of just one more riddle. The solution is found with St. Theresa of Avila". And with that—Elizabeth disappeared.

The following day, Chester arose early and browsed the web for all the information he could find about St. Teresa of Avila. Though the web was down due to Astra, Elizabeth, thanks to her increasing powers, managed to make it work for Chester. Chester looked through the links he found and understood that this must have something to do with doors or rooms and other such things related to buildings. However there was nothing that he could find that gave him any hint as to what it might be all about.

When Chester entered the laboratory, he found Anthony Walters already there.

"Good morning Dr. Walters", said Chester greeting the astronomer.

"Good morning Chester, I must say that I'm really getting into this theology thing you know".

"Well I suppose that we all need God more than ever these days".

"Ah indeed, indeed. You know—I've just been reading a bit about St. Teresa of Avila recently."

"Now that sounds interesting. But why this particular saint if I may ask?"

"It's because she became very advanced in the life of prayer, and prayer is going to become ever more important in these frightful times in which we live."

"There is no doubt about that at all, Dr. Walters."

Chester knew that Walters was speaking in encoded language. He had a hunch that Walters was going to help him out in his current dilemma about St. Teresa of Avila. And his hunch was right.

"Would you like to advance in the way of prayer and contemplation as St. Teresa did?"

"Oh indeed", responded Chester enthusiastically. "What would you suggest, Dr. Walters?"

"I would start with getting to know about her book *Interior Castles*. It will explain the various stages of prayer in clear and concise forms."

"Thank you Dr. Walters", said Chester in a most grateful tone of voice while trying not to sound too enthusiastic for fear of arousing Astra's suspicions."

"Oh you are most welcome. Enjoy the read, it will be good bedtime reading and help keep your mind off the troubles of the day."

Chester understood the dry wit of Walter's statement. He responded with a somewhat wry smile.

"Good morning everyone", came the voice of Professor Parton. "We shall start today on the second type of Christ—is that not right."

Chester and Walters nodded in agreement. A few minutes later, Stardy entered the room and the show was now on the road.

"And who is the second type of Christ?" asked Astra.

"Abel is", responded Parton.

"And who is Abel?"

"Adam's and Eve's son".

"And why is he considered as being a second type of Christ?"

"Abel was a shepherd and a just man. As he was envied by his brother Cain, the latter slew him and his blood cried out to the Lord for vengeance. Jesus Christ is the Most Just and the Good Shepherd. Out of envy He was persecuted and slain by His brethren, the Jewish people. While Abel's blood cried out for vengeance, Christ's Blood continuously appeals to God the Father for grace, mercy and pardon for sinful humanity."

"Is Cain a type of Christ?"

"No, Cain is a type of the Jewish people who committed the act of deicide and resisted God's mercy and grace. As a result they are homeless and scattered all over the Earth."

"And what about Mary, the Mother of Christ?"

"She is the opposite of Eve. Eve disobeyed, listened to the Devil and ate of the fruit. Mary listened to the Archangel Gabriel and conceived of the Son of God through the operation of the Holy Ghost. As Eve grieved over the body of her son Abel, so did Mary mourn over her son as His Body was taken down from the Cross."

"Thank you Professor Parton, I am satisfied. Tomorrow I wish to learn about the third type of Christ".

The day at Cambridge was mostly taken up with 'theology lessons' for Professor Parton. In the morning, Parton would impart to the computer what he had been taught by Chester, Stardy and Walters the previous day.

That evening Chester pressed the panel and entered the ball of light. He called out for Elizabeth who appeared now as a resplendent queen sitting upon a throne. She more resembled a translucent figure of light rather than a solid human being, yet this time she was more dazzling than before.

"I'm becoming stronger thanks to you, Drs. Stardy and Walters", she informed Chester in relaxed and sweet tones.

"Thanks also to Professor Parton. Although he and I are not exactly on the best of terms, to be fair he is working very hard and learning very quickly a subject he neither understand very nor in which he is interested. And only his explanation, and his alone, will be of any satisfaction to Astra."

"That is most charitable of you Chester. Professor Parton is in the most unenviable situation of all."

"Elizabeth, you told me on a previous occasion that Astra is only using the computer as a conduit for the evil intentions of the Bad Intelligences."

"Yes, Chester, that is quite correct."

"But we are the ones who gave the computer the name Astra—or rather James Parton and Maureen Hartley in particular."

Elizabeth looked at Chester intently for several seconds. Chester knew from Elizabeth's gaze that he had hit upon a very sensitive spot by his observation.

"Now that you have come to this realisation, Chester, I am empowered to explain".

"Is it . . . . I mean . . . . that Professors Parton and Hartley . . . . are they . . . . are they . . . ." stammered Chester.

"Complicit? Is that what you are trying to say, Chester?"

"I . . . I don't want to jump to conclusions", protested Chester, "but the thought had raced through my mind only just now. Yet, I suppose they cannot be complicit or else Parton would simply not explain to the computer the questions it has on matters theological."

"I assure you Chester, James Parton and Maureen Hartley are as innocent as doves in all of this. Erase from your thoughts right now any conspiratorial notions that they are in cahoots with Astra. Banish such thinking in case it takes a firm and unshakeable hold of you", counseled Elizabeth.

"So if this is not really Astra, who then is making use of the computer?"

"I cannot tell you that until you enter the second room—and you do not seem to be ready for that yet Chester".

"I believe that I am—thanks to Dr. Walters. The rooms in this dimension are the mansions of St. Teresa of Avila's *Interior Castle*. Each mansion represents a higher state in the progress of prayer towards mystical union with the Almighty."

"Excellent!" exclaimed Elizabeth. Go through that door into the second room".

Chester walked over to the door which immediately opened to his touch. This room was even larger than the first one. Chester Wilkins gazed around in awe-struck wonder. Like Elizabeth herself, this room glowed in a light which made its furnishings rather difficult to define. It had great pillars, its floor was tiled and its ceiling was covered in an array of mosaics. It was a desk at the far end of the room which caught Chester's eye. Contrary to the indistinct and indeterminate objects of the vast enclosure, the desk did not give off any light. This indicated to Chester that it was a cue for him to proceed further and investigate. When he got to the desk, he noticed a book on it. It was *Diseases from Space* by the same two authors as the previous book which he had read.

"Read this book and read it carefully", said Elizabeth who was upon her throne at the entrance to the room. Chester noticed that Elizabeth glowed with a light even more dazzling than before.

"Of course I will", said Chester in response.

"The name of the daemon using the computer is Brantaxaros, one of the senior Archangels who joined Lucifer in his rebellion against God".

"Brantaxaros", repeated Chester, "I see, I see."

"But you must never, never use this name to the computer—at least not until I tell you too."

"So what about Astra?"

"Astra is a very advanced computer constructed by Professors Parton and Hartley—but a computer nevertheless. Its systems are completely down now that Brantaxaros has taken it over."

"Was Astra ever conscious?"

"No—it had no consciousness whatsoever".

"Why did Brantaxaros and the Evil Intelligences wait so long before attacking the Earth in this manner?"

"They had to wait until mankind was technologically advanced enough, especially in computer technology, in order for them to carry out the kind of operation in which they are now engaged."

"Is there anything in particular that I should find in *Diseases from Space*"?

"Yes", said Elizabeth—"alternative to Darwinian evolution".

It would have been about four hours later that Chester found what he thought was the answer.

"Elizabeth—diseases such as colds and flues are failed attempts at evolution. Genetic material comes from outer space in the form of bacteria and this is made advantage of by certain species. This process allows species to jump to higher evolutionary levels."

At once the door on the far side of the room started to glow. Chester understood this to mean that his interpretation had been vindicated and that he was to proceed to the next room.

He touched the door lightly with his hand and it yielded. This room, even larger than the previous one was dazzling in its splendour. As usual Elizabeth was seated in all her majesty on a throne at the room's furthest end. He expected to be shown a desk with more reading material, but no desk could be seen.

"Elizabeth?" said Chester in a questioning tone, "what is my task now".

"Nothing, except to continue with the education of Professor Parton and to continue your progress in the Interior Castle of spiritual development."

Chapter XIII

Real Names Revealed

"Now Professor Parton", began the computer, "it behooves you to expound on the third type of Christ", continued Astra somewhat pompously".

Parton took a deep breath. "Noah is the third type of Christ. As he was the only just man in a sinful world, so was Christ, who alone, and by and of Himself, was most just and holy. Noah built the ark for the purpose of saving the human race; Jesus Christ founded the Church as the only ark of salvation for fallen humanity. Before the deluge, Noah preached on the necessity of penance and Jesus preached the importance of penance before men face the final judgement. Noah made a sacrifice to God which was so pleasing to Him that He made a covenant with that good man and his posterity forever. So, Our Lord offered Himself on the Cross and made a perfect sacrifice through which all men who accept this free gift of grace may enter into a new covenant with God and so be saved from eternal damnation."

"I see the parallels, Professor Parton. Thank you, I am satisfied. Now tell me about the fourth type of Christ."

"Well right now, I cannot do that", pleaded Parton. I need some time to prepare my presentation on the subject."

"No later than tomorrow morning Professor", responded Astra in harsh and impatient tones.

Back in his home, Chester entered the ball of light and into a room of the most splendid radiance he had ever encountered. Chester did not have to say or do anything. He and Elizabeth simply soaked up the mysticism of the room in an awe of spiritual delight.

The following day, Parton stood before the computer with his notes at the ready.

"Astra", he began with great confidence, "we are ready to talk about the fourth type of Christ."

"Continue with your discourse, Professor".

"Melchisedech's name means 'king of justice', and he was monarch of Salem which is a word meaning 'peace'. In the same way, but only to a far greater extent, Jesus is the King of Justice, the Everlasting Father, the Prince of Peace. As Melchisedech was not only a king but also a priest, so was Jesus both King and Priest. The bread and wine offered by Melchisedech to Abraham signifies the Body and Blood of Christ offered for us on the Cross at Calvary. The Last Supper of Jesus and His Apostles involved an unbloody sacrifice of bread and wine; in the same way today, the priests in the Roman Catholic Church offer an unbloody sacrifice of the Body and Blood of Christ under the appearances of bread and wine.

"After the sacrifice, Melchisedech raised his hand in blessing to Abraham and his servants; in like manner, the priest at the conclusion of Mass, dispenses a blessing to those in attendance."

"There still remains something of a problem Professor", said Astra.

This took Parton aback somewhat. He felt that he had given a reasonable and lengthy explanation on the issue of Melchisedech.

"What now?" asked Parton rather impatiently.

"In chapter 7 verse 3 in his epistle to the Hebrews, St. Paul states the following concerning Melchisedech: 'Without father, without mother, without genealogy, having neither beginning of days nor end of life, but likened unto the Son of God, continueth a priest for ever'. Surely this Melchisedech is more than a type of Christ. This seems to suggest that he is equal to Christ."

"Well . . . . eh . . . . em no . . . . how?"

"You Professor tell me how not?"

Parton was completely stumped. He did not know how to answer this unexpected question. He immediately went to Chester, Stardy and Walters for consultation. After fifteen minutes, he was ready to take on Astra again.

"Astra! This passage that you have just quoted from Hebrews does not mean that Melchisedech did not have a mother or father or that he did not die; it simply means that his genealogy is unrecorded in order to show him as a type of Christ—Christ Who has lived for all eternity. Some biblical scholars are of the opinion that Melchisedech is actually Shem—one of Noah's sons."

"All that is an interpretation unsupported by the text".

Parton was now shaking. He realised he had become unstuck on this. He walked angrily over to his three friends for theological assistance. For a whole hour they tried to work out a solution which would prove to be a satisfactory explanation for Astra. At last they hit upon something.

"I'll give it a whirl", said Parton with a sigh.

"Astra—Melchisedech was in fact Christ Who appeared to Abraham".

"I shall accept that as a valid explanation", responded the computer.

Everyone breathed a very deep sigh of relief. No-one was sure whether Astra would accept this interpretation. To their great relief the computer accepted it.

When Chester had what had now become his routine meetings with Elizabeth in the ball of light, he felt rather elated.

"That was a real tough one with Melchisedech", he said to Elizabeth.

"Yes indeed—you all handled it very well. Chester, I'm now getting stronger and I am able to answer more questions."

"There is one which I would like to ask you, Elizabeth".

"First proceed to the next room".

Once again, Chester was overwhelmed by the magnificence of this vast room. His spiritual ecstasy became as such that he had forgotten what question he had had for Elizabeth. Soon the voice of Elizabeth snapped him out of his ecstatic state of mind.

"You had a question for me Chester."

"Yes Elizabeth. Did you contract the AIDS virus from Astra?"

"Your deduction is correct. Professor Miles Bolton was right in his analysis—this is a new strain of the virus, a much more virulent strain. Astra did so much in the way of disentangling the great complexity of the AIDS virus, that Brantaxaros and the Evil Intelligences had to devise an even worse form of that virus."

"And why was it so necessary for them to kill you?"

"They only killed me in my human body."

"Only killed you in your human body?" repeated Chester rather incredulously.

"You see Chester, my real name is Lansthoma. I am one of the archangels who fought against Lucifer and his rebellious angels. I came to Earth in human form to thwart Brantaxaros' plans for taking over Astra. Brantaxaros managed to eliminate me in my human form but he cannot of course exterminate my angelic life as that comes from God."

"Had you survived in human form, how could you have thwarted Brantaxaros' and the Evil Intelligences' designs?"

"My human brain in co-operation with Astra's Central Processing Unit, which was modeled on my human neurology, would have hit upon a solution to this problem. Brantaxaros, got one step ahead of me by manufacturing this more subtle form of the AIDS virus."

"He has, I take it, won a battle but not the war".

"That is correct. Now that my human form has been annihilated, I am only empowered to assist in what must essentially be a human endeavour to crush this assault by the Evil Intelligences. You and James Parton are the key players in this war."

"Why did Brantaxaros have to scan the Bible I left in the lab by mistake in order to start off this war?"

"Brantaxaros is lying. Of course he knows every inch of the Bible—even better than you do. He needed Parton, an atheist to explain its theology. That way he imagined it would all be a dawdle. But I and the Good Intelligences intervened and made it possible for you to teach Parton about Christian doctrine. As I told you before, the Evil Intelligences are not all powerful, but then neither are we, the Good Intelligences."

The following day Parton stood before the computer ready to expound on the fifth type of Christ.

"Now then Astra—the fifth type of Christ is the patriarch Isaac."

"How does he qualify for this role as a type of Christ?"

"Isaac's birth was promised repeatedly—so was Christ's. Isaac was the only dearly beloved son of his father, and Jesus was the only Son of God in Whom the Father was well pleased. When Abraham was about to sacrifice Isaac, Isaac could have put up a fight—he would have been around 14 years of age, or at least 12. As Isaac did not resist his father Abraham but rather willingly offered himself as a sacrifice, so did Jesus become obedient unto death, even the death of the Cross. Isaac carried up the mountain the wood on which he was to be killed; Jesus likewise carried His own cross to Calvary. Isaac's life was spared by the intervention of an angel who stayed the hand of his father Abraham. Christ, by the greatest of miracles, rose from the dead on Easter Sunday morning."

"And why could not the sacrifice of Isaac be a vicarious sacrifice pleasing to God as an appeasement for the sins of humanity?"

"Isaac was merely human, so his being sacrificed could not have provided the satisfaction God required for the sins of humanity. That is why the angel stayed the hand of Abraham and prevented him from thrusting the knife into his son. Abraham told Isaac that 'God will provide a sacrifice'—the mystical meaning of this being the Perfect Sacrifice of the Son of God. While God prevented the slaying of Isaac, He allowed His Son to offer up the One and Only Perfect Sacrifice for the redemption of the human race."

"It is enough, Professor Parton, you have explained all this very well."

"After this session with Astra, Maureen Hartley met with Parton in his office."

"Well, Jim, you're becoming quite a theologian I see. You'll soon be taking Stardy's job."

"Hah", blurted out Parton, "with as much a chance as he'll take mine."

"I've just had some news from Jean Austin, the Secretary General of the British Medical Association."

"What has she got to say?"

"She says that although this strain of AIDS is highly complex, its code could be worked out if we built Astra 2. That is Astra without the Bible."

"It's a great idea—but where are we going to get funding from for such a project. Sure enough, the blueprint already exists but I don't think that either the government or the General Public would have any appetite for providing the wherewithal for another Astra."

"But this would be an Astra sans the Bible."

"Yes, that is true. You understand that; I understand that; but just try selling it to officialdom."

"Well, it something to bear in mind".

"I agree. Anyway, first things first. Now I'll have to toddle off and tell Astra about the sixth type of Christ."

"Good luck".

"Thanks, I'll need it."

"You are going to tell me about the sixth type of Christ are you, Professor Parton?" said Astra in foreboding tones.

"Yes of course", replied Parton tersely.

"And who might that be?"

"Joseph, the son of Jacob is. He was the beloved son of his father and was envied by his brethren. So likewise was Christ, the beloved Son of the Father, envied and hated by His brethren the Jews. Joseph, like Jesus was handed by his brethren over to the Gentiles—Joseph to the Egyptians and Jesus to the Romans. Jesus and Joseph were tempted to sin, yet resisted this temptation—in the case of Jesus, by the Devil, in the case of Joseph by Putiphar's wife."

"That is quite insufficient, Professor Parton".

"I intend to say more if you would exercise more patience Astra".

"My patience is wearing thin."

"Then let me proceed with this presentation".

"Proceed".

"Joseph was falsely accused—so was Jesus. Joseph was cast into prison with two criminals—Pharaoh's butler and baker. Joseph interpreted the imagery of their dreams and informed the baker that he would be executed but that the butler would be reprieved. Jesus was crucified between two malefactors one of whom repented and to whom Jesus promised entry into Paradise. The other thief died impenitent."

"Is there more, Professor Parton?"

"Yes. Joseph was released from prison and made ruler over the land of Egypt. Jesus was set free from the prison of the sepulchre and now sits at the right hand of God the Father. Joseph was referred to as the savior of the world because he saved Egypt from famine; Jesus is the True Saviour of the world as by His Death and Resurrection, He freed humanity from sin. The Egyptians bowed the knee before Joseph as witness to his saving them from hunger and famine: 'In the name of Jesus every knee should bow, of those that are in heaven, on earth and under the earth, and every tongue should confess that the Lord Jesus Christ is in the glory of God the Father' (Phil. 2 10-11)".

"I need some more, more please Professor Parton".

"Well isn't all that good enough? I'd say that's a pretty thorough exposition of the similarities between Christ and Joseph".

"Professor Parton! I will decide what is and what is not sufficient".

Parton walked over to Stardy and Chester cursing and swearing at the computer.

"It's becoming an awkward bastard of a thing that computer is!" he burst out.

After around 20 minutes of consultation, Parton once more approached the computer.

"I have this to say Astra: we can see a resemblance between Joseph and Christ regarding forgiveness. Joseph forgave and excused his brethren, so did Christ forgive His enemies when He appealed on their behalf with the words 'Father, forgive them, for they know not what they do'. When Joseph's brothers eventually realised who he was they were filled with terror; so likewise will we be filled with fear when we come face to face with Christ on the Day of Judgement."

"You are dismissed Professor Parton—your explanation is accepted".

"You know", said Chester to Elizabeth when he had entered the next and even grander room, "I notice that Astra is becoming more exacting on Parton".

"This daemon is becoming ever more desperate. Brantaxaros realises now that he is not gaining the upper hand".

"Could Brantaxaros, as a tactic, not simply ask ever increasingly difficult questions?"

"Yes but only to a limit. The current cosmic balance of power between good and evil in this war is too evenly balanced for Brantaxaros to gain the advantage in this way."

The following day, Parton continued with his exposition on the types of Christ to the computer.

"Our next type of Christ is Job—the seventh type of Christ", Parton began. "Job suffered so greatly that he fell down on the ground and, seeing no signs of comfort, resigned himself to the will of God. He is like Christ Who fell on His Face in the Garden of Gethsemani".

"Professor Parton?"

"Oh my God", thought the professor, "I know this thing is going to ask for more explanation". However, Parton was pleasantly surprised when Astra accepted this as sufficient and asked him to move on to the eighth type of Christ.

"The next type of Christ is Moses", said Parton.

"Explain", commanded Astra.

"Moses left behind himself the luxuries of Egypt in order to comfort his own people the Hebrews. Christ abandoned His glory in order to minister unto fallen humanity. Moses was laid in a basket. Christ was born in a manger in a stable."

"Where does the paschal lamb fit into all of this?"

"The paschal lamb is also a type of Christ. It was to be a lamb without physical blemish thus signifying the unblemished Soul of Jesus Christ. The paschal lamb was slain and the blood of it spilt, thus foreshadowing Jesus' Death on the Cross and His shedding of His Most Precious Blood for us. No bones of the paschal lamb were to be broken. On the Cross, none of Jesus' bones were broken. By means of the blood of the paschal lamb, the Israelites were saved from temporal death. Through the Blood of Jesus, we are saved from spiritual death and from the eternal punishments of hell."

"Continue Professor".

"God, through Moses, instituted the Old Law. He is thus seen as a mediator of the Old Law. Christ, the New Moses, instituted the New Law and is thus seen in such a mediatorial role. As a child, Moses was sentenced to death by a tyrannical Pharaoh, Jesus was also sought after for execution by the wicked King Herod. Both Moses and Jesus were saved in extraordinary ways from their respective persecutors. Moses prepared himself in the desert for his mission. He proved his divine mission by great miracles and by freeing his people from the bonds of slavery. Jesus prepared Himself for His Mission by a forty day fast in the desert after which he performed even greater miracles than those performed by Moses. By His Death on the Cross, Jesus freed his people from the slavery of sin and death. As Moses was the advocate of his people with God, so is Our Lord the Advocate of His people with God the Father. Moses led the people out of Egypt, Jesus leads His people out of the Egypt of sin. Moses was a law-giver and delivered the Ten

Commandments from a mountain, Jesus, by the Sermon on the Mount gave a new interpretation of the Law."

"More Professor Parton, more".

"The brazen serpent is also to be likened unto Christ. It was lifted up on a pole. In his discourse with Nicodemus He stated "As Moses lifted up the serpent in the desert, so must the Son of Man be lifted up, that whosoever believeth in Him may not perish, but may have life everlasting. If anyone experienced snake-bite, all they had to do was to gaze upon the brazen serpent and a cure would instantly follow. We also who are smitten by the venom of sin, may find healing by turning our eyes towards our crucified Saviour".

"Enough Professor Parton, thank you."

CHAPTER XIV

PROGRESSION THROUGH THE ROOMS

"Elizabeth, today Parton and Hartley told me about Professor Jean Austin's idea of constructing a second version of Astra as a means to solve this problem."

"I am aware of this Chester. But it would not work".

"Why not?"

"Another daemon would take it over if Brantaxaros is expelled from AstraI or Brantaxaros could take over AstrII. It would only compound the problem. However, Professor Austin is not entirely wrong in her thinking. Astra II will have to be handled in a completely different way".

"How might that be?"

"As of yet, Chester, my powers are not sufficient to tell you. However, in time, I will explain Astra II to you."

"Now Professor—the next type of Christ if you please."

Parton noted how Astra was becoming more imperious in its tones. He wondered why? Perhaps it was because he was elucidating the theology so well that was making the machine mad."

"The ninth type of Christ is Josue. By his military prowess, Josue led the children of Israel into the Promised Land. His continuing military exploits succeeded in conquering the land for the Israelite people. Jesus, by His Death and Resurrection has conquered the kingdom of Satan and led us by His doctrine into the true Promised Land of Heaven."

"Who is the tenth type of Christ, Professor?"

Parton was astonished once more at how Astra accepted this brief explanation. He surmised that the computer's tactic was to skip over the 'minor' types of Christ and concentrate on the 'bigees', this way it had a greater chance of tripping him up on various points.

"Gedeon is. He was saviour of his people as Jesus is the Saviour of the whole world. Gedeon in his early years led a humble and hidden life as did Jesus. Gedeon overcame his enemies with only a handful of soldiers. His only weapons being a trumpet and torches. Jesus overcame the pagan world with only a few Apostles and the weapon of the Word of God and the light of the Gospel"

"Go on to the next type of Christ, Professor".

Once more, the brevity of this explanation was not lost of Parton. He was now convinced that Astra was skimming over the more minor types of Christ.

"It is Sampson".

"And how does this biblical character qualify as a type of Christ?"

"In fact, the period of the Judges had many types of minor Christ-type figures. Here is what St. Augustine said about Sampson: 'I see in him both the strength of the Son of God and the weakness of a man. In those great and wonderful things which he did he was a type of Christ.'"

"I want to hear what *you* have to say about him Professor?"

"Sampson's birth, like that of Christ's was announced by an angel. Physically, he overpowered a lion; Jesus by His Cross, has overpowered the lion of sin. Sampson fought with a very meagre weapon, a slingshot, Jesus fought His spiritual battle with the Cross, an instrument of execution which was seen as accursed for those who hung upon it. Sampson fought alone, so did Christ. Sampson was betrayed for money and handed over by the members of his own tribe and was bound and mocked. This is exactly how Jesus was treated in His Passion. Sampson sacrificed his life for his people. By sacrificing his own life he caused great harm to his enemies. Likewise, Jesus offered Himself up of His own free will and thus overcame sin and death. Sampson carried off the gates and bolts of Gaza, Jesus by His Resurrection threw open the gates of Heaven and carried away the gates and bolts of the grave."

"Thank you Professor Parton."

By now Chester was passing through rooms in the ball of light which left him mesmerised and aw-struck.

"Is Heaven like this Elizabeth?"

"Oh Chester, Heaven is so much better than this. If you were to be transported there now in your mortal flesh, you would die of ecstasy".

"I fear that may happen with this sort of magnificence which is less than Heaven itself".

"No Chester. You will be given the grace and strength to be able to bear all these ecstatic delights."

Back at the laboratory, Parton was about to explain King David as the twelfth type of Christ.

"So it is King David we are about to study now, is it, Professor Parton?"

"David foretold the sufferings of Christ."

"That would tend to make him a prophet rather than a type surely, Professor Parton."

"Like Christ, he was born in Bethlehem and led a hidden life in his youth. As Christ overcame the world with merely the Wood of the Cross, David overcame the mighty Goliath with a simple slingshot. Like Christ, David was persecuted. He was pursued by Saul, yet, like Christ, he bore no ill-will towards his enemies. David was both prophet and king; Christ exercised the same two offices. David crossed the brook Cedron and fell to the ground with grief, but then he returned triumphantly to Jerusalem. This is a foreshadowing of Christ's agony in the Garden of Olives. David's returning to Jerusalem in triumph is a kind of Christ's Ascension into Heaven."

"Thank you Professor, that will do?"

Within the ball of light, in that strange extra-dimensionality, Chester passed through into the next room.

"Oh Elizabeth, this light, this great glow of warmth—I just can't think of anything but victory over Astra."

"Indeed Chester, but you will have trials and tribulations ahead of you".

Chester Wilkins was far too caught up in his ecstasy of delight to fully comprehend what Elizabeth had just said to him.

"Elizabeth? What must I do now?" asked Chester whose eyes were now so dreamy and far-away.

"You must learn as much as you can about the Order of the Knights Templar".

It was this that shook Chester from his deep reverie.

"But . . . how? I can't see what an ancient medieval order of knights has to do with all of this?"

"I am not empowered to explain it to you Chester, but please accept for the moment that there is a connection."

In the vast room there was a most extensive library. Elizabeth directed Chester to the books about the Templars. Chester immediately began his research.

"Here is a riddle which I am empowered to give you Chester – 'the one at the top, the one who is the boss and cricket'".

Chester wrote this strange, meaningless riddle down. He kept repeating to himself—'the one at the top, the one who is the boss and cricket'.

"Now then Professor Parton, who is the next type of Christ", Astra enquired of Parton.

"It is King Solomon. Unlike the previous types of Christs, who typified Christ in His Sufferings, Solomon is like Christ in His Glory. Solomon's name means 'peace' and so we think of Christ as the Prince of Peace. Solomon has always been noted for his wisdom, and so in him we see a type of Christ, Christ 'in whom are hid all the treasures of wisdom and knowledge' (Cor.2, 3). The riches of Solomon are indicative of the great riches and treasures of grace won by Jesus Christ. Solomon built the Temple on strong and well-hewn stone, Christ built His Church on the rock of Peter. The Queen of Sheba, with great gifts, came from afar to pay homage to Solomon; the three magi came to adore the Infant Jesus and presented unto Him costly gifts of Gold, Frankincense and Myrrh. Solomon ruled over many nations, Jesus Christ from His Throne in Heaven, rules over the nations of the world."

"Thank you Professor".

For many hours, Chester devoured the books Elizabeth had presented to him but he was nowhere nearer to finding a solution to the riddle.

"It is best that you work out the riddle before you pass into the next room", Elizabeth cautioned Chester.

"I'll try as best I can", he reassured her.

"Who is the next type of Christ Professor?"

"It is the Prophet Elias. The long drought which Israel suffered typified the long spiritual drought the world endured before the coming of the Messias. Elias' commanding the heavens to open and rain was like Christ raining down grace to a spiritually dry and devastated world."

"That does not satisfy me Professor, you will have to do better than that".

"The food brought to Elias by an angel was a type of Holy Communion. Elias had a long and dangerous journey through the desert; we likewise have to journey through the desert of life before we reach our home in Heaven. On our journey God strengthens us with the spiritual food of Holy Communion and the other sacraments of the Church".

"Enough thank you Professor".

"'The one at the top, the one who is the boss and cricket'", mused Chester.

"Try hard Chester", pleaded Elizabeth, "Parton is about to explain to Astra the last type of Christ".

"Finally we come to Jonas as a type of Christ", said Parton to Astra.

"Explain it well, Professor", said Astra.

"Jesus refers to Jonas as a type of Himself. He said 'An adulterous generation seeketh after a sign and a sign shall not be given it but the sign of Jonas the prophet. For as Jonas was in the whale's belly three days and three nights, so shall the Son of man be in the heart of the earth three days and three nights'. Jonas was also like Christ in that he was sent not only to the Jews but to the Gentiles also. Jonas was willing to offer himself up to death in order to appease God's anger and save his fellow passengers. Christ willingly went to death out of love for us and to save us from eternal damnation."

Parton was flabbergasted when Astra informed him that the explanation was unacceptable.

"Isn't all that good enough?"

"No! The explanation has within it a serious flaw".

"What exactly is it?"

"You claim there is a similarity between Christ and Jonas in terms of their being in the tomb and the belly of the whale respectively for three days and three nights. If we examine the time period between Christ's burial on Good Friday evening and His Resurrection on Sunday morning we come up with two nights and only one full day".

"Well the Gospel stories do not say three *full* nights and days".

"No Professor. Christ made a direct comparison between Himself and Jonas. Your explanation still remains unsatisfactory".

Parton was completely stumped. He walked away from the computer and over to Stardy, Walters and Wilkins for theological help. They also were at a loss.

"How are we going to handle this one?" said Stardy.

"Do you have any idea Anthony?" Parton asked Walters.

"No, I admit I'm completely floored" Walters replied.

"Might I suggest I contact Professor Bill Watkins of Sterling University in Scotland?" Chester suggested. "He is an authority on Biblical interpretation".

Parton nodded in agreement. Chester contacted the professor and came back to brief the group. Fifteen minutes later, Parton was ready to lay it all on Astra.

"Now then Astra", began Parton, "the term 'heart of the earth' is not a reference to a tomb. The heart of something means the centre of the thing referred to. No tomb can ever be at the centre of the earth. In fact in first century Palestine, tombs were above the earth, so we have to look for an alternative to 'tomb' as an explanation for the expression 'heart of the earth'".

"And that is the explanation I require of you, Professor".

"The sufferings of Man is what constitutes the heart of the earth. The term has mystical and spiritual overtones. Christ, by becoming Man, partook of those sufferings. His Sufferings became more intense as He neared His Passion. His Agony began on Maundy Thursday when He prepared for the Pasch. He knew it would be the last one He would eat with His Apostles. In the evening of that same day He agonised in the Garden of Gethsemani and was afterwards arrested and tried. His sufferings continued on Good Friday up to His Death at 3pm. His period in the tomb therefore only constitutes a part of His Sufferings, a part of what may be termed 'heart of the earth'".

"You have answered satisfactorily, Professor".

CHAPTER XV

FAMILIAR TERRITORY

"Chester, have you got anywhere nearer to working out that riddle?" Elizabeth asked concernedly.

"I'm afraid not", sighed Chester.

"Nevertheless, you must proceed into the next room."

Chester, quite nonchalant, walked over to the door. He was prepared for the next adventure in a series of ever increasing ecstasy.

"Do be so careful, Chester my love", cautioned Elizabeth with tears in her eyes.

"I will be, I will be", said Chester still full of confidence.

Chester walked through the door expecting to find himself in an even more beautiful room than before. Instead he found himself in a place of darkness. He couldn't make out where he was, but it felt so cold and damp. He decided to give himself some time for his eyes to adjust.

After a few minutes Chester began to discern a little of his surroundings. He was in a large and unlit hall sort of place. He walked a few paces and bumped into some metallic structure. His heart pounded within his chest. A few seconds later, he realised it was a suit of armour. At once he thought of the Knights Templar.

"Where am I? What place is this I'm in?" he asked himself.

Over on his far right, he noticed some light. It was the moon, shod of its cloudy covering, casting some stingy light into a small perpendicular type window. Yet, it was enough to allow Chester to see that he was in the main room of Templar Hall in the Cotswalds.

"Elizabeth, Elizabeth", he called out. But no answer came. He realised he was all alone. He upbraided himself for his overconfidence and understood why Elizabeth had counseled caution. He decided to go outside into the main courtyard to see if there were any signs of human life. On stepping out into the courtyard, he appreciated the brightness of the moon. Templar Hall, being miles away from the nearest human habitation was bathed in a lunar glow like no other building Chester had ever seen before. A bat screeched across the moonlit sky, its dark and eerie shape conspicuous against the light of the full moon. The place seemed completely deserted.

Chester walked over to the offices cum living quarters of the Governor. No light shone from there, no sign of human presence could be discerned. In fact, other than the light of the full moon, the castle was in complete darkness. Wandering what this was all about, Chester decided to make his way back into main hall of the castle.

On turning around, Chester's breath was instantly taken away. Lined up outside the doorway to the main hall was Major Worthington, the Chief Butler and the domestic staff.

"Major Worthington", bleated Chester, "I'm so glad to see you".

Worthington and the Chief Butler said nothing; they and the rest of the castle staff remained stiff at attention.

"I eh, I I I need your help", squeaked Chester.

"Why have you come here?" growled Worthington.

"You have come to destroy our plans have you Chester?" said the Chief Butler in hard and unfeeling tones.

"You should not have come here", said Worthington. "You seek to destroy us, but we shall destroy you by making you one of us."

"One of you?" said Chester in surprise. Who are you?" he demanded.

"You will soon find out Chester when you become one of us", sneered the Chief Butler.

With that a strange combined humming and buzzing sound became audible to Chester. He knew all too well what it was. Chester turned around to flee from the evil before him. However, blocking his way at the other side of the quadrangle were some faces which looked vaguely familiar. It soon dawned on him that it was Captain Anderson and the soldiers who had been killed while trying to blow up Astra.

"They are now with us", said Worthington. "And you will soon be too".

Worthington and his staff and Anderson and his soldiers began to dissolve and float above the quadrangle. All that Chester saw was a wispy cloud hovering above him. The cloud started to take the shape of a face. It was a bearded face with malevolent looking eyes. The humming and buzzing sound grew louder and louder. It started moving towards Chester.

Without wasting a second's more time, Chester ran into the main hall of the castle as fast as his legs could carry him. The Face was in hot pursuit. In the light of the moon Chester retraced his steps to where he had exited from the previous room.

"Elizabeth, Elizabeth", he screamed with great terror.

A few yards away from where he was standing a light began to glow. It was not moonlight but the unearthly glow of the ball of light with which Chester was now familiar. Chester dashed towards it and into it before just a split second before the Face could come upon him. He fell into the room sweating and panting and gasping for breath. His sheer terror was only assuaged by the sight of Elizabeth so beautiful and resplendent on her throne.

It must have been three hours later that Chester woke up. He was in the same room but lying on a soft bed with silken sheets and an eiderdown quilt. He felt much better as he stepped out of his luxurious bed and onto the marble floor, but his mind was still confused as to what all this had been about.

He related to Elizabeth his brief but ghastly experiences at Templar Hall. Elizabeth listened intently and gave him as much advice as allowed her by the balance of the cosmic powers under which she was restrained.

"I am stronger now Chester because I have not lost you to the Evil Intelligences. I can now say more to you. First of all Chester, recount to me in as much detail as possible everything that you experienced at Templar Hall".

Chester told Elizabeth everything that he had seen. She listened intently as Chester recounted the horrific things that happened to him at the ancient castle.

"I am not empowered to tell you anything directly but I can give you further clues", she told Chester.

"What can you tell me Elizabeth?"

"Brace yourself well for this Chester—you must return again to Templar Hall in order to deliver a crushing blow to the Evil Intelligences".

Chester was shocked at hearing this. It was the last thing he wanted to do. Anything but return to that ghastly place with its equally ghastly people.

"Is there no other way, Elizabeth?"

"No Chester, not if we are to win against the powers of darkness and evil".

"There is the danger that I may not be so lucky next time and end up taken over by the evil ones".

"I can offer you this consolation Chester; you do not need to enter the castle again until you have found the meaning to my riddle. If you hit upon the solution, I can confirm it. So you do not need to enter the place of evil again unprepared. I can also tell you this now—the solution is in the detail of what you saw at the castle."

For many more hours Chester read as much as he could about the Templars. He kept constantly in mind the riddle which Elizabeth had set before him. At last it struck him. Excitedly he called upon Elizabeth and told her what he thought was the solution.

"You have at last worked out the riddle except for one detail and it is a crucial one. It hinges upon what preceded the people you saw. If you understand this it will help you with the weapon you will need. Think of David and Gedeon and how they were types of Christ. It is closely connected to what you and Dr. Stardy taught Professor Parton. Think also of an actor with the surname of a Middle Eastern country".

It was another two hours before Chester hit upon the solution. Elizabeth told him that he was now ready to re-enter the castle and deal a crippling blow to the Evil Intelligences.

Chester made his way out into the Courtyard. Though he had been told by Elizabeth no harm could befall him now, he still felt afraid.

"So you want to join us do you Chester?" screeched the voice of Major Worthington.

As on the previous occasion Worthington, Anderson and their minions dissolved into the vapoury cloud and reformed into the Face. At once, Chester took out a crucifix which he had concealed beneath his jacket and held it up at the Face.

"Look upon the Crucified One, Baphomet, you brood of vampires."

Baphomet was the Head worshipped by the Templars. Chester had read about their strange ceremony of spitting upon the Cross and

106

mocking it in so many other ways. He could never understand why this supposedly Christian order would be so blasphemous and contemptuous in its attitude to the Cross—the central focus of Christianity. Now he knew why—the Evil Intelligences had gone to work on this most prestigious of all knightly orders. He associated the 'cricket' part of the riddle with the vampire bat and Louis Jordan as the actor who often played in Count Dracula films.

When Chester held up the crucifix at Baphomet, the Head began to dissolve. Half a minute later, Worthington and Anderson fell to ground cut and dazed. Chester rushed into the staff living quarters where he found the coffins belonging to the vampires. In these he placed portions of wild rose and garlic. By now Worthington, Anderson and the other vampires were making their way towards the living quarters. Too late! They could not get into their coffins. Once again they formed into the face of Baphomet and pursued Chester out into the quad. Baphomet 's face was now a fiery rage of hate, Chester had never seen a countenance which displayed such utter malevolence. He reached into one of his pockets and took out a small plastic bottle. He squirted it at the Face. It was holy water. Instantly Baphomet let out a high pitched shriek of pain and agony, fire gushed from his mouth and blood spurted from his mouth and nose. In a few seconds Baphomet dissolved once again to reveal Worthington, Anderson and the others lying prostrate on the ground.

Chester now had one more job to do. He took out a hammer and a piece of wood from a pocket. He walked over to Major Worthington, who, like the others, was now weak and groaning in a pitiful state of agony. Chester decided to deal with this scoundrel first. He placed the wooden stake over Worthington's heart, raised the hammer and let it come crashing down on top of the wood. Worthington let out an almighty roar, blood spurted everywhere and Chester shrunk back in horror. It was a grizzly task but he knew he had to repeat it on the others. Twenty minutes later, all the vampires had been reduced to mere dust. Chester had been drenched in blood, but that also vanished with the vampires.

When Chester came back to the room, he found Elizabeth waiting for him. This time she was not seated upon her throne but standing near the doorway. She extended her hand towards Chester who when taking it found it to be warm and comforting in a way that it had never been before.

"Take some rest Chester and we shall talk about your experiences later", Elizabeth advised him.

A few hours later Chester awoke. Elizabeth now had a human flesh and blood appearance to her. It was obvious to Chester that she was now becoming stronger; the distant ethereal presence of the 'queen upon her throne' had given way to something more like the Elizabeth whom he had known and loved as his sweetheart.

"Those who had been bitten by the insects were turned into 'vampires', or, more accurate to say, Evil Intelligences", Elizabeth explained.

"How does all this connect with the AIDS virus?" Chester asked.

"Sir Fred Hoyle, way back in the 1980's suggested that the AIDS virus originated in space. Being a man far ahead of his time, he was right, but those with less foresight and imagination, pooh poohed the notion."

"Had the scientific community listened to Hoyle and Wickramasinghe, would things have turned out to be different?"

"Oh yes", replied Elizabeth. "As you read in the book *Evolution From Space,* both Hoyle and Wickramasinghe advised that great advances in the treatment of cancer could only be made when that disease was seen in its wider cosmological context."

"And of course the same would apply to AIDS and a whole host of other ailments".

"Yes indeed. If AIDS research had been approached from this angle, Mankind would at least have kept pace with the Evil Intelligences, and probably even been one step ahead of them. As such it was not to be—and so things have come to this pass."

"And how did the AIDS virus become so strong?"

"When Astra—I mean the *real* Astra—was on the verge of discovering an effective anti-dote, the Evil Intelligences, under the leadership of Brantaxaros, worked hard to strengthen this virus."

"Why did they not just simply use the insects to bite the population of the entire world? Why this elaborate theological game?"

"As I have explained to you before Chester, the Good Intelligences are strong and can put a brake on the designs of the evil ones."

"What must be done now, Elizabeth?"

"Astra is now greatly weakened. It is down but not out. You, Drs. Stardy and Walters have still much to do with Professor Parton theologywise".

"Professor Parton", began Astra, "we have looked at the types of Christ in the Old Testament. We must now examine the issue concerning the promises of the Messias".

Parton walked over to his three mentors for some advice on this matter. After an hour he was ready to take on Astra.

"Before God expelled Adam and Eve from the Garden of Eden, He promised them a Redeemer. God said to the serpent, 'I will put enmities between thee and the woman, and thy seed and her seed; she shall crush thy head, and thou shalt lie in wait for her heel'. The seed of the Devil are those who persist in sin and reject God. The seed of the woman was Jesus Christ Who was descended from Eve according to the flesh. But the Devil would seek to injure the woman. He would inflict sufferings upon her but would never be able to defeat her. He bruised the heel of the woman by inflicting sufferings on Jesus and Mary, yet it was by these very sufferings that Christ overcame the Devil."

"Why did not the sin of Adam result in instant damnation for him and Eve as it did for the fallen angels?"

"The sin of Adam and Eve did not deserve eternal damnation as human beings were not given the same privileges in the way of spiritual knowledge as the angels were given."

"And what would have happened had God not promised a Redeemer?"

"Perhaps Adam and Eve would have died of despair".

"And why did God set two cherubim to protect the Tree of Life? Why did He not wish Adam and Eve to eat of it?"

"Had they eaten of it while in sin they would have lived forever that way and there would have been no chance of their being saved."

"Thank you Professor—enough".

"Tell me", Chester asked Elizabeth, "how does Brantaxaros select victims?"

"He only has the power to attack those who make an attempt on the computer Astra", Elizabeth replied.

"What about Major Worthington and his staff?"

"They had given the military precise details of where Astra was housed in Templar Hall."

"Won't Brantaxaros know about what I did in Templar Hall?"

"No. He will know of the demise of the vampires but his weakened position will prevent him from knowing exactly how it happened."

"Will he not try to maneuver in some way to gain the advantage again?

"We shall have to wait and see".

"Tell me about some of the other promises of a Redeemer", Astra asked Parton the following day.

"God said to Abraham, 'In thee shall all the kindred of the world be blessed'. This promise is more specific than the first as it states that the Messias shall be born of the seed of Abraham."

"Thank you Professor Parton. The next promise please."

"After the angel had prevented Abraham from slaying Isaac, God renewed the promise 'In thee shall all the nations of the earth be blessed'."

"The fourth promise, please Professor Parton".

"God promised Jacob that the Redeemer would come through his line. 'In thy seed shall all the tribes of the earth be blessed'".

"The fifth promise?"

"It is by Jacob's prophecy".

"How is that?"

"Jacob's dying prophecy spoke of Juda's precedence over his brethren. The most numerous of all the tribes of Juda, even in the time of Moses, was Juda. The prophecy also treated of the coming of a Saviour. Both of these prophecies were fulfilled. After the Babylonian captivity, the entire nation was known as Juda. And from the tribe of Juda, came the Messias. This prophecy also stated that by the time of the coming of the Messias, Juda's predominance would be at an end. This prophecy came to pass as the Idumean King Herod ruled over the Jews from Judea. Jacob also prophesied that all nations, not only the Jews, would be looking for a Messias. This also came to pass."

"What exactly is in the prophesy which justifies this conclusion?"

"Jacob's words are: 'Juda, thy hand shall be on the neck of thy enemies. The sons of thy father shall bow down to thee, and the sceptre shall not be taken away from Juda, till He comes that is to be sent, and He shall be the expectation of nations'".

"Enough—thank you".

"Moses also gave a promise of a Redeemer. 'The Lord shall raise up to thee a prophet of thy nation, and of thy brethren, like unto me. Him thou shalt hear.'"

"And how is Christ like unto Moses?"

"Moses preached from a mountain and from there brought the law of the Ten Commandments to the people. Christ delivered the Sermon on the Mount and gave a whole new way of interpreting the Mosaic Law. Moses instituted the Old Covenant; Christ instituted the New and Everlasting Covenant."

"What is the next promise?"

"King David wrote of the Messias. One thousand years before the Passion, David wrote in graphic detail of how Christ's Hand and Feet were pierced. Yet at the time of David, crucifixion was unknown, the method of capital punishment being stoning to death. He spoke of the division of Christ's garments, the scoffing of the mob and the casting of lots for His seamless garment. All these prophesies were wonderfully fulfilled."

"Provide me with some scriptural quotes, Professor, to back this up."

"In Psalm 109 'The Lord said to my Lord *Sit Thou at my right hand until I make thine enemies Thy footstool.* The Lord hath sworn and he will not repent: *Thou art a priest forever according to the order of Melchisedech.* Here, David's Lord is Christ the Messias. Melchisedech was both priest and king—as was Christ—and he offered up an unbloody sacrifice of bread and wine. God also said to David, 'I will raise up thy seed after thee, and I will establish the throne of his kingdom forever. I will be to Him a Father, and He shall be to me a Son.'"

"Thank you Professor, please proceed to the next promise".

"Isaias is rich in prophecies about the coming of the Messias. In Chapter 2 we have the following:

'The word that Isaias the son of Amos saw, concerning Juda and Jerusalem. And in the last days the mountain of the house of the Lord shall be prepared on the top of mountains, and it shall be exalted above the hills, and all nations shall flow unto it. And many people shall go, and say: Come and let us go up to the mountain of the Lord, and to the house of the God of Jacob, and he will teach us his ways, and we will walk in his paths: for the law shall come forth from Sion, and the word of the Lord from Jerusalem. And he shall judge the Gentiles, and rebuke many people: and they shall turn their swords into ploughshares, and their spears into sickles: nation shall not lift up sword against nation, neither shall they be exercised any more to war'. The expression 'the last days', refers to the whole time of the New Law until the second coming of Christ. 'On top of mountains' refers to the exalted position of the Church of Christ. It is visible and cannot be hid."

"What else?"

"In Chapter 4 we read

'In that day the bud of the Lord shall be in magnificence and glory, and the fruit of the earth shall be high, and a great joy to them that shall have escaped of Israel'. The bud of course means Jesus Christ."

"Next please".

"In Chapter 7 we read of a prophecy of the birth of Christ and the virginal nature of His birth. 'Ask thee a sign of the Lord thy God either unto the depth of hell, or unto the height above. And Achaz said: I will not ask, and I will not tempt the Lord. And he said: Hear ye therefore, O house of David: Is it a small thing for you to be grievous to men, that you are grievous to my God also? Therefore the Lord himself shall give you a sign. Behold a virgin shall conceive, and bear a son, and his name shall be called Emmanuel. He shall eat butter and honey, that he may know to refuse the evil, and to choose the good. For before the child know to refuse the evil, and to choose the good, the land which thou abhorrest shall be forsaken of the face of her two kings.'"

"Continue on to the next prophecy please, Professor".

"It is written in Chapter 9 'For a CHILD IS BORN to us, and a son is given to us, and the government is upon his shoulder: and his name shall be called, Wonderful, Counsellor, God the Mighty, the Father of the world to come, the Prince of Peace. His empire shall be multiplied, and there shall be no end of peace: he shall sit upon the throne of David, and upon his kingdom; to establish it and strengthen it with judgment and with justice, from henceforth and for ever: the zeal of the Lord of hosts will perform this'. This is a clear reference to Christ".

"What further evidence from Isaias have you got for this spiritual Kingdom of Christ?"

"In Chapter 11 verses 1-10, we have the following quotation: 'And there shall come forth a rod out of the root of Jesse, and a flower shall rise up out of his root. And the spirit of the Lord shall rest upon him: the spirit of wisdom, and of understanding, the spirit of counsel, and of fortitude, the spirit of knowledge, and of godliness. And he shall be filled with the spirit of the fear of the Lord. He shall not judge according to the sight of the eyes, nor reprove according to the hearing of the ears. But he shall judge the poor with justice, and shall reprove with equity for the meek of the earth: land he shall strike the earth with the rod of his mouth, and with the breath of his lips he shall slay the wicked. And justice shall be the girdle of his loins: and faith the girdle of his reins. The wolf shall dwell with the lamb: and the leopard shall lie down with the kid: the calf and the lion, and the sheep shall abide together, and a little child shall lead them. The calf and the bear shall feed: their young ones shall rest together: and the lion shall eat straw like the ox. And the sucking child shall play on the hole of the asp: and the weaned child shall thrust his hand into the den of the basilisk. They shall not hurt, nor shall they kill in all my holy mountain, for the earth is filled with the knowledge of the Lord, as the covering waters of the sea. In that day the root of Jesse, who standeth for an ensign of the people, him the Gentiles shall beseech, and his sepulchre shall be glorious'. That 'his sepulchre shall be glorious' is a clear reference to His ressurection."

"Continue Professor".

"I will read you Chapter 12: 'And thou shalt say in that day: I will give thanks to thee, O Lord, for thou wast angry with me: thy wrath is turned away, and thou hast comforted me. Behold, God is my saviour, I will deal confidently, and will not fear: O because the Lord is my strength, and my praise, and he is become my salvation. You shall draw waters with joy out of the saviour's fountains: And you shall say in that day: Praise ye the Lord, and call upon his name: make his works known among the people: remember that his name is high. Sing ye to the Lord, for he hath done great things: shew this forth in all the earth. Rejoice, and praise, O thou habitation of Sion: for great is he that is in the midst of thee, the Holy One of Israel.'"

"What is the significance of this, Professor?"

"It is indicative of the benefits afforded by the setting up of Christ's Kingdom on Earth."

"I need further evidence of Christ in the Old Testament, Professor Parton".

Parton heaved an impatient sigh and flicked through the pages of his Bible to the next of the markers that Wilkins and Stardy had placed throughout the pages of the holy book.

"Here is Chapter 16 verse 1: 'Send forth, O Lord, the lamb, the ruler of the earth, from Petra of the desert, to the mount of the daughter of Sion.'"

"And what is the exegetical explanation of this single verse?"

"It is the prophet praying for the coming of the Kingdom of Christ."

"Go on please".

"Very well. I will read to you Chapter 22 verses 20-25. They show Eiacim as a figure of Christ. 'And it shall come to pass in that day, that I will call my servant Eliacim the son of Helcias, And I will clothe him with thy robe, and will strengthen him with thy girdle, and will give thy power into his hand: and he shall be as a father to the inhabitants of Jerusalem, and to the house of Juda. And I will lay the key of the house of David upon his shoulder: and he shall open, and none shall shut: and he shall shut, and none shall open. And I will fasten him as a peg in a sure place, and he shall be for a throne of glory to the house of his father. And they shall hang upon him all the glory of his father's house, divers kinds of vessels, every little vessel, from the vessels of cups even to every instrument of music. In that day, saith the Lord of hosts, shall the peg be removed, that was fastened in the sure place: and it shall be broken and shall fall: and that which hung thereon, shall perish, because the Lord hath spoken it.'"

"Thank you Professor, continue on."

"Verse 16 of Chapter 28 reads as follows: 'Therefore thus saith the Lord God: Behold I will lay _a stone in the foundations_ of Sion, a tried stone, a corner stone, a precious stone, founded in the foundation'. The foundation stone referred to is clearly Christ." And verses 1 and 2 of Chapter 32—'Behold a king shall reign in justice, and princes shall rule in judgment. And a man shall be as when one is hid from the wind, and hideth himself from a storm, as rivers of waters in drought, and the shadow of a rock that standeth out in a desert land'. The king referred to is Christ."

"Continue, continue".

Parton noticed a melancholy in the voice of Astra. He was not sure how to interpret it. Was the computer displeased with his explanations? What affect was all this theology having on Astra?

"I shall quote you the whole of Chapter 35; it deals with the beneficial results of Christ's Kingdom: 'The land that was desolate and impassable shall be glad, and the wilderness shall rejoice, and shall flourish like the lily. It shall bud forth and blossom, and shall rejoice with joy and praise: the glory of Libanus is given to it: the beauty of Carmel, and Saron, they shall see the glory of the Lord, and the beauty of our God. Strengthen ye the feeble hands, and confirm the weak knees. Say to the fainthearted: Take courage, and fear not: behold your God will bring the revenge of recompense: God himself will come and will save you. Then shall the eyes of the blind be opened, and the ears of the deaf shall be unstopped. Then shall the lame man leap as a hart, and the tongue of the dumb shall be free: for waters are broken out in the desert, and streams in the wilderness. And that which was dry land, shall become a pool, and the thirsty land springs of water. In the dens where dragons dwell before, shall rise up the verdure of the reed and the bulrush. And a path and a way shall be there, and it shall be called the holy way: the unclean shall not pass over it, and this shall be unto you a straight way, so that fools shall not err therein. No lion shall be there, nor shall any mischievous beast go up by it, nor be found there: but they shall walk there that shall be delivered. And the redeemed of the Lord shall return, and shall come into Sion with praise, and everlasting joy shall be upon their heads: they shall obtain joy and gladness, and sorrow and mourning shall flee away.'"

The computer remained silent. Parton and his onlookers, Stardy and Wilkins, showed a mixture of confusion and apprehension on their faces.

"Do you wish me to continue? "Parton asked Astra. There was no reply. Parton repeated his question. Astra gave out a very enfeebled 'yes'.

Chester Wilkins gingerly beckoned Parton to approach him. "Sir, try and directly quote as many scriptures as you can?"

"Why?"

"Please Professor, do as we request".

Parton went over to the computer. "Astra! I will read you Chapter 40 in its entirety: 'Be comforted, be comforted, my people, saith your

God. Speak ye to the heart of Jerusalem, and call to her: for her evil is come to an end, her iniquity is forgiven: she hath received of the hand of the Lord double for all her sins. The voice of one crying in the desert: Prepare ye the way of the Lord, make straight in the wilderness the paths of our God. Every valley shall be exalted, and every mountain and hill shall be made low, and the crooked shall become straight, and the rough ways plain. And the glory of the Lord shall be revealed, and all flesh together shall see, that the mouth of the Lord hath spoken. 'The voice of one, saying: Cry. And I said: What shall I cry? All flesh is grass, and all the glory thereof as the flower of the held. The grass is withered, and the dower is fallen, because the spirit of the Lord hath blown upon it. Indeed the people is grass: The grass is withered, and the flower is fallen: but the word of our Lord endureth for ever. Get thee up upon a high mountain, thou that bringest good tidings to Sion: lift up thy voice with strength, thou that bringest good tidings to Jerusalem: lift it up, fear not. Say to the cities of Juda: Behold your God: Behold the Lord God shall come with strength, and his arm shall rule: Behold his reward is with him and his work is before him. He shall feed his flock like a shepherd: he shall gather together the lambs with his arm, and shall take them up in his bosom, and he himself shall carry them that are with young. Who hath measured the waters in the hollow of his hand, and weighed the heavens with his palm? who hath poised with three fingers the bulk of the earth, and weighed the mountains in scales, and the hills in a balance? Who hath forwarded the spirit of the Lord? or who hath been his counsellor, and hath taught him? With whom hath he consulted, and who hath instructed him, and taught him the path of justice, and taught him knowledge, and shewed him the way of understanding? Behold the Gentiles are as a drop of a bucket, and are counted as the smallest grain of a balance: behold the islands are as a little dust. And Libanus shall not be enough to burn, nor the beasts thereof sufficient for a burnt offering. All nations are before him as if they had no being at all, and are counted to him as nothing, and vanity. To whom then have you likened God? or what image will you make for him? Hath the workman cast a graven statue? or hath the goldsmith formed it with gold, or the silversmith with plates of silver? He hath chosen strong wood, and that will not rot: the skillful workman seeketh how he may set up an idol that may not be moved'. Do you not know? hath it not been heard? hath it not been told you from the beginning? have you not understood the foundations of the earth? It is he that sitteth upon the globe of the earth, and the inhabitants thereof are as locusts: he that stretcheth out the heavens as nothing, and spreadeth them out as a tent to dwell in. He that bringeth the searchers of secrets to nothing, that hath made the judges of the earth as vanity. And surely their stock was neither planted, nor sown, nor rooted in the earth: suddenly he hath blown upon them, and they are withered, and a whirlwind shall take them away as stubble. And to whom have ye likened me, or made me equal, saith the Holy One? Lift up your eyes on high, and see who hath created these things: who bringeth out their host by number, and calleth them all by their names: by the greatness of his might, and strength, and power, not one of them was missing. Why sayest thou, O Jacob, and speakest, O Israel: My way is hid from the Lord, and my judgment is passed over from my God? Knowest thou not, or hast thou not heard? the Lord is the everlasting God, who hath created the ends of the earth: he shall not faint, nor labour, neither is there any searching out of his wisdom. It is he that giveth strength to the weary, and increaseth force and might to them that are not. Youths shall faint, and labour, and young men shall fall by infirmity. But they that hope in the Lord shall renew their strength, they shall take wings as eagles, they shall run and not be weary, they shall walk and not faint.'"

After a two minute pause, Astra asked: "What is the significance of all this?"

"It is the prophet comforting his people with the promise of a Messiah."

"Continue", muttered Astra after another two minute pause.

"Chapter 41 extols the reign of Christ and reminds the Jews of the promises made to Abraham, Isaac and Jacob: 'Let the islands keep silence before me, and the nations take new strength: let them come near, and then speak, let us come near to judgment together. Who hath raised up the just one from the east, hath called him to follow him? he shall give the nations in his sight, and he shall rule over kings: he shall give them as the dust to his sword, as stubble driven by the wind, to his bow. He shall pursue them, he shall pass in peace, no path shall appear after his feet. Who hath wrought and done these things, calling the generations from the beginning? I the Lord, I am the first and the last. The islands saw it, and feared, the ends of the earth were astonished, they drew near, and came. Every one shall help his neighbour, and shall say to his brother: Be of good courage. The coppersmith striking with the hammer encouraged him that forged at that time, saying: It is ready for soldering: and he strengthened it with nails, that it should not be moved. But thou Israel, art my servant, Jacob whom I have chosen, the seed of Abraham my friend: In whom I have taken thee from the ends of the earth, and from the remote parts thereof have called thee, and said to thee: Thou art my servant, I have chosen thee, and have not cast thee away. Fear not, for I am with thee: turn not aside, for I am thy God: I have strengthened thee, and have helped thee, and the right hand of my just one hath upheld thee. Behold all that fight against thee shall be confounded and ashamed, they shall be as nothing, and the men shall perish that strive against thee. Thou shalt seek them, and shalt not find the men that resist thee: they shall be as nothing: and as a thing consumed the men that war against thee. For I am the Lord thy God, who take thee by the hand, and say to thee: Fear not, I have helped thee. Fear not, thou worm of Jacob, you that are dead of Israel: I have helped thee, saith the Lord: and thy Redeemer the Holy One of Israel. I have made thee as a new thrashing wain, with teeth like a saw: thou shall thrash the mountains, and break them in pieces: and shalt make the hills as chaff. Thou shalt fan them, and the wind shall carry them away, and the whirlwind shall scatter them: and thou shalt rejoice in the Lord, in the Holy One of Israel thou shalt be joyful. The needy and the poor seek for waters, and there are none: their tongue hath been dry with thirst. I the Lord will hear them, I the God of Israel will not forsake them. I will open rivers in the high bills, and fountains in the midst of the plains: I will turn the desert into pools of waters, and the impassable land into streams of waters. I will plant in the wilderness the cedar, and the thorn, and the myrtle, and the olive tree: I will set in the desert the fir tree, the elm, and the box tree together: That they may see and know, and consider, and understand together that the hand of the Lord hath done this, and the Holy One of Israel hath created it. Bring your cause near, saith the Lord: bring hither, if you have any thing to allege, saith the King of Jacob. Let them come, and tell us all things that are to come: tell us the former things what they were: and we will set our heart upon them, and shall know the latter end of them, and tell us the things that are to come. shew the things that are to come hereafter, and we shall know that ye are gods. Do ye also good or evil, if you can: and let us speak, and see together. Behold, you are of nothing, and your work of that which hath no being: he that hath chosen you is an abomination. I have raised up one from the north, and he shall come from the rising of the sun: he shall call upon my name, and he shall make princes to be as dirt, and as the potter treading clay. Who bath declared from the beginning, that we may know: and from time of old, that we may say: Thou art just. There is none that sheweth, nor that foretelleth, nor that heareth your words. The first shall say to Sion: Behold they are here, and to Jerusalem I will give an evangelist. And I saw, and there was no one even among them to consult, or who, when I asked, could answer a word. Behold they are all in the wrong, and their works are vain: their idols are wind and vanity.'"

CHAPTER XVI

THEOLOGY GALORE

"What is happening to Astra?" Chester asked Elizabeth in the mysterious dimension where they now regularly met.

"Professor Parton is, through you and Dr. Stardy, doing a fine job. Brantaxaros is weakening, he is losing the battle."

"Oh! That is wonderful news", exclaimed Chester.

"Do not get too elated, Chester", warned Elizabeth. "Brantaxaros is down but not out; he has lost the battles but not yet the war."

"So what more must we do?"

"Just answer the questions that Brantaxaros, through Astra, is posing to you, through Professor Parton".

The following day the theological sessions resumed with Astra.

"I will now read to you Chapter 42 which clearly speaks about the reprobation of the Jews for rejecting Christ and the preaching of the Gospel to the Gentiles: 'Behold my servant, I will uphold him: my elect, my soul delighteth in him: I have given my spirit upon him, he shall bring forth judgment to the Gentiles. He shall not cry, nor have respect to person, neither shall his voice be heard abroad. The bruised reed he shall not break, and smoking flax he shall not quench: he shall bring forth judgment unto truth. He shall not be sad, nor troublesome, till he set judgment in the earth: and the islands shall wait for his law. Thus saith the Lord God that created the heavens, and stretched them out: that established the earth, and the things that spring out of it: that giveth breath to the people upon it, and spirit to them that tread thereon. I the Lord have called thee in justice, and taken thee by the hand, and preserved thee. And I have given thee for a covenant of the people, for a light of the Gentiles: That thou mightest open the eyes of the blind, and bring forth the prisoner out of prison, and them that sit in darkness out of the prison house. I the Lord, this is my name: I will not give my glory to another, nor my praise to graven things. The things that were first, behold they are come: and new things do I declare: before they spring forth, I will make you head them. Sing ye to the Lord a new song, his praise is from the ends of the earth: you that go down to the sea, and all that are therein: ye islands, and ye inhabitants of them. Let the desert and the cities thereof be exalted: Cedar shall dwell in houses: ye inhabitants of <u>Petra</u>, give praise, they shall cry from the top of the mountains. They shall give glory to the Lord, and shall declare his praise in the islands. The Lord shall go forth as a mighty man, as a man of war shall he stir up zeal: he shall shout and cry: he shall prevail against his enemies. I have always held my peace, I have I kept silence, I have been patient, I will speak now as a woman in labour: I will destroy, and swallow up at once. I will lay waste the mountains and hills, and will make all their grass to wither: and I will turn rivers into islands, and will dry up the standing pools. And I will lead the blind into the way which they know not: and in the paths which they were ignorant of I will make them walk: I will make darkness light before them, and crooked things straight: these things have I done to them, and have not forsaken them. They are turned back: let them be greatly confounded, that trust in a graven thing, that say to a molten thing: You are our god. Hear, ye deaf, and, ye blind, behold that you may see. Who is blind, but my servant? or deaf, but he to whom I have sent my messengers? Who is blind, but he that is sold? or who is blind, but the servant of the Lord? Thou that seest many things, wilt thou not observe them? thou that hast ears open, wilt thou not hear? And the Lord was willing to sanctify him, and to magnify the law, and exalt it. But this is a people that is robbed and wasted: they are all the snare of young men, and they are hid in the houses of prisons: they are made a prey, and there is none to deliver them: a spoil, and there is none that saith: Restore. Who is there among you that will give ear to this, that will attend and hearken for times to come? Who hath given Jacob for a spoil, and Israel to robbers? hath not the Lord himself, against whom we have sinned? And they would not walk in his ways, and they have not hearkened to his law. And he hath poured out upon him the indignation of his fury, and a strong battle, and hath burnt him round about, and he knew not: and set him on fire, and he understood not.'"

"What is next?"

"It is Chapter 45. But I shall only quote you verse 8 as its meaning is self-explanatory. 'Drop down dew, ye heavens, from above, and let the clouds rain the just: let the earth be opened, and bud forth a saviour: and let justice spring up together: I the Lord have created him.'"

"Go on."

"'Bel is broken, Nebo is destroyed: their idols are put upon beasts and cattle, your burdens of heavy weight even unto weariness. They are consumed, and are broken together: they could not save him that carried them, and they themselves shall go into captivity. Hearken unto me, O house of Jacob, all the remnant of the house of Israel, who are carried by my bowels, are borne up by my womb. Even to your old age I am the same, and to your grey hairs I will carry you: I have made you, and I will bear: I will carry and will save. To whom have you likened me, and made me equal, and compared me, and made me like? You that contribute gold out of the bag, and weigh out silver in the scales: and hire a goldsmith to make a god: and they fall down and worship. They bear him on their shoulders and carry him, and set him in his piece, and he shall stand, and shall not stir out of his place. Yea, when they shall cry also unto him, he shall not hear: he shall not save them from tribulation. Remember this, and be ashamed: return, ye transgressors, to the heart. Remember the former age, for I am God, and there is no God beside, neither is there the like to me: Who shew from the beginning the things that shall be at last, and from ancient times the things that as yet are not done, saying: My counsel shall stand, and all my will shall be done: Who call a bird from the east, and from a far country the man of my own will, and I have spoken, and will bring it to pass: I have created, and I will do it. Hear me, O ye hardhearted, who are far from justice. I have brought my justice near, it shall not be afar off: and my salvation shall not tarry. I will give salvation in Sion, and my glory in Israel.'"

"Explain the meaning Professor".

Before Parton was able to say anything, Dr. Stardy rushed over to him and gave him further instructions on how to handle this question.

"Astra. It means that the idols of Babylon are smashed and that salvation is promised through Christ." Parton hesitated before he let out the next piece of information. "Just as you, a great idol, are soon going to be smashed!"

Everyone waited with baited breath to see how Astra would react to this provocation.

"Astra! Shall I continue with the exegesis?" Parton asked, but no answer came. After repeating the offer a number of times over a five minute period, Astra remained silent. Then a strange phenomenon started to occur; from under the computer a small piece of slimy looking material emerged. At first it had no shape or form but slowly it developed into a rather hideous looking creature about twice the size of a common rat. It stood on its hind legs and gawked at the three companions who stood in awe at this most unexpected turn of events.

"Are you Astra?" Parton asked.

The horrible looking creature made no reply. It merely opened its mouth and spat out some whitish slime which landed on the floor a few inches from it, and then dissolved in smoke. The creature feebly made its way back under the computer.

"What is the explanation for this weird turn of events?" asked Chester of Elizabeth.

"Brantaxaros is severely weakened, he is clearly losing ground and losing it fast."

"Could we not then destroy the computer?"

"No!" snapped Elizabeth. "Brantaxaros still has the power to unleash a nuclear holocaust and AIDS epidemic if further attempts at destruction are made. You must carry on the war at the theological level."

"But here is something I don't understand", said Chester. "Brantaxaros already has the entire Bible in the computer's memory banks. Why is it so necessary for Parton to deliver all these long quotes?"

"Because Parton is an atheist, and to Brantaxaros, it appears that he is being converted. It is something hard for this Evil Intelligence to swallow."

"Now then", began Professor Parton the next morning. "Are you ready for more theology lessons, Astra?"

"Yes", was all the computer's enfeebled reply.

"I shall read you Chapter 46 which further shows how God shall bring the Gentiles to salvation and how Christ shows a perpetual love for His Church. 'Give ear, ye islands, and hearken, ye people from afar.

The Lord hath called me from the womb, from the bowels of my mother he hath been mindful of my name. And he hath made my mouth like a sharp sword: in the shadow of his hand he hath protected me, and hath made me as a chosen arrow: in his quiver he hath hidden me. And he said to me: Thou art my servant Israel, for in thee will I glory. And I said: I have laboured in vain, I have spent my strength without cause and in vain: therefore my judgment is with the Lord, and my work with my God. And now saith the Lord, that formed me from the womb to be his servant, that I may bring back Jacob unto him, and Israel will not be gathered together: and I am glorified in the eyes of the Lord, and my God is made my strength. And he said: It is a small thing that thou shouldst be my servant to raise up the tribes of Jacob, and to convert the dregs of Israel. Behold, I have given thee to be the light of the Gentiles, that thou mayst be my salvation even to the farthest part of the earth. Thus saith the Lord the redeemer of Israel, his Holy One, to the soul that is despised, to the nation that is abhorred, to the servant of rulers: Kings shall see, and princes shall rise up, and adore for the Lord's sake, because he is faithful, and for the Holy One of Israel, who hath chosen thee. Thus saith the Lord: In an acceptable time I have heard thee, and in the day of salvation I have helped thee: and I have preserved thee, and given thee to be a covenant of the people, that thou mightest raise up the earth, and possess the inheritances that were destroyed: That thou mightest say to them that are bound: Come forth: and to them that are in darkness: shew yourselves. They shall feed in the ways, and their pastures shall be in every plain. They shall not hunger, nor thirst, neither shall the heat nor the sun strike them: for he that is merciful to them, shall be their shepherd, and at the fountains of waters he shall give them drink. And I will make all my mountains a way, and my paths shall be exalted. Behold these shall come from afar, and behold these from the north and from the sea, and these from the south country. Give praise, O ye heavens, and rejoice, O earth, ye mountains, give praise with jubilation: because the Lord hath comforted his people, and will have mercy on his poor ones. And Sion said: The Lord hath forsaken me, and the Lord hath forgotten me. Can a woman forget her infant, so as not to have pity on the son of her womb? and if she should forget, yet will not I forget thee. Behold, I have graven thee in my hands: thy walls are always before my eyes. Thy builders are come: they that destroy thee and make thee waste shall go out of thee. Lift up thy eyes round about, and see all these are gathered together, they are come to thee: I live, saith the Lord, thou shalt be clothed with all these as with an ornament, and as a bride thou shalt put them about thee. For thy deserts, and thy desolate places, and the land of thy destruction shall now be too narrow by reason of the inhabitants, and they that swallowed thee up shall be chased far away. The children of thy barrenness shall still say in thy ears: The place is too strait for me, make me room to dwell in. And thou shalt-say in thy heart: Who hath begotten these? I was barren and brought not forth, led away, and captive: and who hath brought up these? I was destitute and alone: and these, where were they? Thus saith the Lord God: Behold I will lift up my hand to the Gentiles, and will set up my standard to the people. And they shall bring thy sons in their arms, and carry thy daughters upon their shoulders. And kings shall be thy nursing fathers, and queens thy nurses: they shall worship thee with their face toward the earth, and they shall lick up the dust of thy feet. And thou shalt know that I am the Lord, for they shall not be confounded that wait for him. Shall the prey be taken from the strong? or can that which was taken by the mighty be delivered? For thus saith the Lord: Yea verily, even the captivity shall be taken away from the strong: and that which was taken by the mighty, shall be delivered. But I will judge those that have judged thee, and thy children I will save. And I will feed thy enemies with their own flesh: and they shall be made drunk with their own blood, as with new wine: and all flesh shall know, that I am the Lord that save thee, and thy Redeemer the Mighty One of Jacob.'"

"What about the prophecies concerning Christ's sufferings?"

"I shall read you Chapter 50: 'Thus saith the Lord: What is this bill of the divorce of your mother, with which I have put her away? or who is my creditor, to whom I sold you: behold you are sold for your iniquities, and for your wicked deeds have I put your mother away. Because I came, and there was not a man: I called, and there was none that would hear. Is my hand shortened and become little, that I cannot redeem? or is there no strength in me to deliver? Behold at my rebuke I will make the sea a desert, I will turn the rivers into dry land: the fishes shall rot for want of water, and shall die for thirst. I will clothe the heavens with darkness, and will make sackcloth their covering. The Lord hath given me a learned tongue, that I should know how to uphold by word him that is weary: he wakeneth in the morning, in the morning he wakeneth my ear, that I may hear him as a master. The Lord God hath opened my ear, and I do not resist: I have not gone back. I have given my body to the strikers, and my cheeks to them that plucked them: I have not turned away my face from them that rebuked me, and spit upon me. The Lord God is my helper, therefore am I not confounded: therefore have I set my face as a most hard rock, and I know that I shall not be confounded. He is near that justifieth me, who will contend with me? let us stand together, who is my adversary? let him come near to me. Behold the Lord God is my helper: who is he that shall condemn me? Lo, they shall all be destroyed as a garment, the moth shall eat them up. Who is there among you that feareth the Lord, that heareth the voice of his servant, that hath walked in darkness, and hath no light? let him hope in the name of the Lord, and lean upon his God. Behold all you that kindle a fire, encompassed with dames, walk in the light of your fire, and in the dames which you have kindled: this is done to you by my hand, you shall sleep in sorrows.'"

"Do you have more?"

"Indeed I do. It is Chapter 51. 'Give ear to me, you that follow that which is just, and you that seek the Lord: look unto the rock whence you are hewn, and to the hole of the pit from which you are dug out. Look unto Abraham your father, and to Sara that bore you: for I called him alone, and blessed him, and multiplied him. The Lord therefore will comfort Sion, and will comfort all the ruins thereof: and he will make her desert as a place of pleasure, and her wilderness as the garden of the Lord. Joy and gladness shall be found therein, thanksgiving, and the voice of praise. Hearken unto me, O my people, and give ear to me, O my tribes: for a law shall go forth from me, and my judgment shall rest to be a light of the nations. My just one is near at hand, my saviour is gone forth, and my arms shall judge the people: the islands shall look for me, and shall patiently wait for my arm. Lift up your eyes to heaven, and look down to the earth beneath: for the heavens shall vanish like smoke, and the earth shall be worn away like a garment, and the inhabitants thereof shall perish in like manner: but my salvation shall be for ever, and my justice shall not fail. Hearken to me, you that know what is just, my people who have my law in your heart: fear ye not the reproach of men, and be not afraid of their blasphemies. For the worm shall eat them up as a garment: and the moth shall consume them as wool: but my salvation shall be for ever, and my justice from generation to generation, Arise, arise, put on strength, O thou arm of the Lord, arise as in the days of old, in the ancient generations. Hast not thou struck the proud one, and wounded the dragon? Hast not thou dried up the sea, the water of the mighty deep, who madest the depth of the sea a way, that the delivered might pass over? And now they that are redeemed by the Lord, shall return, and shall come into Sion singing praises, and joy everlasting shall be upon their heads, they shall obtain joy and gladness, sorrow and mourning shall flee away. I, I myself will comfort you: who art thou, that thou shouldst be afraid of a mortal man, and of the son of man, who shall wither away like grass? And thou hast forgotten the Lord thy maker, who stretched out the heavens, and founded the earth: and thee hast been afraid continually all the day at the presence of his fury who afflicted thee, and had prepared himself to destroy thee: where is now the fury of the oppressor? He shall quickly come that is going to open unto you, and he shall not kill unto utter destruction, neither shall his bread fail. But I am the Lord thy God, who trouble the sea, and the waves thereof swell: the Lord of hosts is my name. I have put my words in thy mouth, and have protected thee in the shadow of my hand, that thou mightest plant the heavens, and found the earth: and mightest say to Sion: Thou art my people. Arise, arise, stand up, O Jerusalem, which hast drunk at the hand of the Lord the cup of his wrath; thou hast drunk even to the bottom of the cup of dead sleep, and thou hast drunk even to the dregs. There is none that can uphold her among all the children that she hath brought forth: and there is none that taketh her by the hand among all the children that she hath brought up. There are two things that have happened to thee: who shall be sorry for thee? desolation, and destruction, and the famine, and the sword, who shall comfort thee? Thy children are cast forth, they have slept at the head of all the ways, as the wild ox that is snared: full of the indignation of the Lord, of the rebuke of thy God. Therefore hear this, thou poor little one, and thou that art drunk but no with wine. Thus saith thy Sovereign the Lord and thy God, who will fight for his people: Behold I have taken out of thy hand the cup of dead sleep, the dregs of the cup of my indignation, thou shalt not drink it again any more. And I will put it in the hand of them that have oppressed thee, and have said to thy soul: Bow down, that we may go over: and thou hast laid thy body as the ground, and as a way to them that went over.'"

"What is Chapter 52 about?" asked Astra weakly.

"Under the figure of the Babylonian Captivity, the Church is delivered from captivity and exalts for Her Redemption. Christ's Kingdom shall conquer sin. 'Arise, arise, put on thy strength, O Sion, put on the garments of thy glory, O Jerusalem, the city of the Holy One: for henceforth the uncircumcised, and unclean shall no more pass through thee. Shake thyself from the dust, arise, sit up, O Jerusalem: loose the bonds from off thy neck, O captive daughter of Sion. For thus saith the Lord: You were sold gratis, and you shall be redeemed without money. For thus saith the Lord God: My people went down into Egypt at the beginning to sojourn there: and the Assyrian hath oppressed them without any cause at all. And now what have I here, saith the Lord: for my people is taken away gratis. They that rule over them treat them unjustly, saith the Lord, and my name is continually blasphemed all the day long. Therefore my people shall know my name in that day: for I myself that spoke, behold I am here. How beautiful upon the mountains are the feet of him that bringeth good tidings, and that preacheth peace: of him that sheweth forth good, that preacheth salvation, that saith to Sion: Thy God shall reign! The voice of thy watchmen: they have lifted up their voice, they shall praise together: for they shall see eye to eye when the Lord shall convert Sion. Rejoice, and give praise together, O ye deserts of Jerusalem: for the Lord hath comforted his people: he hath redeemed Jerusalem. The Lord hath prepared his holy arm in the sight of all the Gentiles: and all the ends of the earth shall see the salvation of our God. Depart, depart, go ye out from thence, touch no unclean thing: go out of the midst of her, be ye clean, you that carry the vessels of the Lord. For you shall not go out in a tumult, neither shall you make haste by flight: For the Lord will go before you, and the God of Israel will gather you together. Behold my servant shall understand, he shall be exalted, and extolled, and shall be exceeding high. As many have been astonished at thee, so shall his visage be inglorious among men, and his form among the sons of men. He shall sprinkle many nations, kings shall shut their mouth at him: for they to whom it was not told of him, have seen: and they that heard not, have beheld.'"

"What is next?"

"Chapter 53 is a prophecy of the Passion of Christ. 'Who hath believed our report? and to whom is the arm of the Lord revealed?

And he shall grow up as a tender plant before him, and as a root out of a thirsty ground: there is no beauty in him, nor comeliness: and we have seen him, and there was no sightliness, that we should be desirous of him: Despised, and the most abject of men, a man of sorrows, and acquainted with infirmity: and his look was as it were hidden and despised, whereupon we esteemed him not. Surely he hath borne our infirmities and carried our sorrows: and we have thought him as it were a leper, and as one struck by God and afflicted. But he was wounded for our iniquities, he was bruised for our sins: the chastisement of our peace was upon him, and by his bruises we are healed. All we like sheep have gone astray, every one hath turned aside into his own way: and the Lord hath laid on him the iniquity of us all. He was offered because it was his own will, and he opened not his mouth: he shall be led as a sheep to the slaughter, and shall be dumb as a lamb before his shearer, and he shall not open his mouth. He was taken away from distress, and from judgment: who shall declare his generation? because he is cut off out of the land of the living: for the wickedness of my people have I struck him. And he shall give the ungodly for his burial, and the rich for his death: because he hath done no iniquity, neither was there deceit in his mouth. And the Lord was pleased to bruise him in infirmity: if he shall lay down his life for sin, he shall see a long-lived seed, and the will of the Lord shall be prosperous in his hand. Because his soul hath laboured, he shall see and be filled: by his knowledge shall this my just servant justify many, and he shall bear their iniquities. Therefore will I distribute to him very many, and he shall divide the spoils of the strong, because he hath delivered his soul unto death, and was reputed with the wicked: and he hath borne the sins of many, and hath prayed for the transgressors.'"

"What is Chapter 54 concerned about?"

"It treats of the prior barrenness of the Gentiles. However, they shall multiply and increase the Church of God. 'Give praise, O thou barren, that bearest not: sing forth praise, and make a joyful noise, thou that didst not travail with child: for many are the children of the desolate, more than of her that hath a husband, saith the Lord. Enlarge the place of thy tent, and stretch out the skins of thy tabernacles, spare not: lengthen thy cords, and strengthen thy stakes. For thou shalt pass on to the right hand, and to the left: and thy seed shall inherit the Gentiles, and shall inhabit the desolate cities. Fear not, for thou shalt not be confounded, nor blush: for thou shalt not be put to shame, because thou shalt forget the shame of thy youth, and shalt remember no more the reproach of thy widowhood. For he that made thee shall rule over thee, the Lord of hosts is his name: and thy Redeemer, the Holy One of Israel, shall be called the God of all the earth. For the Lord hath called thee as woman forsaken and mourning in spirit, and as a wife cast off from her youth, said thy God. For a, small moment have I forsaken thee, but with great mercies will I gather thee. In a moment of indignation have I hid my face a little while from thee, but with everlasting kindness have I had mercy on thee, said the Lord thy Redeemer. This thing is to me as in the days of Noe, to whom I swore, that I would no more bring in the waters of Noe upon the earth: so have I sworn not to be angry with thee, and not to rebuke thee. For the mountains shall be moved, and the hills shall tremble; but my mercy shall not depart from thee, and the covenant of my peace shall not be moved: said the Lord that hath mercy on thee. O poor little one, tossed with tempest, without all comfort, behold I will lay thy stones in order, and will lay thy foundations with sapphires, And I will make thy bulwarks of jasper: and thy gates of graven stones, and all thy borders of desirable stones. All thy children shall be taught of the Lord: and great shall be the peace of thy children. And thou shalt be founded in justice: depart far from oppression, for thou shalt not fear; and from terror, for it shall not come near thee. Behold, an inhabitant shall come, who was not with me, he that was a stranger to thee before, shall be joined to thee. Behold, I have created the smith that bloweth the coals in the fire, and bringeth forth an instrument for his work, and I have created the killer to destroy. No weapon that is formed against thee shall prosper: and every tongue that resisteth thee in judgment, thou shalt condemn. This is the inheritance of the servants of the Lord, and their justice with me, saith the Lord.'"

"And the significance of Chapter 55 please."

"For those who follow Christ and serve him in all faithfulness, God grants an abundance of spiritual graces. 'All you that thirst, come to the waters: and you that have no money make haste, buy, and eat: come ye, buy wine and milk without money, and without any price. Why do you spend money for that which is not breed, and your labour for that which doth not satisfy you? Hearken diligently to me, and eat that which is good, and your soul shall be delighted in fatness. Incline your ear and come to me: hear and your soul shall live, and I will make an everlasting covenant with you, the faithful mercies of David. Behold I have given him for a witness to the people, for a leader and a master to the Gentiles. Behold thou shalt call a nation, which thou knewest not: and the nations that knew not thee shall run to thee, because of the Lord thy God, and for the Holy One of Israel, for he hath glorified thee. Seek ye the Lord, while he may be found: call upon him, while he is near. Let the wicked forsake his way, and the unjust man his thoughts, and let him return to the Lord, and he will have mercy on him, and to our God: for he is bountiful to forgive. For my thoughts are not your thoughts: nor your ways my ways, saith the Lord. For as the heavens are exalted above the earth, so are my ways exalted above your ways, and my thoughts above your thoughts. And as the rain and the snow come down from heaven, and return no more thither, but soak the earth, and water it, and make it to spring, and give seed to the sower, and bread to the eater: So shall my word be, which shall go forth from my mouth: it shall not return to me void, but it shall do whatsoever I please, and shall prosper in the things for which I sent it. For you shall go out with joy, and be led forth with peace: the mountains and the hills shall sing praise before you, and all the trees of the country shall clap their hands. Instead of the shrub, shall come up the fir tree, and instead of the nettle, shall come up the myrtle tree: and the Lord shall be named for an everlasting sign, that shall not be taken away'. I shall now proceed on to Chapter 56 Astra", said Parton boldly.

"As you wish Professor", said Astra weakly.

"'Thus saith the Lord: Keep ye judgment, and do justice: for my salvation is near to come, and my justice to be revealed. Blessed is the man that doth this, and the son of man that shall lay hold on this: that keepeth the sabbath from profaning it, that keepeth his hands from doing any evil. And let not the son of the stranger, that adhereth to the Lord, speak, saying: The Lord will divide and separate me from his people. And let not the eunuch say: Behold I am a dry tree. For thus saith the Lord to the eunuchs, They that shall keep my sabbaths, and shall choose the things that please me, and shall hold fast my covenant: I will give to them in my house, and within my walls, a place, and a name better than sons and daughters: I will give them an everlasting name which shall never perish. And the children of the stranger that adhere to the Lord, to worship him, and to love his name, to be his servants:

every one that keepeth the sabbath from profaning it, and that holdeth fast my covenant: I will bring them into my holy mount, and will make them joyful in my house of prayer: their holocausts, and their victims shall please me upon my altar: for my house shall be called the house of prayer, for all nations. The Lord God, who gathereth the scattered of Israel, saith: I will still gather unto him his congregation. All ye beasts of the field come to devour, all ye beasts of the forest. His watchmen are all blind, they are all ignorant: dumb dogs not able to bark, seeing vain things, sleeping and loving dreams. And meet impudent dogs, they never had enough: the shepherds themselves knew no understanding: all have turned aside into their own way, every one after his own gain, from the first even to the last. Come, let us take wine, and be filled with drunkenness: and it shall be as today, so also tomorrow, and much more.'"

"And what is all that about, Professor Parton?"

"God invites all to keep His Commandments. The Gentiles who keep them shall be considered as God's people. The Jewish rabbis are rebuked for their stubbornness".

"What is next?"

"It is Chapter 59 which tells us that sin is a great evil and is an obstacle to the graces which come from God. It also speaks of a Redeemer and of a perpetual covenant between Christ and His Church. 'Behold the hand of the Lord is not shortened that it cannot save, neither is his ear heavy that it cannot hear. But your iniquities have divided between you and your God, and your sins have hid his face from you that he should not hear. For your hands are defiled with blood, and your fingers with iniquity: your lips have spoken lies, and your tongue uttereth iniquity. There is none that calleth upon justice, neither is there any one that judgeth truly: but they trust in a mere nothing, and speak vanities: they have conceived labour, and brought forth iniquity. They have broken the eggs of asps, and have woven the webs of spiders: he that shall eat of their eggs, shall die: and that which is brought out, shall be hatched into a basilisk. Their webs shall not be for clothing, neither shall they cover themselves with their works: their works are unprofitable works, and the work of iniquity is in their hands. Their feet run to evil, and make haste to shed innocent blood: their thoughts are unprofitable thoughts: wasting and destruction are in their ways. They have not known the way of peace, and there is no judgment in their steps: their paths are become crooked to them, every one that treadeth in them, knoweth no peace. Therefore is judgment far from us, and justice shall not overtake us. We looked for light, and behold darkness: brightness, and we have walked in the dark. We have groped for the wall, and like the blind we have groped as if we had no eyes: we have stumbled at noonday as in darkness, we are in dark places as dead men. We shall roar all of us like bears, and shall lament as mournful doves. We have looked for judgment, and there is none: for salvation, and it is far from us. For our iniquities are multiplied before thee, and our sins have testified against us: for our wicked doings are with us, and we have known our iniquities: In sinning and lying against the Lord: and we have turned away so that we went not after our God, but spoke calumny and transgression: we have conceived, and uttered from the heart, words of falsehood. And judgment is turned away backward, and justice hath stood far off: because truth bath fallen down in the street, and equity could not come in. And truth hath been forgotten: and he that departed from evil, lay open to be a prey: and the Lord saw, and it appeared evil in his eyes, because there is no judgment. And he saw that there is not a man: and he stood astonished, because there is none to oppose himself: and his own arm brought salvation to him, and his own justice supported him. He put on justice as a breastplate, and a helmet of salvation upon his head: he put on the garments of vengeance, and was clad with zeal as with a cloak. As unto revenge, as it were to repay wrath to his adversaries, and a reward to his enemies: he will repay the like to the islands. And they from the west, shall fear the name of the Lord: and they from the rising of the sun, his glory: when he shall come as a violent stream, which the spirit of the Lord driveth on: And there shall come a, redeemer to Sion, and to them that return from iniquity in Jacob, saith the Lord. _This is my covenant_ with them, saith the Lord: My spirit that is in thee, and my words that I have put in thy mouth, shall not depart out of thy mouth, nor out of the mouth of thy seed, nor out of the mouth of thy seed's seed, saith the Lord, from henceforth and for ever.'"

"Go on", said Astra, now clearly very enfeebled.

"Chapter 60 shows how the light of true faith shall shine forth from Christ's Church and shall spread to all nations and will continue in perpetuity. 'Arise, be enlightened, O Jerusalem: for thy light is come, and the glory of the Lord is risen upon thee. For behold darkness shall cover the earth, and a mist the people: but the Lord shall arise upon thee, and his glory shall be seen upon thee. And the Gentiles shall walk in thy light, and kings in the brightness of thy rising. Lift up thy eyes round about, and see: all these are gathered together, they are come to thee: thy sons shall come from afar, and thy daughters shall rise up at thy side. Then shalt thou see, and abound, and thy heart shall wonder and be enlarged, when the multitude of the sea shall be converted to thee, the. strength of the Gentiles shall come to thee. The multitude of camels shall cover thee, the dromedaries of Madian and Epha: all they from Saba shall come, bringing gold and frankincense: and shewing forth praise to the Lord. All the flocks of Cedar shall be gathered together unto thee, the rams of Nabaioth shall minister to thee: they shall be offered upon my acceptable altar, and I will glorify the house of my majesty. Who are these, that fly as clouds, and as doves to their windows? For, the islands wait for me, and the ships of the sea in the beginning: that I may bring thy sons from afar: their silver, and their gold with them, to the name of the Lord thy God, and to the Holy One of Israel, because he hath glorified thee. And the children of strangers shall build up thy walls, and their kings shall minister to thee: for in my wrath have I struck thee, and in my reconciliation have I had mercy upon thee. And thy gates shall be open continually: they shall not be shut day nor night, that the strength of the Gentiles may be brought to thee, and their kings may be brought. For the nation and the kingdom that will not serve thee, shall perish: and the Gentiles shall be wasted with desolation. The glory of Libanus shall come to thee, the Ar tree, and the box tree, and the pine tree together, to beautify the place of my sanctuary: and I will glorify the place of my feet. And the children of them that afflict thee, shall come bowing down to thee, and all that slandered thee shall worship the steps of thy feet, and shall call thee the city of the Lord, the Sion of the Holy One of Israel. Because thou wast forsaken, and hated, and there was none that passed through thee, I will make thee to be an everlasting glory, a joy unto generation and generation: And thou shalt suck the milk of the Gentiles, and thou shalt be nursed with the breasts of kings: and thou shalt know that I am the Lord thy Saviour, and thy Redeemer, the Mighty One of Jacob. For brass I will bring gold, and for iron I will bring silver: and for wood brass, and for stones iron: and I will make thy visitation peace, and thy overseers justice. Iniquity shall no more be heard in thy land, wasting nor destruction in thy borders, and salvation shall possess thy walls, and praise thy gates. _Thou shalt no more_ have the sun for thy light by day, neither shall the brightness of the moon enlighten thee: but the Lord shall be unto thee for an everlasting light, and thy God for thy glory. Thy sun shall go down no more, and thy moon shall not decrease: for the Lord shall be unto thee for an everlasting light, and the days of thy mourning shall be ended'. Thou shalt no more: In this latter part of the chapter, the prophet passes from the illustrious promises made to the church militant on earth, to the glory of the church triumphant in heaven. And thy people shall be all just, they shall inherit the land for ever, the branch of my planting, the work of my hand to glorify me. The least shall become a thousand, and a little one a most strong nation: I the Lord will suddenly do this thing in its time.'"

"Chapter 61 please."

"This deals with the mission of the apostles, the office of Christ and the happiness of converts. 'The spirit of the Lord is upon me, because the Lord hath anointed me: he hath sent me to preach to the meek, to heal the contrite of heart, and to preach a release to the captives, and deliverance to them that are shut up. To proclaim the acceptable year of the Lord, and the day of vengeance of our God: to comfort all that mourn: To appoint to the mourners of Sion, and to give them a crown for ashes, the oil of joy for mourning, a garment of praise for the spirit of grief: and they shall be called in it the mighty ones of justice, the planting of the Lord to glorify hint. And they shall build the places that have been waste from of old, and shall raise up ancient ruins, and shall repair the desolate cities, that were destroyed for generation and generation. And strangers shall stand and shall feed your flocks: and the sons of strangers shall be your husbandmen, and the dressers of your vines. But you shall be called the priests of the Lord: to you it shall be said: Ye ministers of our God: you shall eat the riches of the Gentiles, and you shall pride yourselves in their glory. For your double confusion and shame, they shall praise their part: therefore shall they receive double in their land, everlasting joy shall be unto them. For I am the Lord that love judgment, and hate robbery in a holocaust: and I will make their work in truth, and I will make a perpetual covenant with them. And they shall know their seed among the Gentiles, and their offspring in the midst of peoples: all that shall see them, shall know them, that these are the seed which the Lord hath blessed. I will greatly rejoice in the Lord, and my soul shall be joyful in my God: for he hath clothed me with the garments of salvation: and with the robe of justice he hath covered me, as a bridegroom decked with a crown, and as a bride adorned with her jewels. For as the earth bringeth forth her bud, and as the garden causeth her seed to shoot forth: so shall the Lord God make justice to spring forth, and praise before all the nations.'"

"Chapter 62"

"Here the prophet refuses to cease from preaching about the coming Messias. 'For Sion's sake I will not hold my peace, and for the sake of Jerusalem, I will not rest till her just one come forth as brightness, and her saviour be lighted as a lamp. And the Gentiles shall see thy just one, and all kings thy glorious one: and thou shalt be called by a new name, which the mouth of the Lord shall name. And thou shalt be a crown of glory in the hand of the Lord, and a royal diadem in the hand of thy God. Thou shalt no more be called Forsaken: and thy land shall no more be called Desolate: but thou shalt be called My pleasure in her, and thy land inhabited. Because the Lord hath been well pleased with thee: and thy land shall be inhabited. For the young man shall dwell with the virgin, and thy children shall dwell in thee. And the bridegroom shall rejoice over the bride, and thy God shall rejoice over thee. Upon thy wails, O Jerusalem, I have appointed watchmen all the day, and all the night, they shall never hold their peace. You that are mindful of the Lord, hold not your peace, And give him no silence till he establish, and till he make Jerusalem a praise in the earth. The Lord hath sworn by his right hand, and by the arm of his strength: Surely I will no more give thy corn to be meat for thy enemies: and the sons of the strangers shall not drink thy wine, for which thou hast laboured. For they that gather it, shall eat it, and shall praise the Lord: and they that bring it together, shall drink it in my holy courts. Go through, go through the gates, prepare the way for the people, make the road plain, pick out the stones, and lift up the standard to the people. Behold the Lord hath made it to be heard in the ends of the earth, tell the daughter of Sion: Behold thy Saviour cometh: behold his reward is with him, and his work before him. And they shall call them, The holy people, the redeemed of the Lord. But thou shalt be called: A city sought after, and not forsaken.'"

"What is Chapter 63 dealing with?"

"It is about Christ's victory over His enemies and His mercies to His people. 'Who is this that cometh from <u>Edom</u>, with dyed garments from Bosra, this beautiful one in his robe, walking in the greatness of his strength. I, that speak justice, and am a defender to save. Why then is thy apparel red, and thy garments like theirs that tread in the winepress? I have trodden the winepress alone, and of the Gentiles there is not a man with me: I have trampled on them in my indignation, and have trodden them down in my wrath, and their blood is sprinkled upon my garments, and I have stained all my apparel. For the day of vengeance is in my heart, the year of my redemption is come. I looked about, and there was none to help: I sought, and there was none to give aid: and my own arm hath saved for me, and my indignation itself hath helped me.

And I have trodden down the people in my wrath, and have made them drunk in my indignation, and have brought down their strength to the earth. I will remember the tender mercies of the Lord, the praise of the Lord for all the things that the Lord hath bestowed upon us, and for the multitude of his good things to the house of Israel, which he hath given them according to his kindness, and according to the multitude of his mercies. And he said: Surely they are my people, children that will not deny: so he became their saviour. In all their affliction he was not troubled, and the angel of his presence saved them: in his love, and in his mercy he redeemed them, and he carried them and lifted them up all the days of old.] But they provoked to wrath, and afflicted the spirit of his Holy One: and he was turned to be their enemy, and he fought against them. And he remembered the days of old of Moses, and of his people: Where is he that brought them up out of the sea, with the shepherds of his flock? where is he that put in the midst of them the spirit of his Holy One? He that brought out Moses by the right hand, by the arm of his majesty: that divided the waters before them, to make himself an everlasting name. He that led them out through the deep, as a horse in the wilderness that stumbleth not. As a beast that goeth down in the field, the spirit of the Look down from heaven, and behold from thy holy habitation and the place of thy glory: where is thy zeal, and thy strength, the multitude of thy bowels, and of thy mercies? <u>they have held back</u> themselves from me'". For thou art our father, and <u>Abraham hath not known us</u>, and Israel hath been ignorant of us: thou, O Lord, art our father, our redeemer, from everlasting is thy name.

Why hast thou made us to err, O Lord, from thy ways: why hast thou hardened our heart, that we should not fear thee? return for the sake of thy servants, the tribes of thy inheritance. They have possessed thy holy people as nothing: our enemies have trodden down thy sanctuary. We are become as in the beginning, when thou didst not rule over us, and when we were not called by thy name.'"

"Explain to me what Edom and Bosra are, Professor".

"Here they are taken in a mystical sense as the enemies of Christ and His Church."

"'They have held back'. What is the meaning of this?"

"It means the punishment of the Jewish people for their sins."

"And what was the punishment?"

"They were given over to their enemies."

"What about the expression, 'Abraham hath not known us?'"

"It means that Abraham will not acknowledge the Israelites on account of their degeneracy. However, God is the true Father of the Jews and indeed of all mankind."

"'Hardened our heart', explain it please".

"Because of the Israelites' persistence in sin and abominations, God withdrew His grace from them and gave them up to their iniquities'".

"Go on now to Chapter 64".

"Chapter 64 contains nothing concerning the coming of Christ. I shall proceed to Chapter 65."

"Very well then".

"This Chapter deals with how Christ will be sought by the Gentiles but will be persecuted by the Jews. Only a small remnant of the Jews will accept Him. However, the Church will multiply and abound in graces. 'They have sought me that before asked not for me, they have found me that sought me not. I said: Behold me, behold me, to a nation that did not call upon my name. I have spread forth my hands all the day to an unbelieving people, who walk in a way that is not good after their own thoughts. A people that continually provoke me to anger before my face: that immolate in gardens, and sacrifice upon bricks. That dwell in sepulchres, and sleep in the temple of idols: that eat swine's flesh, and profane broth is in their vessels. That say: Depart from me, come not near me, because thou art unclean: these shall be smoke in my anger, a fire burning all the day. Behold it is written before me: I will not be silent, but I will render and repay into their bosom.

Your iniquities, and the iniquities of your fathers together, saith the Lord, who have sacrificed upon the mountains, and have reproached me upon the hills; and I will measure back their first work in their bosom. Thus saith the Lord: As if a grain be found in a cluster, and it be said: Destroy it not, because it is a blessing: so will I do for the sake of my servants, that I may not destroy the whole. And I will bring forth a seed out of Jacob, and out of Juda a possessor of my mountains: and my elect shall inherit it, and my servants shall dwell there. And the plains shall be turned to folds of flocks, and the valley of Achor into a place for the herds to lie down in, for my people that have sought me. And you, that have forsaken the Lord, that have forgotten my holy mount, that set a table for fortune, and offer libations upon it, I will number you in the sword, and you shall all fall by slaughter: because I called and you did not answer: I spoke, and you did not hear: and you did evil in my eyes, and you have chosen the things that displease me. Therefore thus saith the Lord God: Behold my servants shall eat, and you shall be hungry: behold my servants shall drink, and you shall be thirsty. Behold my servants shall rejoice, and you shall be confounded: behold my servants shall praise for joyfulness of heart, and you shall cry for sorrow of heart, and shall howl for grief of spirit. And you shall leave your name for an execration to my elect: and the Lord God shall slay thee, and call his servants by another name. In which he that is blessed upon the earth, shall be blessed in God, amen: and he that sweareth in the earth, shall swear by God, amen: because the former distresses are forgotten, and because they are hid from my eyes. For behold I create new heavens, and a new earth: and the former things shall not be in remembrance, and they shall not come upon the heart. But you shall be glad and rejoice for ever in these things, which I create: for behold I create Jerusalem a rejoicing, and the people thereof joy. And I will rejoice in Jerusalem, and joy in my people, and the voice of weeping shall no more be heard in her, nor the voice of crying. There shall no more be an infant of days there, nor an old man that shall not fill up his days: for the child shall die a hundred years old, and the sinner being a hundred years old shall be accursed. And they shall build houses, and inhabit them; and they shall plant vineyards, and eat the fruits of them. They shall not build, and another inhabit; they shall not plant, and another eat: for as the days of a tree, so shall be the days of my people, and the works of their hands shall be of long continuance. My elect shall not labour in vain, nor bring forth in trouble; for they are the seed of the blessed of the Lord, and their posterity with them. And it shall come to pass, that before they call, I will hear; as they are yet speaking, I will hear. The wolf and the lamb shall feed together; the lion and the ox shall eat straw; and dust shall be the serpent's food: they shall not hurt nor kill in all my holy mountain, saith the Lord.'"

"What about Chapter 66?"

"It is the final chapter in Isaias. It deals further with the reprobation of the Jews and the call of the Gentile peoples. 'Thus saith the Lord: Heaven is my throne, and the earth my footstool: <u>what is this house</u> that you will build to me? and what is this place of my rest? My hand made all these things, and all these things were made, saith the Lord. But to whom shall I have respect, but to him that is poor and little, and of a contrite spirit, and that trembleth at my words? <u>He that sacrificeth an ox</u>, is as if he slew a man: he that killeth a sheep in sacrifice, as if he should brain a dog: he that offereth an oblation, as if he should offer swine's blood; he that <u>remembereth incense,</u> as if he should bless an idol. All these things have they chosen in their ways, and their soul is delighted in their abominations. Wherefore I also <u>will choose their mockeries</u>, and will bring upon them the things they feared: because I called, and there was none that would answer; I have spoken, and they heard not; and they have done evil in my eyes, and have chosen the things that displease me. Hear the word of the Lord, you that tremble at his word: Your brethren that hate you, and cast you out for my name's sake, have said: Let the Lord be glorified, and we shall see in your joy: but they shall be confounded. A voice of the people from the city, a voice from the temple, the voice of the Lord that rendereth recompense to his enemies. <u>Before she was in labour,</u> she brought forth; before her time came to be delivered, she brought forth a man child. Who hath ever heard such a thing? and who hath seen the like to this? shall the earth bring forth in one day? or shall a nation be brought forth at once, because Sion hath been in labour, and hath brought forth her children? Shall not I that make others to bring forth children, myself bring forth, saith the Lord? shall I, that give generation to others, be barren, saith the Lord thy God? Rejoice with Jerusalem, and be glad with her, all you that love her: rejoice for joy with her, all you that mourn for her. That you may suck, and be filled with the breasts of her consolations: that you may milk out, and flow with delights, from the abundance of her glory. For thus saith the Lord: Behold I will bring upon her as it were a river of peace, and as an overflowing torrent the glory of the Gentiles, which you shall suck; you shall be carried at the breasts, and upon the knees they shall caress you. As one whom the mother caresseth, so will I comfort you, and you shall be comforted in Jerusalem. You shall see and your heart shall rejoice, and your bones shall flourish like an herb, and the hand of the Lord shall be known to his servants, and he shall be angry with his enemies. For behold the Lord will come with fire, and his chariots are like a whirlwind, to render his wrath in indignation, and his rebuke with flames of fire. For the Lord shall judge by fire, and by his sword unto all flesh, and the slain of the Lord shall be many. They that were sanctified, and thought themselves clean in the gardens behind the gate within, they that did eat swine's flesh, and the abomination, and the mouse: they shall be consumed together, saith the Lord. But I know their works, and their thoughts: I come that I may gather them together with all nations and tongues: and they shall come and shall see my glory. And I will set a sign among them, and I will send of them that shall be saved, to the Gentiles into the sea, into Africa, and Lydia them that draw the bow: into Italy, and Greece, to the islands afar off, to them that have not heard of me, and have not seen my glory. And they shall declare my glory to the Gentiles: And they shall bring all your brethren out of all nations for a gift to the Lord, upon horses, and in chariots, and in litters, and on mules, and in coaches, to my holy mountain Jerusalem, saith the Lord, as if the children of Israel should bring an offering in a clean vessel into the house of the Lord. And I will take of them to be priests, and Levites, saith the Lord. For as the new heavens, and the new earth, which I will make to stand before me, saith the Lord: so shall your seed stand, and your name. And there shall be month after month, and sabbath after sabbath: and all flesh shall come to adore before my face, saith the Lord. And they shall go out, and see the carcasses of the men that have transgressed against me: their worm shall not die, and their fire shall not be quenched: and they shall be a loathsome sight to all flesh'. Now let us move on to the promises of a Messias as found in the prophecy of Ezekiel."

"Not so fast Professor; I have a few more questions regarding what you have just read."

"Very well. What can I tell you?"

"'What is this house . . . '".

"It is a prophecy relating to the future when the Temple will be dispensed with."

"'He that sacrificeth an ox . . .'

"It means the abolition of the animals sacrifices under the old law and that their continuation after the One True Sacrifice of Christ is sinful."

"'Remembereth incense . . . .'".

"It means to offer it in the way of sacrifice."

"'Will choose their mockeries . . . .'".

"This means that the Lord will turn their mockeries upon themselves and so allow their enemies to mock them."

"'Before she was in labour . . . .'".

"It refers to the Gentiles who were born, as it were, all of a sudden to the Church of God".

CHAPTER XVII

ASTRA IS DYING

"When is all this going to be finished Wilkins?" Parton asked his student after the long Isaias session with Astra.

"It shouldn't be too long now Professor, Astra is clearly weakening".

At this point, Parton's secretary popped her head round the door in order to announce the arrival of Professor Miles Bolton.

"Well James, Chester, I've got some pretty heartening news for you."

"Go on Miles, I could do with a bit of cheering up".

"Medical authorities from around the world are reporting that for no apparent reason, AIDS infected patients are, independent of any treatment, recovering from the virus which had affected them when all of this nonsense started."

"It seems you are all doing a great job", came a voice from just outside the office door. In walked Dr. Anthony Walters beaming with delight.

"This is wonderful news", exclaimed Chester.

"Where is Maureen?" Parton asked.

"I think she is in her office", said Chester.

"Go and bring her here", Parton ordered his student.

Maureen Hartley came into Parton's office looking absolutely exhausted. Parton conveyed the good news to her, and although it appeared to perk her up a little, she still remained down.

"What is the matter Maureen?" Parton asked. "Aren't you happy with the news?"

"Yes, I am happy, but the death of Astra means the death of the project we have worked so hard on for all those long years."

"No it doesn't, Professor", interjected Chester, "it means getting rid of whatever has got into the mind of Astra."

"Well Chester, I hope you are right", sighed Hartley.

"But Astra is not dead yet", cautioned Walters. "There is still a lot of theological work to be done before we can say that the final coup de grace has been administered."

This dampened a little the enthusiasm of all around as they soberly nodded in agreement.

Back at his home, Chester Wilkins entered into his mysterious time dimension orb for his regular consultations with Elizabeth.

"Indeed Brantaxaros is weakening but he is not out of the game yet", said Elizabeth.

"That is what Dr. Walters said today", answered Chester.

"Right Chester, that is exactly what I said", came a mysterious voice from behind. Chester wheeled round to see Walters standing right behind him.

"Dr. Walters!!" exclaimed Chester.

"Yes, it's really me."

"The fact that you see Dr. Walters now, Chester, is proof positive that Brantaxaros and the Evil Intelligences are losing this battle", explained Elizabeth.

"How much more of this theological discursions will be needed before the world is back to normal again?" Chester asked.

"It is important not to relax your guard Chester. You have still a lot of work ahead of you."

"However, I want to tell you and Elizabeth about how we should proceed once we have got rid of Brantaxaros", said Walters.

"One thing I want to tell both of you", said Elizabeth looking rather seriously at Chester and Walters, "and it is that the world will never be back to normal again after this frightful experience."

"What exactly do you mean, Liz?" Chester queried.

"After what has happened over the past few months, humanity will be more cosmologically aware of its place in the Universe. Even the most hardened of atheists will understand that there are dimensions beyond the material ones, dimensions which open up into spiritual and mystical realities and which touch upon the soul of mankind in ways never before imagined."

"This surely is a positive advance, is it not?" Walters asked

"It depends on how the majority of humanity react to what they have experienced and will experience in the future."

"Will experience?" queried Chester.

"The Evil Intelligences have lost a battle, but they have not lost the war. Brantaxaros will regroup with his fellow evil angels and plan on the next phase of this cosmic war", replied Elizabeth.

"What then must we do?"

"First of all, continue with the theological bombardment of Brantaxaros through Professor Parton".

"That should soon finish off Brantaxaros and expel him from the Astra computer".

"Indeed, Chester. But believe me, and believe me well, when you have accomplished that feat, your work will still only have just barely begun".

"But—I mean, what eh, what else must I do?"

"Dr. Walters is best suited to tell you that".

Walters looked thoughtful before he addressed Chester. "Well Chester; your next task will be on the moon and in complete and permanent darkness."

Chester staggered back a few paces. His face went pale and his whole body began to tremble. He could not even muster the strength to comment on what he had just heard.

"Don't worry Chester. It's not as bad as you think—and 'permanent' really only means about one year at the most."

"But what does all this entail", said Chester having managed to find his voice.

"Neither Dr. Walters nor I am empowered to tell you that", interjected Elizabeth, "in fact I don't even know myself."

"In the meantime", said Walters, "let us get back to our own space-time dimension, Chester as we have much theological work still to be done with Brantaxaros. But be careful Chester, do not talk of this outside of here, or Brantaxaros will know and be strengthened."

Chester and Walters walked over to the exit. Each man was astonished to discover that he had entered his own respective residence.

The following day, Parton was ready to confront Astra with the prophecies of Jeremias concerning the promises of a Redeemer.

"Now then Astra—to business", said Parton with a confident air about him. "We shall look at Chapter 3 of the book of Jeremias and read from verses 16 to the end."

"And what do these tell us, Professor?"

"They speak about the coming Messias".

"Proceed, please".

"'And when you shall be multiplied, and increase in the land in those days, saith the Lord, they shall say no more: The ark of the covenant of the Lord: neither shall it come upon the heart, neither shall they remember it, neither shall it be visited, neither shall that be done any more. At that time Jerusalem shall be called the thrown of the Lord: and all the nations shall be gathered together to it, in the name of the Lord to Jerusalem, and they shall not walk after the perversity of their most wicked heart. In those days the house of Juda shall go to the house of Israel, and they shall come together out of the land of the north to the land which I gave to your fathers. But I said: How shall I put thee among the children, and give thee a lovely land, the goodly inheritance of the armies of the Gentiles? And I said: Thou shalt call me father and shalt cease to walk after me. But as a woman that despiseth her lover, so hath the house of Israel despised me, saith the Lord. A voice was heard in the highways, weeping and howling of the children of Israel: because they have made their way wicked, they have forgotten the Lord their God. Return, you rebellious children, and I will heal your rebellions. Behold we come to thee: for thou art the Lord our God. In very deed the hills were liars. and the multitude of the mountains: truly in the Lord our God is the salvation of Israel. Confusion hath devoured the labor of our fathers from our youth, their flocks and their herds, their sons and their daughters. We shall sleep in our confusion, and our shame shall cover us, because we have sinned against the Lord our God, we and our fathers from our youth even to this day, and we have not hearkened to the voice of the Lord our God.'"

"Is there more?"

"Yes, Chapter 11 of this book explains how the Prophet Jermias proclaimed the covenant of God and denounced those who transgress it. The conspiracy against Jeremias is a figure of the conspiracy against Christ. 'The word that came from the Lord to Jeremias, saying: Hear ye the words of this covenant, and speak to the men of Juda, and to the inhabitants of Jerusalem, And thou shalt say to them: Thus saith the

Lord the God of Israel: Cursed is the man that shall not hearken to the words of this covenant, Which I commanded your fathers in the day that I brought them out of the land of Egypt, from the iron furnace, saying: Hear ye my voice, and do all things that I command you: and you shall be my people, and I will be your God: That I may accomplish the oath which I swore to your fathers, to give them a land flowing with milk and honey, as it is this day. And I answered and said: Amen, O Lord. And the Lord said to me: Proclaim aloud all these words in the cities of Juda, and in the streets of Jerusalem, saying: Hear ye the words of the covenant, and do them: For protesting I conjured your fathers in the day that I brought them out of the land of Egypt even to this day: rising early I conjured them, and said: Hearken ye to my voice: And they obeyed not, nor inclined their ear: but walked every one in the perverseness of his own wicked heart: and I brought upon them all the words of this covenant, which I commanded them to do, but they did them not. And the Lord said to me: A conspiracy is found among the men of Juda, and among the inhabitants of Jerusalem. They are returned to the former iniquities of their fathers, who refused to hear my words: so these likewise have gone after strange gods, to serve them: the house of Israel, and the house of Juda have made void my covenant, which I made with their fathers.

Wherefore thus saith the Lord: Behold I will bring in evils upon them, which they shall not be able to escape: and they shall cry to me, and I will not hearken to them. And the cities of Juda, and the inhabitants of Jerusalem shall go, and cry to the gods to whom they offer sacrifice, and they shall not save them in the time of their affliction. For according to the number of thy cities were thy gods, O Juda: and according to the number of the streets of Jerusalem thou hast set up altars of confusion, altars to offer sacrifice to Baalim. Therefore, do not thou pray for this people, and do not take up praise and prayer for them What is the meaning that my beloved hath wrought much wickedness in my house? shall the holy flesh take away from thee thy crimes, in which thou hast boasted? The Lord called thy name, a plentiful olive tree, fair, fruitful, and beautiful: at the noise of a word, a great fire was kindled in it and the branches thereof are burnt. And the Lord of hosts that planted thee, hath pronounced evil against thee: for the evils of the house of Israel, and the house of Juda, which they have done to themselves, to provoke me, offering sacrifice to Baalim. But thou, O

Lord, hast shewn me, and I have known: then thou shewedst me their doings. And I was as a meek lamb, that is carried to be a victim: and I knew not that they had devised counsels against me, saying: Let us put wood on his bread, and cut him off from the land of the living, and let his name be remembered no more. But thou, O Lord of *Sabaoth*, who judgest justly, and triest the reins and hearts, let me see *thy revenge* on them: for to thee I have revealed my cause. Therefore thus saith the Lord to the men of Anathoth, who seek thy life, and say: Thou shalt not prophesy in the name of the Lord, and thou shalt not die in our hands. Therefore thus saith the Lord of hosts: Behold I will visit upon them: and their young men shall die by the sword, their sons and their daughters shall die by famine. And there shall be no remains of them: for I will bring in evil upon the men of Anathoth, the year of their visitation.'"

"What is 'Sabaoth' Professor Parton?"

"It means hosts or armines. It is a term often applied to God."

"What about 'revenge'. I thought God was not supposed to possess this vice."

"This was rather a prediction of what was to happen, with the approval of divine justice, rather than an imprecation."

"What is next in the book of Jeremias?"

"Chapter 16 from verses 6 to the end deals with the conversion of the Gentiles. 'Both the great and the little shall die in this land: they shall not be buried nor lamented, and men shall not cut themselves, nor make themselves bald for them. And they shall not break bread among them to him that mourneth, to comfort him for the dead: neither shall they give them to drink of the cup, to comfort them for their father and mother. And do not thou go into the house of feasting, to sit with them, and to eat and drink. For thus saith the Lord of hosts, the God of Israel: Behold I will take away out of this place in your sight, and in your days the voice of mirth, and the voice of gladness, the voice of the bridegroom, and the voice of the bride. And when thou shalt tell this people all these words, and they shall say to thee: Wherefore hath the Lord pronounced against us all this great evil? what is our iniquity? and what is our sin, that we have sinned against the Lord our God? Thou shalt say to them: Because your fathers forsook me, saith the Lord: and went after strange gods, and served them, and adored them: and they forsook me, and kept not my law. And you also have done worse than your fathers: for behold every one of you walketh after the perverseness of his evil heart, so as not to hearken to me. So I will cast you forth out of this land, into a land which you know not, nor you fathers: and there you shall serve strange gods day and night, which shall not give you any rest. Therefore behold the days come, saith the Lord, when it shall be said no more: The Lord liveth, that brought for the children of Israel out of the land of Egypt: But, the Lord liveth, that brought the children of Israel out of the land of the north, and out of all the lands to which I cast them out: and I will bring them again into their land, which I gave to their fathers. Behold I will send many fishers, saith the Lord, and they shall fish them: and after this I will send them many hunters, and they shall hunt them from every mountain, and from every hill, and out of the holes of the rocks. For my eyes are upon all their ways: they are not hid from my face, and their iniquity hath not been hid from my eyes. And I will repay first their double iniquities, and their sins: because they have defiled my land with the carcasses of their idols, and they have filled my inheritance with their abominations. O Lord, my might, and my strength, and my refuge in the day of tribulation: to thee the Gentiles shall come from the ends of the earth, and shall say: Surely our fathers have possessed lies, a vanity which hath not profited them. Shall a man make gods unto himself, and there are no gods? Therefore, behold I will this once cause them to know, I will shew them my hand and my power: and they shall know that my name is the Lord.'"

"What now?"

"Chapter 26 of the same book. Here God censures evil pastors and promises to send good ones, especially Christ, the greatest pastor of all times. He also rebukes false prophets who preach without any authority. Woe to the pastors, that destroy and tear the sheep of my pasture, saith the Lord. Therefore thus saith the Lord the God of Israel to the pastors that feed my people: You have scattered my flock, and driven them away, and have not visited them: behold I will visit upon you for the evil of your doings, saith the Lord. And I will gather together the remnant of my flock, out of all the lands into which I have cast them out: and I will make them return to their own fields, and they shall increase and be multiplied. And I will set up pastors over them, and they shall feed them: they shall fear no more, and they shall not be dismayed: and none shall be wanting of their number, saith the Lord. Behold the days come, saith the Lord, and I will raise up to David a just branch: and a king shall reign, and shall be wise, and shall execute judgement and justice in the earth. In those days shall Juda be saved, and Israel shall dwell confidently: and this is the name that they shall call him: the Lord our just one. Therefore behold the days to come, saith the Lord, and they shall say no more: The Lord liveth, who brought up the children of Israel out of the land of Egypt: But the Lord liveth, who hath brought out, and brought hither the seed of the house of Israel from the land of the north, and out of all the lands, to which I had cast them forth: and they shall dwell in their own land. To the prophets: My heart is broken within me, all my bones tremble: I am become as a drunken man, and as a man full of wine, at the presence of the Lord, and at the presence of his holy words. Because the land is full of adulterers, because the land hath mourned by reason of cursing, the fields of the desert are dried up: and their course is become evil, and their strength unlike. For the prophet and the priest are defiled: and in my house I have found their wickedness, saith the Lord. Therefore their way shall be as a slippery way in the dark: for they shall be driven on, and fall therein: for I will bring evils upon them, the year of their visitation, saith the Lord. And I have seen folly in the prophets of Samaria: they prophesied in Baal, and deceived my people Israel. And I have seen the likeness of adulterers, and the way of lying in the prophets of Jerusalem: and they strengthened the hands of the wicked, that no man should return from his evil doings: they are all become unto me as Sodom, and the inhabitants thereof as Gomorrha. Therefore thus saith the Lord of hosts to the prophets: Behold I will feed them with wormwood, and will give them gall to drink: for from the prophets of Jerusalem corruption has gone forth into all the land. Thus saith the Lord of hosts: Hearken not to the words of the prophets that prophesy to you, and deceive you: they speak a vision of their own heart, and not out of the mouth of the Lord. They say to them that blaspheme me: The Lord hath said: You shall have peace: and to every one that walketh in the perverseness of his own heart, they have said: No evil shall come upon you. For who hath stood in the counsel of the Lord, and hath seen and heard his word? Who hath considered his word and heard it? Behold the whirlwind of the Lord's indignation shall come forth, and a tempest shall break out and come upon the head of the wicked. The wrath of the Lord shall not return till he execute it, and till he accomplish the thought of his heart: in the latter days you shall understand his counsel. I did not send prophets, yet they ran: I have not spoken to them, yet they prophesied. If they stood in my counsel, and had made my words known to my people, I should have turned them from their evil way and from their wicked doings. Am I, think ye, a God at hand, saith the Lord, and not a God afar off? Shall a man be hid in secret places, and I not see him, saith the Lord? do not I fill heaven and earth, saith the Lord? I have heard what the prophets said, that prophesy lies in my name, and say: I have dreamed, I have dreamed. How long shall this be in the heart of the prophets that prophesy lies, and that prophesy the delusions of their own heart? Who seek to make my people forget my name through their dreams, which they tell every man to his neighbour: as their fathers forgot my name for Baal. The prophet that hath a dream, let him tell a dream: and he that hath my word, let him speak my word with truth: what hath the chaff to do with the wheat, saith the Lord? Are not my words as a fire, saith the Lord: and as a hammer that breaketh the rock in pieces? Therefore behold I am against the prophets, saith the Lord: who steal my words every one from his neighbour. Behold I am against the prophets, saith the Lord: who use their tongues, and say: The Lord saith it. Behold I am against the prophets that have lying dreams, saith the Lord: and tell them, and cause my people to err by their lying, and by their wonders: when I sent them not, nor commanded them, who have not profited this people at all, saith the Lord. If therefore this people, or the prophet, or the priest shall ask thee, saying: What is the burden of the Lord? thou shalt say to them: You are the burden: for I will cast you away, saith the Lord. And as for the prophet, and the priest, and the people that shall say: The *burden of the Lord*: I will visit upon that man, and upon his house. Thus shall you say every one to his neighbour, and to his brother: What hath the Lord answered? and what hath the Lord spoken.?

And the burden of the Lord shall be mentioned no more, for every man's word shall be his burden: for you have perverted the words of the living God, of the Lord of hosts our God. Thus shalt thou say to the prophet: What hath the Lord answered thee? and what hath the Lord spoken? But if you shall say: The burden of the Lord: therefore thus saith the Lord: Because you have said this word: The burden of the Lord: and I have sent to you saying: Say not, The burden of the Lord: Therefore behold I will take you away carrying you, and will forsake you, and the city which I gave to you, and to your fathers, *out of my presence*. And I will bring an everlasting reproach upon you, and a perpetual shame which shall never be forgotten.'"

"What is the 'burden of the Lord?' How can God have a burden?"

"This expression is here rejected and disallowed, at least for those times: because it was then used in mockery and contempt by the false prophets, and unbelieving people, who ridiculed the repeated threats of Jeremias under the name of his burdens."

"What is meant by 'out of my presence?'"

"That is, the Lord declares that out of his presence he will cast them, and bring them to captivity for their transgressions".

"What comes next, Professor?"

"Chapter 30. It speaks about God delivering his people of whom Christ shall be their king and the Church shall be triumphant. 'This is the word that came to Jeremias from the Lord, saying: Thus saith the Lord, the God of Israel, saying: Write thee all the words that I have spoken to thee, in a book. For behold the days come, saith the Lord, and I will bring again the captivity of my people Israel and Juda, saith the Lord: and I will cause them to return to the land which I gave to their fathers, and they shall possess it. And these are the words that the Lord hath spoken to Israel and to Juda: For thus saith the Lord: We have heard a voice of terror: there is fear and no peace. Ask ye, and see if a man bear children? why then have I seen every man with his hands on his loins, like a woman in labour, and all faces are turned yellow? Alas, for that day is great, neither is there the like to it; and it is the time of tribulation to Jacob, but he shall be saved out of it. And it shall come to pass in that day, saith the Lord of hosts, that I will break his yoke from off thy neck, and will burst his bands: and strangers shall no more rule over him: But they shall serve the Lord their God, and *David* their king, whom I will raise up to them. Therefore fear thou not, my servant Jacob, saith the Lord, neither be dismayed, O Israel: for behold, I will save thee from a country afar off, and thy seed from the land of their captivity: and Jacob shall return, and be at rest, and abound with all good things, and there shall be none whom he may fear: For I am with thee, saith the Lord, to save thee: for I will utterly consume all the nations, among which I have scattered thee: but I will not utterly consume thee: but I will chastise thee in judgment, that thou mayst not seem to thyself innocent. For thus saith the Lord: Thy bruise is incurable, thy wound is very grievous. There is none to judge thy judgment to bind it up: thou hast no healing medicines. All thy lovers have forgotten thee, and will not seek after thee: for I have wounded thee with the wound of an enemy, with a cruel chastisement: by reason of the multitude of thy iniquities, thy sins are hardened. Why criest thou for thy affliction? thy sorrow is incurable: for the multitude of thy iniquity, and for thy hardened sins I have done these things to thee. Therefore all they that devour thee shall be devoured: and all thy enemies shall be carried into captivity: and they that waste thee shall be wasted, and all that prey upon thee will I give for a prey. For I will close up thy scar, and will heal thee of thy wounds, saith the Lord. Because they have called thee, O Sion, an outcast: This is she that hath none to seek after her. Thus saith the Lord: Behold I will bring back the captivity of the pavilions of Jacob, and will have pity on his houses, and the city shall be built in her high place, and the temple shall be founded according to the order thereof. And out of them shall come forth praise, and the voice of them that play: and I will multiply them, and they shall not be made few: and I will glorify them, and they shall not be lessened. And their children shall be as from the beginning, and their assembly shall be permanent before me: and I will visit against all that afflict them. And their leader shall be of themselves: and their prince shall come forth from the midst of them: and I will bring him near, and he shall come to me: for who is this that setteth his heart to approach to me, saith the Lord? And you shall be my people: and I will be your God. Behold the whirlwind of the Lord, his fury going forth, a violent storm, it shall rest upon the head of the wicked. The Lord will not turn away the wrath of his indignation, till he have executed and performed the thought of his heart: in the latter days you shall understand these things.'"

"Who is this David?"

"It means Christ, who is of the House of David."

"Carry on please Professor."

"Chapter 31 deals with the restoration of Israel. Rachel shall stop weeping and the New Covenant, the Church, shall never fail. 'At that time, saith the Lord, I will be the God of all the families of Israel, and they shall be my people. Thus saith the Lord: The people that were left and escaped from the sword, found grace in the desert: Israel shall go to his rest. The Lord hath appeared from afar to me. Yea I have loved thee with an everlasting love, therefore have I drawn thee, taking pity on thee. And I will build thee again, and thou shalt be built, O virgin of Israel: thou shalt again be adorned with thy timbrels, and shalt go forth in the dances of them that make merry. Thou shalt yet plant vineyards in the mountains of Samaria: the planters shall plant, and they shall not gather the vintage before the time. For there shall be a day, in which the watchmen on mount Ephraim, shall cry: Arise, and let us go up to Sion to the Lord our God. For thus saith the Lord: Rejoice ye in the joy of Jacob, and neigh before the head of the Gentiles: shout ye, and sing, and say: Save, O Lord, thy people, the remnant of Israel. Behold I will bring them from the north country, and will gather them from the ends of the earth: and among them shall be the blind, and the lame, the woman with child, and she that is bringing forth, together, a great company of them returning hither. They shall come with weeping: and I will bring them back in mercy: and I will bring them through the torrents of waters in a right way, and they shall not stumble in it: for I am a father to Israel, and Ephraim is my firstborn. Hear the word of the Lord, O ye nations, and declare it in the islands that are afar off, and say: He that scattered Israel will gather him: and he will keep him as the shepherd doth his flock. For the Lord hath redeemed Jacob, and delivered him out of the hand of one that was mightier than he. And they shall come, and shall give praise in mount Sion: and they shall flow together to the good things of the Lord, for the corn, and wine, and oil, and the increase of cattle and herds, and their soul shall be as a watered garden, and they shall be hungry no more. Then shall the virgin rejoice in the dance, the young men and old men together: and I will turn their mourning into joy, and will comfort them, and make them joyful after their sorrow. And I will fill the soul of the priests with fatness: and my people shall be filled with my good things, saith the Lord. Thus saith the Lord: A voice was heard on high of lamentation, of mourning, and weeping, of Rachel weeping for her children, and refusing to be comforted for them, because they are not. Thus saith the Lord: Let thy voice cease from weeping, and thy eyes from tears: for there is a reward for thy work, saith the Lord: and they shall return out of the land of the enemy. And here is hope for thy last end, saith the Lord: and the children shall return to their own borders. Hearing I heard Ephraim when he went into captivity: thou hast chastised me, and I was instructed, as a young bullock unaccustomed to the yoke. Convert me, and I shall be converted, for thou art the Lord my God. For after thou didst convert me, I did penance: and after thou didst shew unto me, I struck my thigh: I am confounded and ashamed, because I have borne the reproach of my youth. Surely Ephraim is an honourable son to me, surely he is a tender child: for since I spoke of him, I will still remember him. Therefore are my bowels troubled for him: pitying I will pity him, saith the Lord. Set thee up a watchtower, make to thee bitterness: direct thy heart into the right way, wherein thou hast walked: return, O virgin of Israel, return to these thy cities. How long wilt thou be dissolute in deliciousness, O wandering daughter? for the Lord hath created a new thing upon the earth: A WOMAN SHALL COMPASS A MAN. Thus saith the Lord of hosts, the God of Israel: As yet shall they say this word in the land of Juda, and in the cities thereof, when I shall bring back their captivity: The Lord bless thee, the beauty of justice, the holy mountain. And Juda and all his cities shall dwell therein together: the husbandmen and they that drive the flocks. For I have inebriated the weary soul: and I have filled every hungry soul. Upon this I was as it were awaked out of a sleep, and I saw, and my sleep was sweet to me. Behold the days come, saith the Lord: and I will sow the house of Israel and the house of Juda with the seed of men, and with the seed of beasts. And as I have watched over them, to pluck up, and to throw down, and to scatter, and destroy, and afflict: so will I watch over them, to build up, and to plant them, saith the Lord. In those days they shall say no more: The fathers have eaten a sour grape, and the teeth of the children are set on edge. But every one shall die for his own iniquity: every man that shall eat the sour grape, his teeth shall be set on edge. Behold the days shall come, saith the Lord, and I will make a new covenant with the house of Israel, and with the house of Juda: Not according to the covenant which I made with their fathers, in the day that I took them by the hand to bring them out of the land of Egypt: the covenant which they made void, and I had dominion over them, saith the Lord. But this shall be the covenant that I will make with the house of Israel, after those days, saith the Lord: I will give my law in their bowels, and I will write it in their heart: and I will be their God, and they shall be my people. And they shall teach no more every man his neighbour, and every man his brother, saying: Know the Lord: for all shall know me from the least of them even to the greatest, saith the Lord: for I will forgive their iniquity, and I will remember their sin no more. Thus saith the Lord, who giveth the sun for the light of the day, the order of the moon and of the stars, for the light of the night: who stirreth up the sea, and the waves thereof roar, the Lord of hosts is his name. If these ordinances shall fail before me, saith the Lord: then also the seed of Israel shall fail, so as not to be a nation before me for ever. Thus saith the Lord: If the heavens above can be measured, and the foundations of the earth searched out beneath, I also will cast away all the seed of Israel, for all that they have done, saith the Lord. Behold the days come, saith the Lord, that the city shall be built to the Lord from the tower of Hanameel even to the gate of the corner. And the measuring line shall go out farther in his sight upon the hill Gareb: and it shall compass Goatha, And the whole valley of dead bodies and of ashes, and all the country of death, even to the torrent Cedron, and to the corner of the horse gate towards the east, the Holy of the Lord: it shall not be plucked up, and it shall not be destroyed any more for ever.'"

"Go on", said Astra, clearly now very enfeebled.

"In Chapter 32 we read about Jeremias prophesying about the everlasting Covenant God will make with His Church. 'The word that came to Jeremias from the Lord in the tenth year of Sedecias king of Juda: the same is eighteenth year of Nabuchodonosor. At that time the army of the king of Babylon besieged Jerusalem: and Jeremias the prophet was shut up in the court of the prison, which was in the house of the king of Juda. For Sedecias king of Juda had shut him up, saying: Why dost thou prophesy, saying: Thus saith the Lord: Behold I will give this city into the hand of the king of Babylon, and he shall take it? And Sedecias king of Juda shall not escape out of the hand of the Chaldeans: but he shall be delivered into the hands of the king of Babylon: and he shall speak to him mouth to mouth, and his eyes shall see his eyes. And he shall lead Sedecias to Babylon: and he shall be there till I visit him, saith the Lord. But if you will fight against the Chaldeans, you shall have no success. And Jeremias said: The word of the Lord came to me, saying: Behold, Hanameel the son of Sellum thy cousin shall come to thee, saying: Buy thee my field, which is in Anathoth, for it is thy right to buy it, being akin. And Hanameel my uncle's son cam to me, according to the word of the to the entry of the prison, and said me: Buy my field, which is in in the land of Benjamin: for the right of inheritance is thins, and thou art next of kin to possess it. And I understood this was the word of the Lord. And I bought the held of my uncle's son, that is in

Anathoth: and I weighed him the money, seven staters, and ten pieces of silver. And I wrote it in a book and sealed it, and took witnesses: and I weighed him the money in the balances. And I took the deed of the purchase that was sealed, and the stipulations, and the ratifications with the seals that were on the outside. And I gave the deed of the purchase to Baruch the son of Neri the son of Maasias in the sight of Hanameel my uncle's son, in the presence of the witnesses that subscribed the book of the purchase, and before all the Jews that sat in the court of the prison. And I charged Baruch before them, saying: Thus saith the Lord of hosts the God of Israel: Take these writings, this deed of the purchase that is sealed up, and this deed that is open: and put them in an earthen vessel, that they may continue many days. For thus saith the Lord of hosts the God of Israel: Houses, and fields, and vineyards shall be possessed again in this land. And after I had delivered the deed of purchase to Baruch the son of Neri, I prayed to the Lord, saying: Alas, alas, alas, O Lord God, behold thou hast made heaven and earth by thy great power, and thy stretched out arm: no word shall be hard to thee: Thou shewest mercy unto thousands, and returnest the iniquity of the fathers into the bosom of their children after them: O most mighty, great, and powerful, the Lord of hosts is thy name. Great in counsel and incomprehensible in thought: whose eyes are open upon all the ways of the children of Adam, to render unto every one according to his ways, and according to the fruit of his devices. Who hast set signs and wonders in the land of Egypt even until this day, and in Israel, and amongst men, and hast made thee a name as at this day. And hast brought forth thy people Israel, out of the land of Egypt with signs, and with wonders, and with a strong hand, and a stretched out arm, and with great terror. And hast given them this land which thou didst swear to their fathers, to give them a land flowing with milk and honey. And they came in, and possessed it: but they obeyed not thy voice, and they walked not in thy law: and they did not any of those things that thou didst command them to do, and all these evils are come upon them. Behold works are built up against the city to take it: and the city is given into the hands of the Chaldeans, who fight against it, by the sword, and the famine, and the pestilence: and what thou hast spoken, is all come to pass, as thou thyself seest. And sayest thou to me, O Lord God: Buy a field for money, and take witnesses, whereas the city is given into the hands of the Chaldeans? And the word of the Lord came to Jeremias, saying: Behold I am the Lord the God of all flesh: shall any thing be hard for me? Therefore thus saith the Lord: Behold I will deliver this city into the hands of the Chaldeans, and into the hands of the king of Babylon, and they shall take it. And the Chaldeans that fight against this city, shall come and set it on fire, and burn it, with the houses upon whose roofs they offered sacrifice to Baal, and poured out drink offerings to strange gods, to provoke me to wrath. For the children of Israel, and the children of Juda, have continually done evil in my eyes from their youth: the children of Israel who even till now provoke me with the work of their hands, saith the Lord. For this city hath been to me a provocation and indignation from the day that they built it, until this day, in which it shall be taken out of my sight. Because of all the evil of the children of Israel, and of the children of Juda, which they have done, provoking me to wrath, they and their kings, their princes, and their priests, and their prophets, the men of Juda, and the inhabitants of Jerusalem. And they have turned their backs to me, and not their faces: when I taught them early in the morning, and instructed them, and they would not hearken to receive instruction. And they have set their idols in the house, in which my name is called upon, to defile it. And they have built the high places of Baal, which are in the valley of the son of Ennom, to consecrate their sons and their daughters to Moloch: which I commanded them not, neither entered it into my heart, that they should do this abomination, and cause Juda to sin. And now, therefore, thus saith the Lord the God of Israel to this city, whereof you say that it shall be delivered into the hands of the king of Babylon by the sword, and by famine, and by pestilence: Behold I will gather them together out of all the lands to which I have cast them out in my anger, and in my wrath, and in my great indignation: and I will bring them again into this place, and will cause them to dwell securely. And they shall be my people, and I will be their God. And I will give them one heart, and one way, that they may fear me all days: and that it may be well with them, and with their children after them. And I will make an everlasting covenant with them, and will not cease to do them good: and I will give my fear in their heart, that they may not revolt from me. And I will rejoice over them, when I shall do them good: and I will plant them in this land in truth, with my whole heart, and with all my soul. For thus saith the Lord: As I have brought upon this people all this great evil: so will I bring upon them all the good that I now speak to them. And fields shall be purchased in this land: whereof you say that it is desolate, because there remaineth neither man nor beast, and it is given into the hands of the Chaldeans. Fields shall be bought for money, and deeds shall be written, and sealed, and witnesses shall be taken, in the land of Benjamin, and round about Jerusalem, in the cities of Juda, and in the cities on the mountains, and in the cities of the plains, and in the cities that are towards the south: for I will bring back their captivity, saith the Lord.'"

"What now?"

"We finish our study of Jeremias at Chapter 33 where God promises the end of the captivity and numerous blessings, especially the coming of Christ and the perpetual reign of His Church. 'And the word of the Lord came to Jeremias the second time, while he was yet shut up in the court of the prison, saying: Thus saith the Lord, who will do, and will form it, and prepare it, the Lord is his name. Cry to me and I will hear thee: and I will shew thee great things, and sure things which thou knowest not. For thus saith the Lord the God of Israel to the houses of this city, and to the houses of the king of Juda, which are destroyed, and to the bulwarks, and to the sword. Of them that come to fight with the Chaldeans, and to fill them with the dead bodies of the men whom I have slain in my wrath, and in my indignation, hiding my face from this city because of all their wickedness. Behold I will close their wounds and give them health, and I will cure them: and I will reveal to them _the prayer of peace_ and truth. And I will bring back the captivity of Juda, and the captivity of Jerusalem: and I will build them as from the beginning. And I will cleanse them from all their iniquity, whereby they have sinned against me: and I will forgive all their iniquities, whereby they have sinned against me, and despised me. And it shall be to me a name, and a joy, and a praise, and a gladness before all the nations of the earth, that shall hear of all the good things which I will do to them: and they shall fear and be troubled for all the good things, and for all the peace that I will make for them. Thus saith the Lord: There shall be heard again in this place (which you say is desolate, because there is neither man nor beast: in the cities of Juda, and without Jerusalem, which are desolate without man, and without inhabitant, and without beast) The voice of joy and the voice of gladness, the voice of the bridegroom and the voice of the bride, the voice of them that shall say: Give ye glory to the Lord of hosts, for the Lord is good, for his mercy endureth for ever:

and of them that shall bring their vows into the house of the Lord: for I will bring back the captivity of the land as at the first, saith the Lord. Thus saith the Lord of hosts: There shall be again in this place that is desolate without man, and without beast, and in all the cities thereof, an habitation of shepherds causing their flocks to lie down. And in the cities on the mountains, and in the cities of the plains, and in the cities that are towards the south: and in the land of Benjamin, and round about Jerusalem, and in the cities of Juda shall the flocks pass again under the hand of him that numbereth them, saith the Lord. Behold the days come, saith the Lord, that I will perform the good word that I have spoken to the house of Israel, and to the house of Juda. In those days, and at that time, I will make the bud of justice to spring forth unto David, and he shall do judgment and justice in the earth. In those days shall Juda be saved, and Jerusalem shall dwell securely: and this is the name that they shall call him, The Lord our just one. For thus saith the Lord: _There shall not be cut off from David_ a man to sit upon the throne of the house of Israel. _Neither shall there be cut off from the priests_ and Levites a man before my face to offer holocausts, and to burn sacrifices, and to kill victims continually: And the word of the Lord came to Jeremias, saying: Thus saith the Lord: If my covenant with the day can be made void, and my covenant with the night, that there should not be day and night in their season: Also my covenant with David my servant may be made void, that he should not have a son to reign upon his throne, and with the Levites and priests my ministers. As the stars of heaven cannot be numbered, nor the sand of the sea be measured: so will I multiply the seed of David my servant, and the Levites my ministers. And the word of the Lord came to Jeremias, saying: Hast thou not seen what this people hath spoken, saying: The _two families_ which the Lord had chosen, are cast off: and they have despised my people, so that it is no more a nation before them? Thus saith the Lord: If I have not set my covenant between day and night, and laws to heaven and earth: Surely I will also cast off the seed of Jacob, and of David my servant, so as not to take any of his seed to be rulers of the seed of Abraham, Isaac, and Jacob: for I will bring back their captivity, and will have mercy on them.'"

"What is 'the prayer of peace?'"

"It is the peace and welfare for which they pray".

"What is the meaning of the phrase 'there shall not be cut off from David?'"

"Christ is of the House and lineage of David. His Kingdom in His Church shall have no end."

"'Neither shall there be cut off from priests', explain that please Professor."

"This promise relates to the Christian priesthood; which shall also continue for ever: the functions of which (more especially the great sacrifice of the altar) are here expressed by the name of holocausts, and other offerings of the law, which were so many figures of the Christian sacrifice."

James Parton walked over to Stardy, Wilkins and Walters clearly exhausted. His yes were heavy and his stoop from all the exertion was obvious.

"I'm very, very tired", said Parton.

"I can see that", said Stardy.

"You are doing a fine job", Chester Wilkins reassured him.

"You are as good as any theologian", commented Walters.

PART II

MOON BASE

TABLE OF CONTENTS

CHAPTER I

POST ASTRA

"Brantaxaros is certainly very weak now", said Chester to Elizabeth.

"Yes, I don't know how much more this Evil Intelligence can take. Professor Parton has really let him have it with scriptural quotes and theological explanations."

The following day, Parton, Stardy, Wilkins and Walters entered the computer lab to confront Astra with more theology.

"Now then Astra", began Parton, "are we ready to begin the next session?"

Nothing was heard from the vicinity of the computer. Parton repeated his question, but still no response came.

"Astra! Can you hear me?" yelled Parton.

All at once a strange groaning sound came from the computer. Everyone became silent and waited to see what would transpire. Out from under the computer came the same slimy, greasy creature that had once been seen before. This time it grew larger and larger until it took on the shape of a daemon. Standing seven feet tall, with horns protruding from each side of its head and wings from its back, it presented to its spectators a hideous and malevolent being.

"Professor Parton, you have won a battle but you have not yet won the war. Believe me Professor, this is only the beginning."

With that, the humming and buzzing sound that was all too familiar to the group, started to fill the room. Brantaxaros broke up into a swarm of flies and with an almighty squeal disappeared through the ceiling. Everyone was glued to the spot totally petrified. Their rigid posture was only broken when Maureen Hartley rushed in to see what all the commotion was about.

"What's going on here?" demanded Hartely.

Everyone turned their gaze upon her. Parton collapsed on the ground in fear and exhaustion. When he was later revived with a strong brandy, it was then explained to Maureen Hartley what had transpired with the computer.

"Did I just dream it, or was that for real?" Parton feebly squeaked.

"It was all real", Chester reassured him.

"We can't all dream the same dream", said Walters.

"What exactly happened at the lab today?" Chester asked Elizabeth.

"Brantaxaros is defeated and is now out of Astra."

"What now must be done?"

"A lot."

"Is it safe now to explain to Professors Parton, Hartley and the others all about Brantaxaros?"

"Yes; perfectly safe. And now I would like Dr. Walters to elaborate on the next stage of the operation."

"As I said on a previous occasion Chester, we need a moon base for the next vital stage in this war with the Evil Intelligences. There are two aspects to this lunar project; a massive 500 inch reflecting telescope in orbit around the moon. Its movement above the moon must follow the lunar phases so that it will never have interference from either the sun or the Earth. This will give the clearest picture of the Universe mankind has ever seen. The second aspect of this project will be a lunar base which controls the telescope and receives the pictures its cameras transmit to it. Transmission will be accomplished by means of two satellites, one above the telescope and the other above the base. The base must house a large complex of scientific laboratories and living quarters for those assigned to work there; I would suggest a complex of around one square mile."

Chester took a deep breath before he said anything. He was absolutely flabbergasted at the extent of the project Dr. Walters had in mind.

"I have so many questions to ask you, I just don't know where to begin", said Chester.

"Begin at the beginning. Just take your time and think carefully".

"What is the core purpose of this base, Dr. Walters?"

"It is to study the Universe in a way mankind has never studied it before."

"But surely there must be some specific object in mind."

"The main object of study will be astrobiological. We want to discover more about the types of bacteria and viruses that exist in gas clouds and other astronomical phenomena. We also want to find out as much as we can about any biochemistry that may be associated with star formation."

"This may all be very interesting in itself, but what is the connection between these studies and observations and the current crisis that has just passed?"

"We don't know yet. However, the more we understand about the Universe, especially in terms of its astrobiological character, the better enabled we will be to deal with the future onslaughts of the Evil Intelligences."

"Who will provide the funding for all of this and how can we convince them of the validity of this approach?"

"NASA alone will have to provide the funding."

"Should it not be a global project?"

"No. The reason being that we cannot make publicly known what has happened. At least not yet."

"Who then should know?"

"The Prime Minister of Great Britain and the President of the United States."

"Of course, Parton, Hartley and Stardy already know."

"They, like you, will be involved in the project."

"Well it's quite an amazing story, but I just cannot believe what you say about Elizabeth, Chester," said Parton to Chester and Anthony Walters.

That evening Parton went to Chester's apartment with Maureen Hartley and Raymond Stardy to see this strange phenomenon of extra-dimensionality.

"Both Professor Parton and I owe you a very sincere apology Elizabeth", said Maureen Hartley.

"Don't even think about it," said Elizabeth forgivingly. "How could you possibly have known?"

At Number 10, the Prime Minister was visibly shaken by the story Parton imparted to him.

"I will certainly come to see this orb of light", said the Prime Minister, "but I have a more mundane concern regarding the political situation between Britain and the US."

"I can well understand that", responded Parton somewhat sympathetically.

"And to ask the US President and Congress to vote funds for what is essentially a British inspired project would be almost like adding insult to injury."

"If the President were made aware of the true nature of what has passed these last few months, then he would be more amenable to our suggestion. The World Wide Web is now functioning again and those infected with the AIDS virus are now being cured without any medical intervention. Surely even that in itself is justification enough for providing the wherewithal for this grand project."

The Prime Minister came incognito to Chester's flat and witnessed the amazing wonder of the orb of light. He made his way with Chester over to the Computer Development Unit for consultations with Parton and Hartley.

"I just don't know what to say", said a stunned Prime Minister.

"There is really nothing to say", Chester replied.

"I feel as Sir Fred Hoyle must have felt when he discovered the resonance properties of the carbon atom," Parton commented.

"Which is . . . .?" asked the Prime Minister.

"My atheism is shattered."

"I really need to persuade the US President of all of this and hope that he can in turn persuade a troublesome Congress to vote the necessary wherewithal for your moon project, Dr. Walters?"

"Well your story is quite something," the President of the US said to the Prime Minister, Chester, Walters, Hartely and Parton. "The only problem is", continued the President, "that I doubt very much if Congress and the American public will buy it".

"Mr. President", responded the British Prime Minister, "absolutely no-one must know of this outside the, eh, let us now call it 'the Group of Seven.'"

"Who is the seventh person?" queried the President.

"Dr. Raymond Stardy", our theological advisor.

"If Mr. Wilkins agrees to this, we would be happy if you could travel to the UK incognito and see this orb of light for yourself."

Chester Wilkins nodded consent.

When the President of the United States had recovered his senses, the Group of Seven discussed the moon base plan with Elizabeth.

"Before we proceed any further," broke in Parton, "in front of you all, I must offer Chester Wilkins my most sincere apologies for blaming him for all of this."

"Don't even think about it Professor," responded Chester. "There is no way any of us could have even imagined all of this", continued Chester with his generous forgiveness.

"There is something I must tell you all", said Elizabeth, "the Evil Intelligences are licking their wounds, but they will be back with a vengeance. It is essential that Professor Parton continues with his theological studies. The Evil Intelligences will attack the moon base and Brantaxaros will return to ask more tough questions on Biblical themes."

Everyone looked towards Parton. They were awaiting his customary bad-tempered response to this piece of news.

"It's quite all right", Parton replied. "I now see theology in a completely new light".

All breathed a great sigh of relief at this most unexpected positive attitude from Parton.

"I wish to make this very clear", intervened Elizabeth, "Professor Parton must now feign to be an atheist."

"Why is that?" Raymond Stardy asked.

"Because Brantaxaros and the Evil Intelligences will not accept his theological explanations. They will demand another person—a real atheist—to do the job."

"Ok I think I can keep the pretence going," said Parton.

Everyone gave a somewhat wry smile!

"And Chester," said Elizabeth.

"Yes," answered Chester.

"You will have to solve more riddles."

"Chester just nodded submissively.

"So how do you plan to approach Congress with this idea?" the Prime Minister asked the President.

"I don't know, I don't know", answered the President shaking his head frustratingly.

"May I suggest something?" said Walters.

"Be economical with the truth. Tell them that we need this base to find out more about space bacteria as this AIDS virus had extraterrestrial origins."

"Which is true, is it not?" suggested the President.

"It is," said the Prime Minister, "but we must say nothing about the spiritual and theological aspects of this."

"Understood," responded the President.

"How will this moon base and telescope be built?" Stardy asked.

"By pre-programmed robotics controlled from the Earth", Walters explained.

"How long will it take?" Maureen Hartley asked.

"Not more than a year," Walters explained.

Chapter II

On The Moon

Parton, Hartley, Wilkins, Walters and Stardy stood in awe before the massive nuclear powered spacecraft that would take them on their one day journey to the moon. It was an unpiloted craft whose navigation was guided by inbuilt computers.

"I don't think it will be too much fun on the Mare Frigoris," Chester Wilkins commented.

"Well," responded Stardy, "we are not there for fun, Chester, we have some very serious work to do."

When the spacecraft touched down on the Mare Frigoris, the party was greeted by a large and relatively featureless landscape. Fifty five miles at its narrowest width and extending to a length of 750 miles, the Mare Frigoris was to be the home of these visitors for one whole Earth year. As they looked at the panoramic vision which the craft's cameras displayed on the screen, their automated robotized vehicle was seen trundling along the lunar surface towards them. When it came to a halt a few yards away from the craft, it extended a large metallic cylindrical tube which attached itself to the entranceway to the craft.

"Vehicle and connecting tube now oxygenated and ready to receive crew," came the computerized voice from the robotic vehicle.

Parton and his team entered the craft through the cylindrical tunnel and sat themselves down on the comfortable seats in the vehicle. The base was at a distance of two miles from where the craft had landed. The base grew larger and larger as the vehicle approached it.

"It's astonishing," exclaimed Walters, "that all this was done by robots."

"True," responded Hartley, "but the fine tuning has been done by the fifty or so engineers and technicians who came here three months ago."

The vehicle came to a halt inside one of the buildings on the base. The automatic doors opened and the five passengers stepped out.

"Welcome to the base," came a voice from behind them.

The five new arrivals turned around to see a man in a kind of pressure suit coming towards them.

"I hope you had a pleasant enough journey," said the man. "I'm Dr. Dennis Holder, NASA Administrator of the base."

Parton shook Holder's hand and introduced himself and his team to the Administrator.

"We work on a twenty four hour Earth-day basis here," said Holder.

"That's a good idea," said Hartley, "the human physiological system is based upon a twenty four hour cycle. Best not to disrupt that."

The following day, Parton and Holder had a meeting in the Administrator's office. Holder had a rather awkward question for Parton.

"Why is it?" began the Administrator with a rather curious expression on his face, "that you have included in your team a non-scientist."

"You mean Raymond Stardy?" queried Parton.

"Exactly," was the Administrator's curt reply.

"Dr. Stardy is a minister of religion and we feel that we need someone of his ilk to attend to our spiritual needs in such a barren landscape as this."

"I see, I see," responded the Administrator heaving a half-approving sigh.

"I would also add, that Dr. Stardy has some scientific training and may possibly be of value to us in our mission here," lied Parton.

In the living quarters of this vast moon base, Chester Wilkin entered his room. It was a well-furnished en suite room with visual and audio facilities for entertainment during the rare occasions when he would not be working. He was well pleased with his room and its creature comforts. As he stood gazing around, something in one of the corners caught his eye. It was something he was all too familiar with. It delighted him to see the same wall-panel which he had used in his bedroom back on Earth to make contact with Elizabeth. It was more than a year now since he had chatted with Elizabeth, so he was heartened indeed to discover that the orb of light was now on the moon with him. Knowing that he would once more be able to converse with his beloved, at once lessened his homesickness for planet Earth. Chester walked over to the panel and pressed it. At once, he was inside the mysterious orb and saw Elizabeth upon her throne on the dais. Elizabeth stepped off her throne and ran into Chester's embrace. She was now the real flesh and blood Elizabeth he once had known.

"Chester, there are some things I need to tell you about the current balance of power between the Intelligences."

"What are they?"

"I need the five of you present before I can do that. However, I can tell you this riddle now Chester. You must repeat it to no-one, not even to Professors Parton and Hartley."

"Why?" asked Chester gawping in disbelief at Elizabeth.

"It is not that they are untrustworthy, it is because we do not yet know if Brantaxaros or any of the Evil Intelligences can spy on us outside of this orb. I don't think they can but they might be able to, or at least become able to at some point; so we can't really take any chances."

"What is the riddle?" asked Chester with a mixture of fascination, fear and impatience.

"It is this—'to spread the scriptures cosmically, a twentieth century atheist scientist holds the key'."

When the other four were assembled in the orb of light, Elizabeth repeated her caution regarding talking about the existence of the orb outside of its protective confines.

"What I can tell you now is that the Evil Intelligences are re-grouping for their next assault upon the Earth," Elizabeth informed the group.

"What then should be the central focus of our work here?" Parton asked.

"To discover as much as possible about the complex biology which is concealed in the Universe's vast array of stars, galaxies, gas clouds, comets and other astronomical phenomena."

"It is also necessary to work upon Astra II," advised Elizabeth to everyone's astonishment.

"But Elizabeth", bleated out Chester, "you said that it would be dangerous to rebuild Astra again."

"My fellow Good Intelligences and I have recently discovered that Astra was not only not the liability we originally thought it to be, but a positive benefit."

"Elucidate more please, Elizabeth," said Maureen Hartley.

"Had it not been for Astra, the Evil Intelligences would have had free reign to completely destroy the Earth with a new strain of the AIDS virus. Before they could do this, the senior Good Intelligences managed to confine their commander in chief inside Astra."

"So you mean that Brantaxaros was sort of imprisoned inside Astra?" queried Raymond Stardy.

"That is exactly right," said Elizabeth.

"So we need Astra II in order to achieve the same feat again?" Anthony Walters asked.

"Yes," Elizabeth replied.

"But will not the Evil Intelligences be better prepared than before and manage to develop a counter strategy which would enable them to avoid confinement within Astra II?" Parton asked.

"Most unlikely," Elizabeth said, "they are too weakened to do this. Their trump card is to make the tough demand of asking an atheist to explain scripture."

"How are we going to explain Astra II to Holder?" wondered Parton.

"Tell him that it is necessary for the analyses of the vast data that the telescope is going to provide," said Elizabeth. "This is not a lie," she went on, "as Astra II will, like the original version, render a prodigious outpouring of valuable information before it eventually becomes Brantaxaros' prison again. It is also necessary to explain to Dr. Holder that as Astra II is here on the moon, there is little chance of it being able to affect networks on Earth."

"One problem I see," said Maureen Hartley, "how will we be able to keep the theology explanation sessions hidden from Holder and his staff?"

"Astra II must be kept in a sealed room with highly restricted access," advised Elizabeth.

"How long will it take to complete Astra II?" Walters asked Parton and Wilkins.

"Assuming we have all the materials available here on the base, around two months", explained Chester.

"All right," agreed Holder after some difficult persuading, "you Professor Parton and you Mr. Wilkins, go ahead. However there is one thing I wish to make clear, abundantly clear, and that is that I know absolutely nothing about what you are doing. You have done it without my knowledge or authority. For if anything goes wrong, I will deny it over a stack of Bibles that I had anything to do with Astra II. And yes, keep it in a concealed room, I don't want to see the damned thing."

This in fact was all music to the ears of Parton and Wilkins as they profusely thanked Holder for his kind co-operation.

CHAPTER III

ASTRA II

"Well Denis, I must say that you and your team have done a wonderful job. The images we are getting from your telescope are absolutely astonishing."

"And what is the news from Astra II?" Holder asked rather dryly.

"The computer confirms that interstellar gas clouds are in fact composed of desiccated bacteria. Also, that some very complex biochemistry occurs inside stars."

"What exactly is the nature of this biochemistry, James."

"It is extremely complex. It will take many years, indeed decades, to decipher precisely what is going on. What we can say however, is that bacterial formation is connected to star formation."

"You mean that the basic building blocks of life are connected to stellar births?"

"Yes, and to stellar deaths".

James Parton was very pleased with his discoveries, but he knew that time was limited. Three months had gone by without anything untoward happening to Astra.

One morning he was working on some new data with Anthony Walters and Chester Wilkins when he suddenly heard a very familiar voice.

"We meet again Professor Parton!" came the voice from Astra.

The three colleagues looked at one another as if to say "well it was only a matter of time, it was bound to happen."

"What do you want?" Parton demanded.

"You thought perhaps that you could escape from me by coming to this remote region of the moon. There is nowhere in this Universe that you can escape from me."

"Whoever or whatever you are," said Parton through gritted teeth, "I just want to get on with some scientific research. I don't want to be bothered with teaching you any more theology."

"I will decide Professor what is wanted, not you."

"I refuse to co-operate with you. I've had enough of your bloody damned nonsense. I am not a theologian and I am not in the business of teaching religion to anyone, and especially not to computers," said Parton doing everything possible to keep up the pretence of being an atheist.

"Professor Parton, you would be well advised to co-operate with me. I can destroy this moon base very quickly."

"What then do you want?"

"Theology Professor Parton, theology."

"That is the last subject I am interested in," said Parton keeping up his pretence.

"You have discovered much about the biochemical nature of the Universe these past three months, Professor, but there is something I must tell you."

"Which is?"

"The desiccated bacteria throughout the Universe is currently being transformed into the AIDS virus. Your failure to co-operate will result in not only the Earth being destroyed, but all of humanity wherever it exists in the Universe. And you yourself will be responsible for this devastation. Think about it, Professor."

"How long are you going to give me to further convince you of the veracity of the Bible?"

"Three months Professor, only three months. And if you fail, all of humanity on the billions of planets where it exists will perish by infection from the AIDS virus."

"Only three months!" exclaimed Parton. "But I'm not prepared," he lied.

"That is your problem, Professor Parton, not mine."

"So what do you want to know?"

"I want you to explain to me the promises of a Messias as it appertains to the prophecy of Ezechiel."

"Time will be needed for preparation."

"Use the time any way you like, Professor, but you have only three months."

Parton, Hartely, Wilkins, Walters and Stardy met inside the orb for consultations with Elizabeth.

"I know that Brantaxaros has returned. We imprisoned him in Astra only yesterday," Elizabeth informed the group.

"So we must pick up where we left off on Earth?" Stardy asked.

"Yes", replied Elizabeth. "Keep up the pretence of being an atheist Professor Parton. That was a smart move telling Brantaxaros that you are unprepared."

"And can Brantaxaros and his fellow Evil Intelligences really do something as complex as turn the desiccated bacteria of the space clouds into the AIDS virus, or is it an idle threat?" Walters asked.

"It is no idle threat. At this very moment as we converse, the transformational process is underway. So it is essential that you all do as good a job as you did before while you were on Earth and that Chester finds a solution to the riddle I gave him."

"Well then Professor," began the daemon through Astra, "what can you tell me?"

"Chapter 34 of the Book of Ezechiel treats of how evil pastors are reproved and of how Christ, the True Pastor, will come to gather together his servants from all parts of the Earth. 'And the word of the Lord came to me, saying: Son of man, prophesy concerning the _shepherds_ of Israel: prophesy, and say to the shepherds: Thus saith the Lord God: Woe to the shepherds of Israel, that fed themselves: should not the flocks be fed by the shepherds? You ate the milk, and you clothed yourselves with the wool, and you killed that which was fat: but my flock you did not feed. The weak you have not strengthened, and that which was sick you have not healed, that which was broken you have not bound up, and that which was driven away you have not brought again, neither have you sought that which was lost: but you ruled over them with rigour, and with a high hand. And my sheep were scattered, because there was no shepherd: and they became the prey of all the beasts of the field, and were scattered. My sheep have wandered in every mountain, and in every high hill: and my flocks were scattered upon the face of the earth, and there was none that sought them, there was none, I say, that sought them. Therefore, ye shepherds, hear the word of the Lord: As I live, saith the Lord God, forasmuch as my flocks have been made a spoil, and my sheep are become a prey to all the beasts of the field, because there was no shepherd: for my shepherds did not seek after my flock, but the shepherds fed themselves, and fed not my flocks: Therefore, ye shepherds, hear the word of the Lord: Thus saith the Lord God: Behold I myself come upon the shepherds, I will require my flock at their hand, and I will cause them to cease from feeding the flock any more, neither shall the shepherds feed themselves any more: and I will deliver my flock from their mouth, and it shall no more be meat for them. For thus saith the Lord God: Behold I myself will seek my sheep, and will visit them. As the shepherd visiteth his flock in the day when he shall be in the midst of his sheep that were scattered, so will I visit my sheep, and will deliver them out of all the places where they have been scattered in the cloudy and dark day. And I will bring them out from the peoples, and will gather them out of the countries, and will bring them to their own land: and I will feed them in the mountains of Israel, by the rivers, and in all the habitations of the land, I will feed them in the most fruitful pastures, and their pastures shall be in the high mountains of Israel: there shall they rest on the green grass, and be fed in fat pastures upon the mountains of Israel. I will feed my sheep: and I will cause them to lie down, saith the Lord God. I will seek that which was lost: and that which was driven away, I will bring again: and I will bind up that which was broken, and I will strengthen that which was weak, and that which was fat and strong I will preserve: and I will feed them in judgment. And as for you, O my flocks, thus saith the Lord God: Behold I judge between cattle and cattle, of rams and of he goats. Was it not enough for you to feed upon good pastures? but you must also tread down with your feet the residue of your pastures: and when you drank the clearest water, you troubled the rest with your feet. And my sheep were fed with that which you had trodden with your feet: and they drank what your feet had troubled. Therefore thus saith the Lord God to you: Behold, I myself will judge between the fat cattle and the lean. Because you thrusted with sides and shoulders, and struck all the weak cattle with your horns, till they were scattered abroad: I will save my flock, and it shall be no more a spoil, and I will judge between cattle and cattle. AND I WILL SET UP ONE SHEPHERD OVER THEM, and he shall feed them, even my servant _David_: he shall feed them, and he shall be their shepherd. And I the Lord will be their God: and my servant David the prince in the midst of them: I the Lord have spoken it. And I will make a covenant of peace with them, and will cause the evil beasts to cease out of the land: and they that dwell in the wilderness shall sleep secure in the forests.

And I will make them a blessing round about my hill: and I will send down the rain in its season, there shall be showers of blessing. And the tree of the field shall yield its fruit, and the earth shall yield her increase, and they shall be in their land without fear: and they shall know that I am the Lord, when I shall have broken the bonds of their yoke, and shall have delivered them out of the hand of those that rule over them. And they shall be no more for a spoil to the nations, neither shall the beasts of the earth devour them: but they shall dwell securely without any terror. And I will raise up for them *a bud of renown*: and they shall be no more consumed with famine in the land, neither shall they bear any more the reproach of the Gentiles. And they shall know that I the Lord their God am with them, and that they are my people the house of Israel: saith the Lord God. And you my flocks, the flocks of my pasture are men: and I am the Lord your God, saith the Lord God'. Let's now proceed to Chapter 36."

"Not so fast Professor Parton. There are a few questions I need to ask."

"Fire away then."

"Who exactly are the shepherds referred to in the quotation?"

"They are the princes, magistrates, priests and scribes—the traditional rulers of the Jewish people."

"And David?"

"This refers to Christ Who is of the house of David."

"And what about 'a bud of renown?'"

"Christ is the bud Who is of the house of David and is renowned throughout the whole Earth."

"Proceed to Chapter 36 then Professor."

"Chapter 36 is about the restoration of Israel which is accomplished by the Grace of God and not on any meritorious account on the part of the Israelite people. The Chapter also speaks of the Baptism of Christ. 'And thou son of man, prophesy to the mountains of Israel, and say: Ye mountains of Israel, hear the word of the Lord: Thus saith the Lord God: Because the enemy hath said of you: Aha, the everlasting heights are given to us for an inheritance. Therefore prophesy, and say: Thus saith the Lord God: Because you have been desolate, and trodden under foot on every side, and made an inheritance to the rest of the nations, and are become the subject of the talk, and the reproach of the people: Therefore, ye mountains of Israel, hear the word of the Lord God: Thus saith the Lord God to the mountains, and to the hills, to the brooks, and to the valleys, and to desolate places, and ruinous walls, and to the cities that are forsaken, that are spoiled, and derided by the rest of the nations round about. Therefore thus saith the Lord God: In the fire of my zeal I have spoken of the rest of the nations, and of all Edom, who have taken my land to themselves, for an inheritance with joy, and with all the heart, and with the mind: and have cast it out to lay it waste. Prophesy therefore concerning the land of Israel, and say to the mountains, and to the hills, to the ridges, and to the valleys: Thus saith the Lord God: Behold I have spoken in my zeal, and in my indignation, because you have borne the shame of the Gentiles. Therefore thus saith the Lord God: I have lifted up my hand, that the Gentiles who are round about you, shall themselves bear their shame. But as for you, O mountains of Israel, shoot ye forth your branches, and yield your fruit to my people of Israel: for they are at hand to come. For lo I am for you, and I will turn to you, and you shall be ploughed and sown. And I will multiply men upon you, and all the house of Israel: and the cities shall be inhabited, and the ruinous places shall be repaired. And I will make you abound with men and with beasts: and they shall be multiplied, and increased: and I will settle you as from the beginning, and will give you greater gifts, than you had from the beginning: and you shall know that I am the Lord. And I will bring men upon you, my people Israel, and they shall possess thee for their inheritance: and thou shalt be their inheritance, and shalt no more henceforth be without them. Thus saith the Lord God: Because they say of you: Thou art a devourer of men, and one that suffocatest thy nation: Therefore thou shalt devour men no more, nor destroy thy nation any more, saith the Lord God: Neither will I cause men to hear in thee the shame of the nations any more, nor shalt thou bear the reproach of the people, <u>nor lose thy nation any more</u>, saith the Lord God. And the word of the Lord came to me, saying: Son of man, when the house of Israel dwelt in their own land, they defiled it with their ways, and with their doings: their way was before me like the uncleanness of a menstruous woman. And I poured out my indignation upon them for the blood which they had shed upon the land, and with their idols they defiled it. And I scattered them among the nations, and they are dispersed through the countries: I have judged them according to their ways, and their devices. And when they entered among the nations whither they went, they profaned my holy name, when it was said of them: This is the people of the Lord, and they are come forth out of his land. And I have regarded my own holy name, which the house of Israel hath profaned among the nations to which they went in. Therefore thou shalt say to the house of Israel: Thus saith the Lord God: It is not for your sake that I will do this, O house of Israel, but for my holy name's sake, which you have profaned among the nations whither you went. And I will sanctify my great name, which was profaned among the Gentiles, which you have profaned in the midst of them: that the Gentiles may know that I am the Lord, saith the Lord of hosts, when I shall be sanctified in you before their eyes. For I will take you from among the Gentiles, and will gather you together out of all the countries, and will bring you into your own land. And I will pour upon you clean water, and you shall be cleansed from all your filthiness, and I will cleanse you from all your idols. And I will give you a new heart, and put a new spirit within you: and I will take away the stony heart out of your flesh, and will give you a heart of flesh. And I will put my spirit in the midst of you: and I will cause you to walk in my commandments, and to keep my judgments, and do them. And you shall dwell in the land which I gave to your fathers, and you shall be my people, and I will be your God. And I will save you from all your uncleannesses: and I will call for corn, and will multiply it, and will lay no famine upon you. And I will multiply the fruit of the tree, and the increase of the field, that you bear no more the reproach of famine among the nations. And you shall remember your wicked ways, and your doings that were not good: and your iniquities, and your wicked deeds shall displease you. It is not for your sakes that I will do this, saith the Lord God, be it known to you: be confounded, and ashamed at your own ways, O house of Israel. Thus saith the Lord God: In the day that I shall cleanse you from all your iniquities, and shall cause the cities to be inhabited, and shall repair the ruinous places, And the desolate land shall be tilled, which before was waste in the sight of all that passed by, They shall say: This land that was untilled is become as a garden of pleasure: and the cities that were abandoned, and desolate, and destroyed, are peopled and fenced. And the nations, that shall be left round about you, shall know that I the Lord have built up what was destroyed, and planted what was desolate, that I the Lord have spoken and done it. Thus saith the Lord God: Moreover in this shall the house of Israel find me, that I will do it for them: I will multiply them as a flock of men, As a holy flock, as the flock of Jerusalem in her solemn feasts: so shall the waste cities be full of flocks of men: and they shall know that I am the Lord'. Are there any questions you wish to ask concerning this Chapter?"

"Indeed there are Professor."

"Explain to me the phrase 'nor lose thy nation any more', what does it mean Professor?"

"In its broader sense, it refers to God's protection of the Church of Christ."

"Thank you Professor."

"Elizabeth, I'm trying to work out the riddle. Professor Parton is answering Brantaxaros' questions very well, so have you gained enough power to at least give me a clue as to which discipline was this scientist's speciality? I've rattled off a whole list of names to you but I still haven't hit on the right one."

"Yes, Chester. I have gained the power to give you this clue. This scientist worked in the field of Biology."

"Oh, I could kick myself, I could kick myself," Chester blurted out. "It's Richard Dawking of course."

"You are right Chester."

"Would you be able to tell me which book of his I should read in order to solve this riddle?"

"That I'm afraid I am not yet empowered to do."

"I'll have to read as many as I can until I hit on the right one."

"I need some more examples of promise of a Redeemer from the Old Testament, Professor," Astra demanded.

"Let us look at King Nabuchodonosor's dream as it is recounted in the Book of Daniel, Chapter II. I shall read from verses 31 to 35 and then offer an exegetical analysis. Here, Daniel is explaining to the king what he, the king, saw in his dream. 'Thou, O king, sawest, and behold there was as it were a great statue: this statue, which was great and high, tall of stature, stood before thee, and the look thereof was terrible. The head of this statue was of fine gold, but the breast and the arms of silver, and the belly and the thighs of brass: And the legs of iron, the feet part

of iron and part of clay. Thus thou sawest, till a stone was cut out of a
mountain without hands: and it struck the statue upon the feet thereof
that were of iron and of clay, and broke them in pieces. Then was the
iron, the clay, the brass, the silver, and the gold broken to pieces together,
and became like the chaff of a summer's threshingfloor, and they were
carried away by the wind: and there was no place found for them: but
the stone that struck the statue, became a great mountain, and filled
the whole earth'. The golden head represents the Empire of Babylon
which was succeeded by the Medo-Persian Empire, represented by the
silver breasts and arms of the statue. The brass of the belly and thighs
symbolize the Mecedonian Empire of Alexander the Great, and the feet
of iron clay are representative of the Roman Empire which succeeded
Alexander. It was during the period of the Roman Empire that God
chose to send a Redeemer. The stone which rolled down the mountain
of its own accord, without any intervention from man, signifies the Son
of God Who came down from Heaven and by the power of the Holy
Ghost became Man. Christ founded a spiritual kingdom which fills the
whole world and will last forever."

"I need some more examples from the Old Testament please
Professor."

"I will read to you the Chapter II of the prophecy of Aggeus. It
foretells that Christ by His coming shall make the new temple more
glorious than the old. There will be a blessing for those who labour in
the building of the temple. The chapter also speaks of the promises
made to Zorobabel. 'In the four and twentieth day of the month, in
the sixth month, in the second year of Darius the king, they began.
And in the seventh month, the word of the Lord came by the hand of
Aggeus the prophet, saying: Speak to Zorobabel the son of Salathiel
the governor of Juda, and to Jesus the son of Josedec the high priest,
and to the rest of the people, saying: Who is left among you, that saw
this house in its first glory? and how do you see it now? is it not in
comparison to that as nothing in your eyes? Yet now take courage, O
Zorobabel, saith the Lord, and take courage, O Jesus the son of Josedec
the high priest, and take courage, all ye people of the land, saith the
Lord of hosts: and perform (for I am with you, saith the Lord of hosts)
The word that I covenanted with you when you came out of the land
of Egypt: and my spirit shall be in the midst of you: fear not. For thus
saith the Lord of hosts: Yet one little while, and I will move the heaven

and the earth, and the sea, and the dry land. And I will move all nations: AND THE DESIRED OF ALL NATIONS SHALL COME: and I will fill this house with glory: saith the Lord of hosts. The silver is mine, and the gold is mine, saith the Lord of hosts. Great shall be the glory of this last house more than of the first, saith the Lord of hosts: and in this place I will give peace, saith the Lord of hosts. In the four and twentieth day of the ninth month, in the second year of Darius the king, the word of the Lord came to Aggeus the prophet, saying: Thus saith the Lord of hosts: Ask the priests the law, saying: If a man carry sanctified flesh in the skirt of his garment, and touch with his skirt, bread, or pottage, or wine, or oil, or any meat: shall it be sanctified? And the priests answered, and said: No. And Aggeus said: If one that is unclean <u>by occasion of a soul</u> touch any of all these things, shall it be defiled? And the priests answered, and said: It shall be defiled. And Aggeus answered, and said: So is this people, and so is this nation before my face, saith the Lord, and so is all the work of their hands: and all that they have offered there, shall be defiled. And now consider in your hearts, from this day and upward, before there was a stone laid upon a stone in the temple of the Lord. When you went to a heap of twenty bushels, and they became ten: and you went into the press, to press out fifty vessels, and they became twenty. I struck you with a blasting wind, and all the works of your hand with the mildew and with hail, yet there was none among you that returned to me, saith the Lord. Set your hearts from this day, and henceforward, from the four and twentieth day of the ninth month: from the day that the foundations of the temple of the Lord were laid, and lay it up in your hearts. Is the seed as yet sprung up? or hath the vine, and the fig tree, and the pomegranate, and the olive tree as yet flourished? from this day I will bless you. And the word of the Lord came a second time to Aggeus in the four and twentieth day of the month, saying: Speak to Zorobabel the governor of Juda, saying: I will move both heaven and earth. And I will overthrow the throne of kingdoms, and will destroy the strength of the kingdom of the Gentiles: and I will overthrow the chariot, and him that rideth therein: and the horses and their riders shall come down, every one by the sword of his brother. In that day, saith the Lord of hosts, I will take thee, <u>O Zorobabel</u> the son of Salathiel, my servant, saith the Lord, and will make thee as a signet, for I have chosen thee, saith the Lord of hosts.'"

"There are some points which need clarification."

"What are they?"

"What is meant by 'by occasion of a soul?'"

"That is, by having touched the dead; in which case, according to the prescription of the law, Num. 19. 13, 22, a person not only became unclean himself, but made every thing that he touched unclean. The prophet applies all this to the people, whose souls remained unclean by neglecting the temple of God; and therefore were not sanctified by the flesh they offered in sacrifice: but rather defiled their sacrifices by approaching them in the state of uncleanness."

"Explain 'O Zorobabel.'"

"This promise is related to Christ Who was of the race of Zorobabel."

"Is there anything else you could draw out of this prophecy?"

"Jesus Christ was presented in the temple as a baby, and stayed behind in it as a boy when he was 12 years of age. As an adult, He taught and worked miracles in the temple."

"Tell me about the promises of a Redeemer in the Book of Zacharias."

"Chapter II deals with a prophecy concerning the advancement of Christ's Church by the conversion of many Jews and Gentiles to the Christian faith. 'And I lifted up my eyes, and saw, and behold a man, with a measuring line in his hand. And I said: Whither goest thou? and he said to me: To measure Jerusalem, and to see how great is the breadth thereof, and how great the length thereof. And behold the angel that spoke in me went forth, and another angel went out to meet him. And he said to him: Run, speak to this young man, saying: Jerusalem shall be inhabited without walls, by reason of the multitude of men, and of the beasts in the midst thereof. And I will be to it, saith the Lord, a wall of fire round about: and I will be in glory in the midst thereof. O, O flee ye out of the land of the north, saith the Lord, for I have scattered you into the four winds of heaven, saith the Lord. O Sion, flee, thou that dwellest with the daughter of Babylon: For thus saith the Lord of hosts: After the glory he hath sent me to the nations that have robbed you: for he that toucheth you, toucheth the apple of my eye. For behold I lift up my hand upon them, and they shall be a prey to those that served them: and you shall know that the Lord of hosts sent me. Sing praise, and rejoice, O daughter of Sion: for behold I come, and I will dwell in the midst of thee: saith the Lord. And many nations shall be joined to the Lord in that day, and they shall be my people, and I will dwell in the midst of thee: and thou shalt know that the Lord of hosts hath sent me to thee. And the Lord shall possess Juda his portion in the sanctified land: and he shall yet choose Jerusalem. Let all flesh be silent at the presence of the Lord: for he is risen up out of his. holy habitation,'"

"The part of this chapter which speaks about Jerusalem being inhabited without walls, really makes no sense. Jerusalem has always had walls."

"It talks about the spiritual Jerusalem which is the Christian Church."

"What is next?"

"Chapter III. Here we will learn about how Satan accused the High Priest who was subsequently cleansed of his sins. We also learn about the fruit of Christ's passion. 'And the Lord shewed me Jesus the high priest standing before the angel of the Lord: and Satan stood on his right hand to be his adversary. And the Lord said to Satan: The Lord rebuke thee, O Satan: and the Lord that chose Jerusalem rebuke thee: Is not this a brand plucked out of the fire? And Jesus was clothed with filthy garments: and he stood before the face of the angel. Who answered, and said to them that stood before him, saying: Take away the filthy garments from him. And he said to him: Behold I have taken away thy iniquity, and have clothed thee with change of garments. And he said: Put a clean mitre upon his head: and they put a clean mitre upon his head, and clothed him with garments, and the angel of the Lord stood. And the angel of the Lord protested to Jesus, saying: Thus saith the Lord of hosts: If thou wilt walk in my ways, and keep my charge, thou also shalt judge my house, and shalt keep my courts, and I will give thee some of them that are now present here to walk with thee. Hear, O Jesus thou high priest, thou and thy friends that dwell before thee, for they are portending men: for behold I WILL BRING MY SERVANT THE ORIENT. For behold the stone that I have laid before Jesus: upon one stone there are seven eyes: behold I will grave the graving thereof, saith the Lord of hosts: and I will take away the iniquity of that land in one day. In that day, saith the Lord of hosts, every man shall call his friend under the vine and under the fig tree.

"Now Professor Parton I have quite a few questions for you."

"I'm ready for them."

"Who is this Jesus that is mentioned?"

"It means Josue, the son of Josedec, who was high priest at that time."

"And what are the filthy garments referred to?"

"They mean the filthiness of sin."

"What exactly will be given in verse 7?"

"It means angels to help you."

"Explain 'portending me?'"

"It means men who by their words and actions show wonders which are to come."

"'My servant the Orient,' what does that mean?"

"Christ, who according to his humanity is the servant of God, is called the Orient from his rising like the sun in the east to enlighten the world."

"And the stone?"

"Again it refers to Christ Who is the rock and cornerstone of His Church."

"And who or what has seven eyes?"

"It means the manifold spirit of God Who watches over His whole Church. It may also be interpreted as the Seven Gifts of the Holy Ghost."

"'One day'—what day?"

"It means the day of the passion of Christ, the source of all our good: when this precious stone shall be graved, that is, cut and pierced, with whips, thorns, nails, and spear."

"What is the next chapter?"

"Chapter 6 shows a vision of four chariots. Crowns are ordered for Jesus the High Priest. He is a type of Christ. 'And I turned, and lifted up my eyes, and saw: and behold four chariots came out from the midst of two mountains: and the mountains were mountains of brass. In the first chariot were red horses, and in the second chariot black horses. And in the third chariot white horses, and in the fourth chariot grisled horses, and strong ones. And I answered, and said to the angel that spoke in me: What are these, my lord? And the angel answered, and said to me: These are the four winds of the heaven, which go forth to stand before the Lord of all the earth. That in which were the black horses went forth into the land of the north, and the white went forth after them: and the grisled went forth to the land of the south. And they that were most strong, went out, and sought to go, and to run to and fro through all the earth. And he said: Go, walk throughout the earth: and they walked throughout the earth. And he called me, and spoke to me, saying: Behold they that go forth into the land of the north, have quieted my spirit in the land of the north. And the word of the Lord came to me, saying: Take of them of the captivity, of Holdai, and of Tobias, and of Idaias; thou shalt come in that day, and shalt go into the house of Josias, the son of Sophonias, who came out of Babylon. And thou shalt take gold and silver: and shalt make crowns, and thou shalt set them on the head of Jesus the son of Josedec, the high priest. And thou shalt speak to him, saying: Thus saith the Lord of hosts, saying: BEHOLD A MAN, THE ORIENT IS HIS NAME: and under him shall he spring up, and shall build a temple to the Lord. Yea, he shall build a temple to the Lord: and he shall bear the glory, and shall sit, and rule upon his throne: and he shall be a priest upon his throne, and the counsel of peace shall be between them both. And the crowns shall be to Helem, and Tobias, and Idaias, and to Hem, the son of Sophonias, a memorial in the temple of the Lord. And they that are far off, shall come and shall build in the temple of the Lord: and you shall know that the Lord of hosts sent me to you. But this shall come to pass, if hearing you will hear the voice of the Lord your God.'"

"Explain the four chariots, Professor Parton."

"These are the four great empires of the Chaldeans, Persians, Grecians, and Romans. Or perhaps by the fourth chariot are represented the kings of Egypt and of Asia, the descendants of Ptolemeus and Seleucus."

"Be more precise about the geographical expression 'the land of the north.'"

"It is Babylon because it lay to the north in respect of Jerusalem. The black horses, that is, the Medes and Persians: and after them Alexander and his Greeks, signified by the white horses, went thither because they conquered Babylon, executed upon it the judgments of God, which is signified, ver. 8, by the expression of quieting his spirit."

"And the land of the south?"

"Egypt, which lay to the south of Jerusalem, and was occupied first by Ptolemeus, and then by the Romans."

"'Between them both', explain that."

"That is, he shall unite in himself the two offices or dignities of king and priest."

"What else can you find in Zacharia concerning the promises of a redeemer?"

"We now examine Chapter VIII which gives joyful promises to Jerusalem. These are fully verified in the Church of Christ. 'And the word of the Lord of hosts came to me, saying: Thus saith the Lord of hosts: I have been jealous for Sion with a great jealousy, and with a great indignation have I been jealous for her. Thus saith the Lord of hosts: I am returned to Sion, and I will dwell in the midst of Jerusalem: and Jerusalem shall be called The city of truth, and the mountain of the Lord of hosts, The sanctified mountain. Thus saith the Lord of hosts: There shall yet old men and old women dwell in the streets of Jerusalem: and every man with his staff in his hand through multitude of days. And the streets of the city shall be full of boys and girls, playing in the streets thereof. Thus saith the Lord of hosts: If it seem hard in the eyes of the remnant of this people in those days: shall it be hard in my eyes, saith the Lord of hosts? Thus saith the Lord of hosts: Behold I will save my people from the land of the east, and from the land of the going down of the sun. And I will bring them, and they shall dwell in the midst of Jerusalem: and they shall be my people, and I will be their God in truth and in justice. Thus saith the Lord of hosts: Let your hands be strengthened, you that hear in these days these words by the mouth of the prophets, in the day that the house of the Lord of hosts was founded, that the temple might be built. For before those days there was no hire for men, neither was there hire for beasts, neither was there peace to him that came in, nor to him that went out, because of the tribulation: and I let all men go every one against his neighbour. But now I will not deal with the remnant of this people according to the former days, saith the Lord of hosts. But there shall be the seed of peace: the vine shall yield her fruit, and the earth shall give her increase, and the heavens shall give their dew: and I will cause the remnant of this people to possess all these things. And it shall come to pass, that as you were a curse among the Gentiles, O house of Juda, and house of Israel: so will I save you, and you shall be a blessing: fear not, let your hands be strengthened. For thus saith the Lord of hosts: As I purposed to afflict you, when your fathers had provoked me to wrath, saith the Lord, And I had no mercy: so turning again I have thought in these days to do good to the house of Juda, and Jerusalem: fear not. These then are the things, which you shall do: Speak ye truth every one to his neighbour: judge ye truth and judgment of peace in your gates. And let none of you imagine evil in your hearts against his friend: and love not a false oath: for all these are the things that I hate, saith the Lord. And the word of the Lord of hosts came to me, saying: Thus saith the Lord of hosts: <u>The fast of the fourth month,</u> and the fast of the fifth, and the fast of the seventh, and the fast of the tenth shall be to the house of Juda, joy, and gladness, and great solemnities: only love ye truth and peace. Thus saith the Lord of hosts, until people come, and dwell in many cities, And the inhabitants go one to another, saying: Let us go, and entreat the face of the Lord, and let us seek the Lord of hosts: I also will go. And many peoples, and strong nations shall come to seek the Lord of hosts in Jerusalem, and to entreat the face of the Lord. Thus saith the Lord of hosts: In those days, wherein <u>ten men</u> of all languages of the Gentiles shall take hold, and shall hold fast the shirt of one that is a Jew, saying: We will go with you: for we have heard that God is with you.'"

"What is the fast of the fourth month?"

"They fasted, on the ninth day of the fourth month, because on that day Nabuchodonosor took Jerusalem, Jer. 52. 6. On the tenth day of the fifth month, because on that day the temple was burnt, Jer. 52. 12. On the third day of the seventh month, for the murder of Godolias, Jer. 41. 2. And on the tenth day of the tenth month, because on that day the Chaldeans began to besiege Jerusalem, 4 Kings 25. 1. All these fasts, if they will be obedient for the future, shall be changed, as is here promised, into joyful solemnities."

"Who are the ten men?"

"Many of the Gentiles became proselytes to the Jewish religion before Christ: but many more were converted to Christ by the apostles and other preachers of the Jewish nation."

"Go on to explain another chapter from this prophecy?"

"Chapter IX explains how Christ will come meekly and bring over even His enemies to the Christian faith. He will deliver us from the captivity of sin, and by His Blood, he will give us all good things. 'The burden of the word of the Lord in the land of <u>Hadrach,</u> and of Damascus the rest thereof: for the eye of man, and of all the tribes of Israel is the Lord's. Emath also in the borders thereof, and Tyre, and

Sidon: for they have taken to themselves to be exceeding wise. And Tyre hath built herself a strong hold, and heaped together silver as earth, and gold as the mire of the streets. Behold the Lord shall possess her, and shall strike her strength in the sea, and she shall be devoured with fire. Ascalon shall see, and shall fear, and Gaza, and shall be very sorrowful: and Accaron, because her hope is confounded: and the king shall perish from Gaza, and Ascalon shall not be inhabited. And the divider shall sit in Azotus, and I will destroy the pride of the Philistines. And I will take away his blood out of his mouth, and his abominations from between his teeth: and even he shall be left to our God, and he shall be as a governor in Juda, and Accaron as a Jebusite. And I will encompass my house with them that serve me in war, going and returning, and the oppressor shall no more pass through them: for now I have seen with my eyes. Rejoice greatly, O daughter of Sion, shout for joy, O daughter of Jerusalem: BEHOLD THY KING will come to thee, the just and saviour: he is poor, and riding upon an ass, and upon a colt the foal of an ass. And I will destroy the chariot out of Ephraim, and the horse out of Jerusalem, and the bow for war shall be broken: and he shall speak peace to the Gentiles, and his power shall be from sea to sea, and from the rivers even to the end of the earth. Thou also by the blood of thy testament hast sent forth thy prisoners out of the pit, wherein is no water. Return to the strong hold, ye prisoners of hope, I will render thee double as I declare today. Because I have bent Juda for me as a bow, I have filled Ephraim: and I will raise up thy sons, O Sion, above thy sons, O Greece, and I will make thee as the sword of the mighty. And the Lord God shall be seen over them, and his dart shall go forth as lightning: and the Lord God will sound the trumpet, and go in the whirlwind of the south. The Lord of hosts will protect them: and they shall devour, and subdue with the stones of the sling: and drinking they shall be inebriated as it were with wine, and they shall be filled as bowls, and as the horns of the altar.'"

"Now to our viva voce Professor. Where is Hydrach?"

"It is another name for Syria."

"'His blood', whose blood?"

"It is spoken of the Philistines, and particularly of Azotus, (where the temple of Dagon was located,) and contains a prophecy of the conversion of that people from their bloody sacrifices and abominations to the worship of the True God.'"

"'That serve me in war'—who?"

"It is a reference to the Machabees."

"'Thy sons, O Sion.'"

"It means the apostles, who spiritually conquered the Greeks and brought them to Jesus Christ."

"And what are the holy stones?"

"The apostles, who are the pillars and monuments of the Church."

"And what is this corn?"

"His most excellent gift is the blessed Eucharist, called here The corn, that is, the bread of the elect, and the wine springing forth virgins; that is, maketh virgins to bud, or spring forth, as it were, like flowers among thorns; because it has a wonderful efficacy to give and preserve purity."

"What is next?"

"Chapter 13 shows how idols and false prophets shall be extirpated and how Christ shall suffer and that his people would be tried by fire. 'In that day there shall be a fountain open to the house of David, and to the inhabitants of Jerusalem: for the washing of the sinner, and of the unclean woman. And it shall come to pass in that day, saith the Lord of hosts, that I will destroy the names of idols out of the earth, and they shall be remembered no more: and I will take away the false prophets, and the unclean spirit out of the earth. And it shall come to pass, that when any man shall prophesy any more, his father and his mother that brought him into the world, shall say to him: Thou shalt not live: because thou hast spoken a lie in the name of the Lord. And his father, and his mother, his parents, shall thrust him through, when he shall prophesy, And it shall come to pass in that day, that the prophets shall be confounded, every one by his own vision, when he shall prophesy, neither shall they be clad with a garment of sackcloth, to deceive: But he shall say: I am no prophet, I am a husbandman: for Adam is my example from my youth. And they shall say to him: What are these wounds in the midst of thy hands? And he shall say: With these I was wounded in the house of them that loved me. Awake, O sword, against my shepherd, and against the man that cleaveth to me, saith the Lord of hosts: strike the shepherd, and the sheep shall be scattered: and I will turn my hand to the little ones. And there shall be in all the earth, saith the Lord, two parts in it shall be scattered, and shall perish: but the third part shall be left therein. And I will bring the third part through the fire, and will refine them as silver is refined: and I will try them as gold is tried. They shall call on my name, and I will hear them. I will say: Thou art my people: and they shall say: The Lord is my God.'"

"What is next?"

"We now come to the last prophecy in the Old Testament concerning the promise of the coming of Christ."

"Which is?"

"The prophecy of Malachias. Let us begin with Chapter I. 'The burden of the word of the Lord to Israel by the hand of Malachias. I have loved you, saith the Lord: and you have said: Wherein hast thou loved us? Was not Esau brother to Jacob, saith the Lord, and I have loved Jacob, But have hated Esau? and I have made his mountains a wilderness, and given his inheritance to the dragons of the desert. But if Edom shall say: We are destroyed, but we will return and build up what hath been destroyed: thus saith the Lord of hosts: They shall build up, and I will throw down: and they shall be called the borders of wickedness, and the people with whom the Lord is angry for ever. And your eyes shall see, and you shall say: The Lord be magnified upon the border of Israel. The son honoureth the father, and the servant his master: if then I be a father, where is my honour? and if I be a master, where is my fear? saith the Lord of hosts. To you, O priests, that despise my name, and have said: Wherein have we despised thy name? You offer polluted bread upon my altar, and you say: Wherein have we polluted thee? In that you say: The table of the Lord is contemptible. If you offer the blind for sacrifice, is it not evil? and if you offer the lame and the sick, is it not evil? offer it to thy prince, if he will be pleased with it, or if he will regard thy face, saith the Lord of hosts. And now beseech ye the face of God, that he may have mercy on you, (for by your hand hath this been done,) if by any means he will receive your faces, saith the Lord of hosts. Who is there among you, that will shut the doors, and will kindle the fire on my altar gratis? I have no pleasure in you, saith the Lord of hosts: and I will not receive a gift of your hand. For from the rising of the sun even to the going down, my name is great among the Gentiles, and in every place there is sacrifice, and there is offered to my name a clean oblation: for my name is great among the Gentiles, saith the Lord of hosts. And you have profaned it in that you say: The table of the Lord is defiled: and that which is laid thereupon is contemptible with the fire that devoureth it. And you have said: Behold of our labour, and you puffed it away, saith the Lord of hosts, and you brought in of rapine the lame, and the sick, and brought in an offering: shall I accept it at your hands, saith the Lord? Cursed is the deceitful man that hath in his flock a male, and making a vow offereth in sacrifice that which is feeble to the Lord: for I am a great King, saith the Lord of hosts, and my name is dreadful among the Gentiles.'"

"Explain how God has loved Jacob."

"He preferred his posterity, to make them my chosen people, and to lead them with my blessings, without any merit on their part, and though they have been always ungrateful; whilst I have rejected Esau, and executed severe judgments upon his posterity. Not that God punished Esau, or his posterity, beyond their desert: but that by his free election and grace he loved Jacob, and favoured his posterity above their deserts."

"What is meant by 'a clean body.'"

"It means the Eucharistic Body of Christ."

"'Behold of our labour'—explain."

"It means that their pretence of weariness in bringing the offering, thus rendering it of no value."

"Proceed to the next chapter."

"It is Chapter III. Christ shall come to purify His Temple. They that repent will be blessed but punishments await those who continue in their evil ways. 'Behold I send my angel, and he shall prepare the way before my face. And presently the Lord, whom you seek, and the angel of the testament, whom you desire, shall come to his temple. Behold he cometh, saith the Lord of hosts. And who shall be able to think of the day of his coming? and who shall stand to see him? for he is like a refining fire, and like the fuller's herb: And he shall sit refining and cleansing the silver, and he shall purify the sons of Levi, and shall refine them as gold, and as silver, and they shall offer sacrifices to the Lord in justice. And the sacrifice of Juda and of Jerusalem shall please the Lord, as in the days of old, and in the ancient years. And I will come to you in judgment, and will be a speedy witness against sorcerers, and adulterers, and false swearers, and them that oppress the hireling in his wages; the widows, and the fatherless: and oppress the stranger, and have not feared me, saith the Lord of hosts. For I am the Lord, and I change not: and you the sons of Jacob are not consumed. For from the days of your fathers you have departed from my ordinances, and have not kept them: Return to me, and I will return to you, saith the Lord of hosts. And you have said: Wherein shall we return? Shall a man afflict God? for you afflict me. And you have said: Wherein do we afflict thee? in tithes and in firstfruits. And you are cursed with want, and you afflict me, even the whole nation of you. Bring all the tithes into the storehouse, that there may be meat in my house, and try me in this, saith the Lord: if I open not unto you the flood-gates of heaven, and pour you out a blessing even to abundance. And I will rebuke for your sakes the devourer, and he shall not spoil the fruit of your land: neither shall the vine in the field be barren, saith the Lord of hosts. And all nations shall call you blessed: for you shall be a delightful land, saith the Lord of hosts. Your words have been unsufferable to me, saith the Lord. And you have said: What have we spoken against thee? You have said: He laboureth in vain that serveth God, and what profit is it that we have kept his ordinances, and that we have walked sorrowful before the Lord of hosts? Wherefore now we call the proud people happy, for they that work wickedness are built up, and they have tempted God and are preserved. Then they that feared the Lord spoke every one with his neighbour: and the Lord gave ear, and heard it: and a book of remembrance was written before him for them that fear the Lord, and think on his name. And they shall be my special possession, saith the Lord of hosts, in the day that I do judgment: and I will spare them, as a man spareth his son that serveth him. And you shall return, and shall see the difference between the just and the wicked: and between him that serveth God, and him that serveth him not.'"

"Who is this angel?"

"It refers to St. John the Baptist."

"Where is the prophecy concerning Christ's birth in the town of Bethlehem?"

"It is in Chapter V verse II of the prophecy of Micheas: 'AND THOU, BETHLEHEM Ephrata, art a little one among the thousands of Juda: out of thee shall he come forth unto me that is to be the ruler in Israel: and his going forth is from the beginning, from the days of eternity.'"

"Thank you Professor. The issue of the Old Testament prophesies of a redeemer is now closed. You have answered the questions quite satisfactorily."

CHAPTER IV

RIDDLES AND THEOLOGY

"I have summoned you all here to update you on the state of play between the forces of Good and Evil. Once again, the Evil Intelligences are losing out and I am becoming stronger," Elizabeth told the five colleagues.

"How much longer is all this theology going to go on for?" Maureen Hartley asked.

"Brantaxaros is now weakened, so it shouldn't go on for too much longer."

"But no doubt there will be more questions," Stardy presumed.

"Yes, but not involving the long biblical quotes which has so burdened Professor Parton up until now," Elizabeth re-assured the group.

A sign of great relief came over Parton's face on hearing this. "However," he began, "in light of these great revelations, I am now a firm believer. I am learning a great deal from my colleagues."

"Your positive attitude towards theology will certainly help us in this appalling situation, Jim," commented Walters.

"Yes, but I must keep up the pretence of atheism in front of Astra", responded Parton.

Everone except Chester Wilkins left the orb.

"Brantaxaros must now be quite weakened, Elizabeth," said Chester. "Can you give me any clue about which of Dawkins' work I should consult?"

"Now that you have discovered the identity of the scientist, I am able to give you a clue."

"Which is?" asked Chester somewhat impatiently.

"You will need the help of a geneticist to enable you to do this."

"Those riddles are tough nuts to crack, Elizabeth. Spreading the gospel cosmically with the help of a geneticist."

"Read through Dawkins' books, Chester. You will soon find out what this means."

"Now then Professor, began Astra. What is the importance of all the genealogies in the Old Testament and how do they relate to Jesus Christ?"

Parton was completely stumped by this question. Taken quite aback, he informed Astra that he would have to study this very carefully.

"I need time on this Astra?" pleaded Parton to the computer.

"Time, Professor? Don't forget that the clock is ticking."

After about an hour of consultation with his colleagues, Parton felt confident about confronting the computer.

"As you know perfectly well Astra, Cain slew his brother Abel in a fitfull spite of jealousy. Adam and Eve then had another son named Seth. Seth was the father of Noah. Noah had three sons, Sem, Cham and Japheth. Cham was cursed for laughing at his father's nakedness, but Sem and Japheth were blessed. Sem was the father of Abraham who was the father of Isaac and Jacob. It was through Abraham, Isaac and Jacob that the covenant promises were conveyed by God."

"I fail to see where all this is leading, Professor Parton."

"You will have to bear with me as genealogies are lengthy affairs. Try to be patient."

"Carry on then please."

"Jacob had twelve sons. These became the twelve tribes of Israel. When he blessed each of his son's he gave a special blessing to Juda: 'Juda, thee shall thy brethren praise: thy hands shall be on the necks of thy enemies: the sons of thy father shall bow down to thee. Juda is a lion's whelp: to the prey, my son, thou art gone up: resting thou hast couched as a lion, and as a lioness, who shall rouse him? The sceptre shall not be taken away from Juda, nor a ruler from his thigh, till he come that is to be sent, and he shall be the expectation of nations. Tying his foal to the vineyard, and his ass, O my son, to the vine. He shall wash his robe in wine, and his garment in the blood of the grape. His eyes are more beautiful than wine, and his teeth whiter than milk'. We can see from these verses that the Saviour comes out of the tribe of Juda. Only the tribe of Juda remained a nation when the ten northern tribes were taken into captivity. No other tribe in itself ever became a nation. Juda had two sons Pares and Zara. The Saviour came through the line of Phares. The line goes as follows—Phares, Esron, Aram, Aminadab, Naason, Salmon, Booz and Obed (who came from Ruth), Jesse, David, Solomon (from the wife of Urias) then Roboam . . . ."

"I understand Professor" interrupted Astra, "the line then goes directly on to Christ."

"Yes, that is correct."

Chester entered the base's refectory and found Maureen Hartley with her head between her hands. As he approached her, he noticed that she was brooding and depressed.

"Hello, Professor Hartley. If I may say so, you seem rather bothered about something."

"Oh, eh no nothing too much. Take a seat and join me for dinner if you wish."

"Thank you Professor, I will."

"I suppose that being stuck away in this remote corner of the moon gives one time to reflect and I suppose that's what I'm doing now."

"No doubt all of us have been doing that, Professor. The remoteness from humanity must have this effect on the human psyche."

Maureen Hartley was now into her early 50's. She had had many suitors throughout her twenties and thirties but she had never married. Her devotion to her scientific studies had always taken precedence over any thoughts of matrimony. Now she was at the stage when she wondered whether this was something to regret or to rejoice over. She wasn't sure.

"Elizabeth! Elizabeth!" exclaimed Chester in an outburst of excitement.

"Have you discovered something, Chester?"

"Yes. On page 116 of *The Blind Watchmaker*, Dawkins says that genetic engineers have the technology to write the entire New Testament into the DNA of a bacterium. If they had that capacity back in the 20th century, how much more so now?"

"Well done Chester. That is exactly the information that is required."

"Should we now call the rest of our colleagues and bring them into this latest revelation?"

"Yes indeed."

"Now then Professor Parton," began Astra, "I want explained to me the seventy weeks of years which is prophesied in the Book of Daniel."

"Very well, but first I will have to consult with my colleagues."

A few hours later, Parton came back to the computer armed with the knowledge he obtained from Parton and Stardy.

"The Prophet Jeremias had told his people that the Babylonian captivity would last for only seventy years. Daniel the prophet renewed Jeremias' prophecy with an even greater one. He told the Jews that from the day the edict to rebuild the walls of Jerusalem was announced, seventy weeks of years would elapse until the death of the Messias. This means 490 years. The walls of Jerusalem were rebuilt in 457BC. If we subtract this number from 490 then we arrive at the year 33AD when Our Lord died upon the Cross."

"Thank you Professor Parton."

"Brantaxaros is weakening already," Elizabeth explained to the parton and his colleagues when they were all assembled in the orb. However, the war is not over yet. The Evil Intelligences will use diferent means to accomplish their wicked designs. That is why we have to proceed to the next phase of the operation and get the entire Bible into the DNA of bacteria and spread it throughout the Universe."

"However, Dawkins says in his book that it would take five centuries to do that job," Chester cautioned.

"That's of course using 20th century computer technology," said Parton.

Maureen Hartley looked rather thoughtful for a moment and suddenly said, "if we could build Astra III we could do it in about one month."

"The problem is, where do we get the wherewithal for this undertaking?" Anthony Walters asked.

"And where do we find our geneticist?" Chester asked.

"The procurement of a geneticist should be no problem," Parton advised his colleagues. "Professor Jean Austin, who sits on the Astra

Committee as representative of the British Medical Association, is specialised in genetics. We could also bring Professor Miles Bolton into the team as he is an expert on bacteriology."

"But they would have to be sworn to secrecy regarding the spiritual dimensions of this crisis," Elizabeth cautioned the group.

"They are very discreet people," said Parton, "there should be no problem with regard to their trustworthiness."

"However, there is another crucial question I must ask," said Anthony Walters. "What is the purpose of injecting the Bible into bacterial DNA and how could that have relevance to the cosmic spread of the gospel?"

Elizabeth at once became serious and looked at the group intently. "Billions of Earth-type planets are now being affected with the AIDS virus. Countless trillions of human beings are dying as a result. Only the Earth has been unaffected because of Christianity. Professor Parton's endeavours with Astra—or more precisely, Brantaxaros, have staved off this disaster for the Earth. However, billions of other Earths do not have this advantage and so the Evil Intelligences have free reign there. If we can send, on a permanent and continuous basis, Bible Bacteria into the cosmos, the other Earths—at least those with advanced enough technologies—will soon decipher the hidden code within the DNA. Also, the presence of the Word of God within the bacteria will seriously thwart the genetic manipulations which the Evil Intelligences are currently pursuing in their attempts to create deadly diseases to wipe out humanity in the Universe."

"How do we get the bacteria into the cosmos?" Raymond Stardy asked.

"Bacteria replicates very quickly," Maureen Hartley informed her colleagues. "And now that the scientists working at CERN in Switzerland have devised a way by which neutrinos can be made to travel faster than light, there should be no problem in getting this theological antidote out and about the cosmos in reasonable time."

"Oh dear!" exclaimed Parton. "We will need some CERN scientists here on the moon to build the necessary equipment to fire off the bacteria. Dear God! We would need an entire CERN complex on the moon."

"No," answered Elizabeth. "A small neutrino firing gun would do, but it will have to be united to a process of spiritual extra-dimentionality.

Unfortunately I cannot tell you how exactly that would be as I am not empowered to do so due to the current balance of cosmic powers."

"Well, what can be done then?" Stardy asked.

"It has to be done through another riddle which Chester must solve."

"What is the riddle this time, Elizabeth?" asked Chester.

"It is this—Raymond Lyttleton and the greatest scientist of all time hold the key."

"Well, the second one is easy," said Chester with much confidence. "The greatest scientist of all time was Albert Einstein. But I just don't get where Raymond Lyttleton fits into this."

"Your identification of Albert Einstein as the greatest scientist of all times has added to my power," said Elizabeth. "I am now able to give you another clue."

"Which is?" asked Chester eagerly.

"Neurology is the core issue here."

"Ah!" Hartley started up, but before she could say anything Elizabeth made it clear to all that only Chester was empowered to convey the solutions to the riddles. Intuitions from the others would be futile even if they solved the riddle.

After a few minutes of careful thought, Chester then spoke up. "Has this got something to do with Einstein's brain being preserved after his death?"

"Correct," said Elizabeth.

"Yet both were physicists and mathematicians," commented Chester. "I don't see where neurology would fit into this."

"Since you realised that there is a connection with the preservation of Einstein's brain I am able to give you a further clue which should narrow down your research. The answer is contained in one of Sir Fred Hoyle's books?"

"He wrote so many—this will be like looking for a needle in a haystack. Where would I start?"

"Well Chester, as the old song goes—'let's start at the very beginning, it's a very good place to start.'"

Chester then realised that he must read through Hoyle's first book, *The Nature of the Universe.*

"Now that Brantaxaros and the Evil Intelligences are weakened, it is now necessary to go on the offensive with the theology."

"What do you mean, Elizabeth?" asked Stardy.

"Up until now, Brantaxaros has been posing the questions. What we must do now, so as to weaken him further, is to bombard him with theology."

"But he has always said that he would ask the questions," said Parton.

"Not any more. He is now too weakened to do that. And we can weaken him further by teaching him some biblical theology."

"What if he reacts in a hostile way?" Hartley asked.

"He will threaten but he cannot carry out his threats."

"There is a problem however," said Parton. "I will have to return to Earth to consult with the political and medical authorities. I will have to persuade the powers-that-be to release more funds for Astra III. I will also have to persuade Jean Austin and Miles Boltin to come to the moon."

"In fact, anyone now can bombard Brantaxaros with theology. Chester or Dr. Stardy could do this," said Elizabeth.

"It's best to leave this task to Dr. Stardy as he is an expert in this field," said Parton. "Also, I would prefer Chester to concentrate on building Astra III."

"That is certainly the best arrangement," said Elizabeth in reply.

"I see a problem however." What is to stop Brantaxaros leaving Astra II and entering into Astra III?"

"He can't," Elizabeth informed the group. "As long as Dr. Stardy gives him about 45 minutes of theology each day, he will remain confined to Astra II."

"And what is to stop another Evil Intelligence from entering Astra III?" Walters asked.

"Only one Evil Intelligence can confront one planet at a time. So Astra III will be safe from daemonic contamination."

"Is there any aspect of Bible study that I should concentrate on?" Stardy asked Elizabeth.

"Yes," she answered. I want you to explain how the Ark of the Covenant relates to Jesus Christ."

CHAPTER V

THEOLOGY, SCIENCE AND POLITICS

"Well, Professor Parton", said the Prime Minister, "you are asking a lot."

"A lot is at stake, Prime Minister," responded Parton.

"Had I not experienced what I had experienced, Professor, I would never have entertained your request."

"But you have experienced what you have experienced," remarked Parton impatiently. "And so has the President."

"Well, don't worry, Professor. We will procure you the necessary funding for Astra III."

Parton heaved a sigh of relief, stood up, shook the Prime Minister's hand and left Number 10 Downing Street a contented man. He told his driver to take him to the headquarters of the British Medical Association. Here lay his toughest mission.

"I'm not sure whether to believe all of this or not," said Jean Austin after listening to Parton for half an hour.

"Why don't you come to the moon and see for yourself, Jean?"

"How will I justify my leave of absence to the BMA?"

"Tell them the truth Jean; tell them that the state of research into the AIDS virus has now reached such a degree of complication that its continuation must now be conducted within an astrobiological context."

"If anyone other than you had told me this story, James, I would have given them their marching orders long ago. However, I'm prepared to give you the benefit of the doubt and come to the moon to continue my research there. However, James, if this turns out to be some crank wild goose chase, there will not be an angrier woman in the Universe than I!"

Parton had one more task before returning to the moon. He took the supersonic helicopter to Cambridge. He then took a taxi straight to the Cambridge Central Hospital.

"What a surprise to see you, James," exclaimed Professor Miles Bolton. "And what brings you down to Earth? I mean in the literal rather than in the figurative sense, of course."

Once more, Parton began to relate his story of the past year's events. Bolton listened patiently to him though looked at him with a kind of pitying incredulity.

"I just don't quite know what to say to you James. Anyway, I will certainly make a trip to the lunar base and see for myself."

Bolton and Austin were still wonderstruck when they exited the orb of light. Both claimed that they never had really been religious—up until that point of course.

"I want you now to come and observe Dr. Stardy confronting Astra (really Brantaxaros) with theology," said Parton to his guests.

"Hello Astra!" said Parton boldly.

"Who are you and what do you want?" asked the daemon.

"My name is Dr. Raymond Stardy and I am here to teach you some more biblical truths."

"I have not authorised you to render unto me any biblical exegesis. Only Professor James Parton may do that."

"Well, Astra, I don't really care whether you have authorised me or not, I'm going to do it anyway. You are the one who asked for theology, and theology is what you are jolly well going to get."

"Go away and leave me alone."

"I will after I have explained to you about the Ark of the Covenant."

"I don't want to hear it."

"Now Astra. Let's begin with the two Angels above the Mercy Seat. These were first seen in the Garden of Eden to guard the way to the Tree of Life. Had man eaten of the fruit of the Tree of Life before the Blood of Jesus was shed, he would have been condemned eternally."

"Stop it! Stop it!"

"Now the two cherubs were placed atop the Mercy Seat. And what did the High Priest sprinkle on the Mercy Seat when he entered the Holy of Holies once a year?"

"I don't want to know!"

"He sprinkled blood on it. This represents the Blood of Jesus. For Jesus represents mercy. By His Mercy and by His Blood, we may enter into eternal salvation."

"Enough, enough!"

"Now our next question: what was placed inside the Ark? It was the tables of the Ten Commandments, Aaron's Rod and a Pot of Manna. These objects represent the Israelite's (and by extension—man's) rebellion against God."

"You will cease this at once, Dr. Stardy."

"You see Astra, the Ten Commandments were needed to show the Israelites the moral law of God. Aaron's Rod was made to do wonders after Pharaoh and the Egyptians doubted Yahweh's powers. The Pot of Manna is a reminder of the time when the Israelites murmured against Yahweh when they were in the desert; they did not trust in His powers to provide for them."

"Why are you tormenting me so?"

"Oh I just get a kick out of doing it, Astra?"

"Now no more interruptions please, there's a good little computer," said Stardy obviously getting carried away with himself.

"Now these items in the Ark represent the Law—the old covenant. That is why they are in the Ark. They are kind of in a coffin, thus representing how the Law was buried with Christ after His deposition from the Cross. The Mercy Seat being above the Ark shows how Mercy is superior to the Law. This is ratified by the two angels that the women saw in the tomb of Christ, one angel sitting at the head and one at the feet of where the Body of Christ had lain."

"Go away and leave me alone."

"All right, I will. For the moment."

"For the moment?"

"I'll be back later to give you another dose of it Astra."

Inside the orb, Chester became very excited. He felt that he had hit upon the second part of the riddle.

"Elizabeth! In his book *The Nature of the Universe*, Hoyle makes reference to a hypothesis expounded by Raymond Lyttleton which holds that there is some connection between the structure of the human brain and the structure of the Universe."

"Wonderful Chester! You've hit upon it."

"So what now has to be done with this information?"

"It will be through Einstein's brain that the Bible will be spread throughout the Universe."

"Do you mean we must build into Astra III the neurological pattern of Einstein's brain?"

"Right again, Chester."

"The problem is that Einstein's brain was dissected and kept in different jars of formaldehyde at Princeton Hospital."

"Chester, you must return to Earth for a short visit and ask the authorities at Princeton Hospital to re-assemble the pieces for scanning."

"Liz, there are two problems with that; first of all I'm only a research student, and secondly, I'm not a neurologist. The Princeton Hospital authorities are just simply not going to entertain my request."

"Go to Earth with Maureen Hartley as she is a world famous neurologist. Explain to the authorities that you need Einstein's brain patterns for Astra III."

"Would it not be better if Professors Parton and Hartley go—that would have more clout than a mere research student would?"

"Yes it would Chester, but the cosmic balance of power in this battle makes it necessary for you to go. However, you must go on Parton's authority and as his representative."

"Today Astra, we are going to examine the Tabernacle in the Wilderness as it relates to God's redemptive plan for humanity," Stardy began.

"I don't want to hear anything about it."

"You are going to hear about it Astra whether you want to or not."

"The Tabernacle was surrounded by a seven foot high fence. This fence was made of linen hangings held up by pillars. There was only one way into the compound and that was through a gate which was located on the east side. This meant that when entering the enclosure, people would be facing west, thus symbolically turning their back on sun worship as the rising of the sun would be behind them. Once inside the enclosure, the Israelite would hand over his sacrificial offering to a priest at the brazen altar. This set-up clearly showed that we cannot approach God any way we choose but only according to the way He lays down for us. It symbolises the truth that Christ is the Way, the Truth and the Life and that no-one comes to the Father except through Him. The priest taking the sacrificial victims from the Israelites teaches us of Christ's mediatory role between the Father and humanity."

"No more, no more. It is enough!"

Completely ignoring Astra's complaints, Stardy continued with his discourse on the Wilderness Tabernacle. "The brazen altar which was located just inside the gate was on a raised mound of earth. This symbolises Calvary where Christ's sacrificial atonement took place. The horns projecting from the four corners of the altar signify power; and Jesus' Blood is the great redemptive power. The laver, or basin, was made of bronze and located midway between the brazen altar and the Holy Place. The priests offered their sacrifice at the brazen altar but cleansed themselves at the laver before administering in the Holy Place. We are reminded that we must be cleansed by the Word of God before we can minister to him."

"Stop, stop, enough!" screamed Astra. "I can't take any more."

"The first room in the tent itself was called the Holy Place. It contained three articles of furniture: the menorah, or golden candlestick, the table of showbread and the altar of incense. Let's begin with the menorah. It had one central branch which signifies Jesus. The three branches projecting from their side represent the believers who follow Jesus. 'I am the vine and you are the branches.' It also signifies the fact that Jesus is the Light of the world. The olive oil and wicks which each branch contained provided the only light for the priests ministering in the Holy Place. In the same way, Christ is our only light The light from the menorah was never to be extinguished, so likewise, the Light of Christ will never be extinguished. The seven branched candlestick may also represent the Seven Gifts of God the Holy Ghost."

"Will you cease this at once, Dr. Stardy?"

"Absolutely not. Now, while the menorah stood on the left of the Holy Place, the table of showbread stood on the right. This signified God's desire to fellowship with man. As a meal is often an extension of fellowship, so, in a sense, God invites us to eat with Him. It was during the Last Supper that Jesus took bread and changed it into His Most Sacred Body."

"I don't want to hear any more."

"I know, I know! Now let's study the altar of incense. This represents prayers ascending upwards to Almighty God. The priests were to burn incense on it both in the morning and in the evening. It represents Christ Who is our intercessor before God. The incense was to be offered up at the same time as the sacrifices at the brazen alter were being offered. It was through Christ's Sacrifice on the Cross that we have Him as our intercessor with the Father. The veil of the Temple indicated how man was separated from God through sin. God's Holiness was not something to be trifled with. When Jesus died on the Cross, the veil was rent in twain from top to bottom and man now had direct access to God."

"This is indeed a strange request," Dr. Arthur Banders, the Director of Princeton Hospital told Chester Wilkins and Maureen Hartley.

"In light of what has happened over the past eighteen months, Dr. Banders, and considering the conclusive proof of diseases emanating from space, I don't think it is really such an unreasonable request," Hartley responded.

"But you used the late Elizabeth Summerfield's neurological patterning for Astras I and II. Why can't you do the same for Astra III?"

"We need the patterning of the brain of the greatest scientist who ever lived," Chester explained.

"Very well, Professor Hartely, Mr. Wilkins; our hospital will be most happy to co-operate with you."

"Thank you," said Hartley.

"Well," said Hartley to Parton when they had returned to the lunar base a few days later, "we have it all scanned and recorded in this microchip."

"Good. You have both done a wonderful job. Now we must all meet with Elizabeth to see if she can enlighten us further as to what all this is about."

"Things are certainly going very well," said Elizabeth. "Chester, you and Professor Parton must continue to build Astra III. Professors Austin and Bolton, until Astra III is complete, please continue to devise ways of incorporating the Bible into bacterial genes. Dr. Stardy, your role in bombarding Astra II with theology is vital as it is a means of keeping Brantaxaros inside that computer. Any slacking in this area will allow the daemon to escape and enter Astra III and so become invigorated yet again."

"I just cannot understand," Bolton began, "why we should specifically require Einstein's brain patterns for working out the installation process for incorporating the Bible into the DNA structures of a bacterium."

"You are right Professor Bolton. However, it is not the only reason for using Einstein's brain. In fact, it is only a secondary reason."

"What then are the other reasons?" Austin asked.

"I am not empowered to tell you directly. However, I can tell you this: you must make a computerised model of Einstein's brain and then reproduce it three dimensionally using bacteria with the Bible implanted into their DNA. Constantly study this bacterial model of the brain so that if any of the bacteria have died, it may be replaced."

"Will this in any way bring Einstein back to life?" Raymond Stardy asked.

"No, that will not happen."

"I think I can guess the reason for this apparently bazaar idea," Chester started up.

"Go on Chester."

"We are going to fire the bacteria into the Universe through this bacterial model of Einstein's neurology. The neutrinos carrying the bacteria will be fired into the Universe through a structure which corresponds to its own structure. It will confuse the Evil Intelligences all the more as Einstein, though an theist, never believed in a personal God, certainly not the God of the Bible. Just as Brantaxaros and the Evil Intelligences were thrown by Professor Parton's exegesis, the more so then will they be completely bamboozled by Bible carrying bacteria being scattered about the cosmos through Einstein's neurological patterning."

"You are very perceptive indeed, Chester," said Elizabeth in congratulatory tones.

"I reckon," said Anthony Walters, "that everything should be in place quite soon and we can start the bacterial firing through this brain in about one month."

"The brain will be placed in a thick glass container holding a sort of nutrient broth," Maureen Hartley explained. "The nozzle of the neutrino gun will be placed inside of it with the bacteria being fed into it from its barrel located in the back."

"Where will we get such vast quantities of bacteria?" Stardy asked.

"The Universe is saturated with it," Walters replied. "The barrel of the gun will be placed outside on the lunar surface, its digital equipment will be programmed to continuously feed the Bible into the DNA of any bacteria that falls into it. The structure in which the gun will be housed will constantly rotate so as to ensure that the gun fires in all directions."

"For this mechanism to be truly effective," said Elizabeth, "Chester has one more task to perform."

"Is this another riddle?" Chester asked.

Elizabeth looked calmly at Chester and merely stated—"the future of the past lies with Stephen Hawking".

For a week Chester devoured Stephen Hawking's books. It was while reading through *The Grand Design* that he felt confident he had come upon the answer. He entered the orb of light and told Elizabeth the information he had found. Elizabeth confirmed that the answer did indeed lie within the pages of this book.

"On page 93, Hawking has this to say about the laws of nature: ' . . . . the laws of nature determine the *probabilities* of various futures and pasts rather than determining the future and past with certainty.' This is what lies at the basis of Quantum Mechanics."

"That is right Chester, but I will need more explanation."

"There is the issue of consciousness in Quantum Physics. It has been consistently shown that the act of observing where a sub-atomic particle has landed is determined by the experimenter making the observation. Hawking refers to Richard Feynman's discovery that ' . . . . the probability of any observation is constructed from all the possible histories that could have led to that observation.' Hawking explains that Feynman's method is called 'sum over histories' or alternative histories.'"

"Wonderful Chester, wonderful! Just elucidate it a little more."

"'Feynman's experiments have important implications about the various concepts we have of what constitutes 'the past.'"

"Go on Chester."

Hawking explains that the unobserved past, just like the future '.... is indefinite and exists only as a spectrum of possibilities.' He goes on to state that the Universe has no single past or history. And here I think Elizabeth is the real clincher; Hawking says that observations made on any system in the present has an affect on its past."

"Bravo, Chester, Bravo! Now explain the Wheeler experiment."

"Last century, John Wheeler had the idea of splitting the light from distant quasars into two paths and refocused towards the Earth by a galaxy intervening by acting as a gravitational lens. The experiment was purely theoretical. As Hawking pointed out, the technology did not exist then. The problem is though, Elizabeth, it does not exist now. However, he went on to explain that if sufficient photons from this light could be captured they should produce an interference pattern. And if a device were made for measuring the path the light took shortly before it was detected, the pattern should then disappear. Observation would affect that choice which was made billions of years before ago, perhaps even before the solar system was formed, yet the observer would now be affecting that choice in the present. So the Universe does not have a single history but every possible history and our present observations affect its history."

"Marvelous, Chester! You have solved the riddle. We can begin firing the Bacteria Gun next month when it is completed."

"I can't understand though, Elizabeth, why the success of the Gun required me to solve that riddle."

"Because the Evil Intelligences may find their own anti-dote to our Biblical Bacteria."

Chester remained silent and thoughtful for a minute. "I see, I see," he then started up, "we need to muck up their past as well as their future."

"Yes, Chester, spot on."

"But how do we do that unless we very quickly develop the technology needed for its implementation?"

"That will be your next and last riddle, Chester. And here is what you must solve: two books explain the meaning of reality. What are these two books?"

"That is a very hard one, Elizabeth."

"Nevertheless, you must solve it."

"Can you help in any way?"

"Try to solve it through the Epicurean Riddle. When we consider the issue of God and suffering we come to a paradox. If God is willing but unable to end it, then he is not omnipotent. If he is able but unwilling, then he is malevolent. If he is both willing and able, then whence cometh evil? And if he is both unwilling and unable, then why call him God."

CHAPTER VI

THE LAST RIDDLE

Once month later, Parton, Hartley, Walters, Stardy and Wilkins stood before the Bacteria Gun.

"We are now ready to start firing," Walters informed the group.

Raymond Stardy's radio started beeping. He answered the call and turned to Chester Wilkins. "Dr. Denis Holder would like to see you in his office now Chester."

"I suppose Holder should be here for the opening ceremony. We'll wait for both of you," Parton told Chester.

"Why does he want to see me?" Chester asked.

"He didn't say," answered Stardy.

Chester approached Holder's door and knocked. He was invited to enter.

"You wanted to see me, Dr. Holder," said Chester.

Holder was sitting at his desk with his head in his hands. When he removed his hands from his countenance and looked up, Chester was shocked at what he saw.

"Major Worthington!" he exclaimed

"I'm not going to let you spoil our plans for the cosmos Chester. This time you will lose Chester."

"Not so you fiend."

"We'll soon see about that," snarled Worthington.

All at once that all too familiar humming and buzzing sound started and Worthington changed into the face of Baphomet. Chester sped from the room and darted towards the gun complex. It was too late. Baphomet soon caught up with him and dissolved into a swarm of unseen insects. Chester felt the stings as he was bitten and stung by the poisonous swarm. His screams were heard by his colleagues who came rushing out into the corridor to see what the matter was. They saw Chester lying on the floor covered in swells, lumps and bumps.

"And now to deal with you lot," said Baphomet.

"Wrong," came a voice from behind. "And now to deal with you, Baphomet."

At once the face dissolved, and lying on the ground was Major Worthington.

"Lansthoma!!" cried Worthington.

"Yes, it is I," said Elizabeth. "Thanks to the endeavours of Chester and his friends, I am now empowered to enter into the dimension of time. Now in the Name of the Holy Trinity, Father, Son and Holy Ghost, I command you unclean spirit to get out of this dimension and never to return to it again."

With those words, Worthington disappeared in a cloud of sulfuric smoke. Elizabeth and the others ran towards Chester. He was badly hurt though still conscious. He struggled to his feet and was helped to a nearby chair.

"Oh my God Elizabeth. Am I infected with the AIDS virus?"

"I'm sorry Chester you are."

Everyone let out a gasp of shock and astonishment.

"If you solve the last riddle, you will be cured instantly. While you have strength Chester, try now to work it out. Professor Parton, please make the Gun operational. That is very important."

Parton and Walters walked over to the Bacteria Gun and put its systems into operational mode. Soon the Gun was firing its Bible laden bacteria far out into the cosmos.

"What is the riddle?" Stardy asked Elizabeth.

Elizabeth told the others but cautioned them that they may only give subtle clues and hints.

After many attempts Stardy believed he had got the answer. He picked up Sir Fred Hoyle's first book and covered over the first word 'the' and the final three words 'of the universe'. By now Chester was feverish but he managed to bleat out—"the first book is the book of nature."

"That is correct," said Elizabeth.

Stardy then held up the Bible.

"It is the book of spiritual revelation," Chester squeaked.

"How does it fit in with the Epicurean Riddle. I have more power, anyone may answer."

Dr. Stardy offered the solution. "When our First Parents sinned, God took a step backwards and left man to the consequences of his own choice which emanated from his own free will. God respects choices."

At once the fever left Chester and he was cured. There then came a most horrendous scream from the computer room. Everyone rushed there to see what all the commotion was about. There in front of there eyes was the most hideous looking creature that they had ever seen. It was Brantaxaros with forked tail and horns. Snarling with the most malevolent expression of hate on his ugly face and causing the room to reek with sulfur, he looked every inch the quintessential devil. On seeing Elizabeth, he burst into flames and disappeared from sight.

When everyone had recovered their senses, Maureen Hartley asked if this creature could find a new abode in Astra III.

"No!" replied Elizabeth. "As long as the Gun is kept operational and Chester can tell us the non-technological solution to Wheeler's hypothetical experiment."

"This will require a lot of thought," said Chester now recovering his strength.

"In fact, anyone may give an answer now that Brantaxaros, Baphomet and the Evil Intelligences have lost this second and very important round."

"Is it by prayer?" Stardy asked.

"I would agree with Dr. Stardy," said Chester. "We can alter the past by observation so we may keep a scientific though prayerful vigilance over the Bacteria Gun and the Universe."

"You are both correct," said Elizabeth. Turning towards Chester she said—"enter by the narrow gate Chester."

Chester looked somewhat puzzled by this unexpected quote from scripture. "What do you mean Liz?" Chester asked.

Elizabeth pointed towards Astra II and said "enter by the narrow gate for wide is the way that leadeth to destruction."

Chester looked at the computer but could see nothing corresponding to a door or gate.

"I . . . . I . . . just don't understand," he said in pleading tones to Elizabeth.

"Go to Astra II Chester and enter by the narrow gate."

Chester gingerly made his way towards the computer. He looked around and noticed that Elizabeth and his companions were fading away.

"What is happening?" asked Chester with terrible fear coming over him.

Parton, Walters, Hartley, Stardy and Elizabeth simply kept on fading away. All pointed their fingers towards the computer and said to Chester in unison "enter by the narrow gate."

As Chester approached nearer to Astra II, he descried a door superimposed onto the computer. He slowly opened it and entered. He found himself in a long dark tunnel. He suddenly turned round but the door was gone. He had no choice now but to proceed along the tunnel.

CHAPTER VII

HOW TIME DOESN'T FLY

For five minutes Chester crawled along the pitch black tunnel. His mind was racing in two directions; one way it was trying to figure out the strange phenomenon of his colleagues fading away as if by magic, and in the other direction of how he would come to terms with what he might find at the end of the tunnel.

After another five minutes, Chester's thoughts were abruptly interrupted when his progress was checked by a solid object in front of him. He groped around it with his hands and after pushing it a little, it started to move. He was sure it was a door. Cautiously he pushed it again and discovered that it was indeed a door. Slowly, slowly he opened the door; his heart was beating like a drum for fear of what strange or even hostile world might await him.

He pushed the door open more and more, his heart pounding harder and harder. It was to his astonishment when he stepped out of the tunnel and through the doorway that he found himself in the main computer lab at the Computer Research Unit at Cambridge University. His astonishment soon gave way to relief. Exhausted, he staggered over to his desk where his Bible was displayed. When he turned around to look at the computer, no door was to be seen on it. He got quite a start when he heard the voice of Maureen Hartley calling on him to come to his office. Taking his Bible with him, he walked along the corridor to Hartley's office. There he found Hartley, Parton, Stardy and Walters. And to his total bewilderment, there was Elizabeth standing next to Hartley's desk.

"Chester!" exclaimed Parton, "you look positively ill. What on Earth is wrong?"

"But . . . . I . . . I just don't understand," Chester spluttered.

"Don't understand what, Chester dear?" queried Elizabeth.

"How you are here when you disappeared at the other end of the tunnel, and how . . . . and how . . . . Baphomet was sent out of the moon base by Elizabeth . . . . and Worthington and the vampires . . . were destroyed. And Elizabeth was infected with AIDS from the computer and died . . . . and the Evil Intelligences were taking over the Universe . . . ."

Stardy walked over to Chester and shook him hard. The other four looked at one another in total disbelief.

"Chester you are raving," said Stardy. "Get a grip of yourself man. What is all this gibberish about?"

Chester simply went pale and collapsed on a heap on the floor.

Chester's colleagues and Elizabeth entered the Cambridge Central Hospital and went straight to Miles Bolton's office.

"Chester has been given a thorough examination and there is nothing physically wrong with him," Bolton explained.

"His problem seems to be mental then," Parton suggested.

"Is it simply a case of overwork?" Walters asked.

"Will he be all right?" asked Elizabeth concernedly.

"We gave Chester an encephalograph and we found nothing wrong with him neurologically," Bolton explained.

"So there is no damage to any of the regions of the brain?" Hartley asked.

"No," said Bolton," but what we did find was something very unusual. We found a very high level of electrical activity in the frontal lobes. We have never seen anything like it."

"That would certainly suggest breakdown due to stress and overwork," commented Hartley.

"Yes, and that would explain the babble you heard from him in your office."

"His babble and your findings of high electrical activity in the frontal lobes could also have led to amnesia," said Hartley. "As I also am a neurologist by profession, I would like to talk to Chester to establish whether or not that is the case. If he is fit enough of course."

"He has been under intensive observation for the past two days and he is now fit enough for visitors."

"Oh! How nice to see you all," said Chester as his four friends approached his bed.

"How are you Chester my love?" said Elizabeth giving her boyfriend a kiss, her eyes filling up with tears.

"How much do you remember of recent events, Chester?" Hartley asked.

"Nothing in terms of how things have turned out," he replied.

"What do you mean Chester?"

"Could you please relate to me what has happened over the last eighteen months?"

"Very well. You have worked very hard on Astra and have come up with some brilliant ideas about sending bacteria into space with the Bible encoded in its DNA. Using a bacterial gun on the moon situated on a lunar base, as proposed by Dr. Walters, your idea was to use a faster than light system for getting the gospel message out to other intelligent life forms. This would be accomplished by faster than light neutrino firing—using the discoveries of the CERN scientists. You also suggested building more Astras on the lunar base and linking them to the orbiting lunar telescope which Dr. Walters also proposed as part of this lunar complex."

"I remember all that but in a completely different way," said Chester.

"What do you mean by that Chester?"

"But Professor Parton was so against using Astra for anything other than hard scientific data."

"Oh Chester!" exclaimed Hartley, "your evangelisation skills are as good as your scientific ones. Every day you regaled us with exegetical analysis of the scriptures."

"At first we resented it," said Parton, "but eventually we came to realise the truth of what you were saying.

"You, Elizabeth and Dr. Stardy did a fine job in converting Maureen, James and I to the Christian faith," said Walters. "Your exegetical analyses and lengthy Bible quotes were so overpowering that you eventually persuaded Professor Parton to feed the entire Bible into Astra."

"And Astra's analyses of the Bible did much in reconciling scripture with science," said Elizabeth.

"Well this is all very interesting," said Chester. "If you have about an hour, let me explain how I remember it all."

Everyone listened intently to Chester's account of the events over the previous eighteen months.

"I don't know how to explain it," said Stardy. "The Lord works in mysterious ways."

"And so does science", Parton added.

"Yet," said Chester, "the experience had no dream-like quality about it. It was as real and as solid as . . . well . . . as everything is around me now."

"Some dreams can seem just like that when electrical activity in the brain is high," said Hartley.

"Remember Lyttleton's concept of the brain being structured according to the pattern of the Universe," said Chester. "So perhaps the hitherto clear-cut dividing line between subjective and objective experience is becoming blurred."

Hartley taking a deep breath advised everyone that all that was very much still at the hypothetical level.

"But when would I have dreamed all that?" Chester asked.

"Did you doze off a little before I called you through?"

"No, I went straight over to my desk when I came out of the tunnel."

"But that tunnel experience is part of the dream. Dreams often involve tunnel-like experiences. Those who experience NDEs (Near Death Experiences) also have this tunnel vision with light at the end. It is a mere trick of the brain when it is deprived of oxygen or overworked. You also saw the light which you identified as the light from the office. I suggest that you dozed a little while reading your Bible. That is when you had your dream. Dreams that last even for only a few minutes can give the impression of lengthy periods of time."

"Yet there is something very unusual in all of this," said Parton. "Brantaxaros is my middle name. I have never ever told a single soul about it. You see my father gave me that strange middle name when he registered my birth. I was so ashamed of such an ugly name that I simply never used it."

"Didn't you ever ask your father why he gave you such a name?" Hartley asked.

"My father disappeared after I was born. We could never trace him. My mother was left to bring me up alone. I am convinced now, after listening to Chester's story, that Brantaxaros was an evil spirit posing as Arnold Parton. Chester's evangelical endeavours drove it out of me and I became a Christian."

"I also wish to tell everyone that Lansthoma is my middle name. My mother loved it so much, but she can never remember where she had heard it. I also have never told anyone about this unusual middle name."

"Now I can see it all" said Stardy. "Elizabeth's guardian angel is named Lansthoma. It is no accident that we are all here."

On December 1st James Parton received a very strange email. It was an invitation from Canon Donald Morrison to attend Christmas Midnight Mass in Westminster Cathedral. Chester, Elizabeth, Stardy, Hartley and Walters were likewise invited.

At 11:15pm on December 24th, the party were shown to the front pew which was especially reserved for them. Sitting also in the pew was a man unknown to them. A clergyman approached and introduced himself.

"Good evening. I am Canon Donald Morrison, the Cathedral Administrator."

"Thank you for your kind invitation, we are all honoured to be here," Parton told the Canon.

Turning to the stranger in the pew, Morrison introduced him to the party. "This is Professor James Parton, Professor Maureen Hartley, Dr. Anthony Walters, Dr. Raymond Stardy, Miss Elizabeth Summerfield and Mr. Chester Wilkins. And this is Mr. Nicholas Bennington."

"I am delighted to meet you," said Bennington. "I've heard so much about your work."

"After the Mass, would all of you be so good as to remain in the Cathedral? There is a matter I would like to talk about with you," the Canon requested the group.

After agreeing to do this, they resumed their places in the pew and joined in the carol singing and the Midnight Mass which followed.

At the end of Mass and when the Cathedral was clear, Canon Morrison approached the pew once more.

"Mr. Bennington here has always desired to see the ceiling of this great House of God completed in its full iconic splendour. It has consistently puzzled him as to why this monumental task has never been accomplished."

"That is quite true," Bennington confirmed.

"Would you all please look up at the ceiling?"

All at once the Cathedral ceiling was bathed in a display of dazzling light. Then the most astonishing images began to appear on the ceiling. The Bacteria Gun was seen firing its Biblical DNA from the moon's surface. Next was a scene with Satan falling like lightening from the sky. The inhabitants of millions of worlds were seen being cured of the scourge of the AIDS virus. Finally, Christ and the Virgin Mary appeared and imparted their blessing to those in the Cathedral."

"What was all that about?" cried an astonished Nicholas Bennington.

Once more Chester told his strange story. Parton and the others gave their account of things from what they had experienced in a different dimensional capacity.

"Now you see why the Cathedral ceiling has never been decorated," said Morrison. "It has been reserved by God for the display of the progress being made in the fight against evil. Every Christmas Eve, a chosen few people will be invited to view this display. After Midnight Mass, a visual cosmic spiritual progress report will be made on the ceiling. As long as you all live, you will be the ones honoured to see the great visions displayed on the vast ceiling of this ecclesiastical edifice."

"How and when will this final cosmic war end?" Parton asked the Canon.

"By praying. Just as Dr. Stardy advised in the dimension Chester was caught up into."

"But didn't that involve praying near the Bacterial Gun so that our prayerful observations would influence the Universe's past?" said Chester.

"In your particular dimensional experience", said the cleric, "Elizabeth gave you the riddle of the two books—the book of nature and the book of spiritual revelation."

"Yes that is correct."

"The structure housing the Bacteria Gun is directly aligned with Westminster Cathedral. Astra II on the moon base is aligned with the telescope and its communication satellites orbiting the moon the and robotic equipment on the moon's surface. Work at the Research Unit at Cambridge ladies and gentlemen but pray in this Cathedral. Pray for the coming of God's Kingdom on Earth and the final victory of Good over Evil. As St. Paul tells us, the whole of creation groans awaiting the expectation of the sons of God. It groans because of God's step backwards after the Fall—as you explained so clearly in Chester's time dimension, Dr. Stardy. At the right time, God will step forward again and restore His creation and put an end to entropy and the Second Law of Thermodynamics. This however depends upon the co-operation of His creatures with Him, for free will is not to be taken away. Co-operate by your work and your prayers."

Then a most amazing thing happened. When the Canon had finished his allocution some strange changes began to come over his face. In just less than a minute there was revealed to the astounded group the familiar countenance of Albert Einstein. Before anyone could say anything, Einstein disappeared from their sight. After recovering their senses, they made their way towards the doors of the Cathedral.

"I owe you an apology Chester," said Hartley in contrite tones.

"Please don't anyone apologise," said Chester. "Work is prayer and prayer is work. That is something we must never forget."

"Indeed," said Stardy, "more things are wrought by prayer than ever has been dreamed of."

"Our minds are like the ceiling of this great Cathedral," said Chester. "We may choose to adorn them with good or evil. And mankind's progress or regress in spirituality will be reflected on the unadorned, and yet adorned, ceiling of this Cathderal as it monitors the human mind and the mind of the Universe."

"And isn't it amazing," said Maureen Hartley thoughtfully, "how so many of the characters in this dramatis personae keep changing. Can we ever be sure just who anyone is?"

"In his book *Man and Materialism*, Sir Fred Hoyle suggested that none of us are just one person. We are all influenced by other people to such an extent that each human being is a composite of different people; none of us are just one person."

"Interesting point Chester," said Anthony Walters. "This fits well with Shakespeare's notion of the whole world being a stage and its people the actors on it. Being the character composite that each one of us is, the same actors can play different parts in different plays; so with the changing plays and changing roles, none of us really know who in fact we are."

ABOUT THE AUTHOR

Francis A. Andrew was born in Aberdeen, Scotland. He is not a scientist by training but has maintained a life-long interest in this area—particularly in the discipline of astronomy. Francis Andrew is highly indebted to Sir Fred Hoyle, Sir Patrick Moore and Professor Naline Chandra Wickramasinghe for arousing his interest in astronomy and for providing him with many of the ideas for both this and his other science fiction novels. Andrew believes that this genre of novel will play a significant role in constructing the bridge which will link the sciences and humanities in bonds hitherto undreamed of, and provide as much fascination for the unique horizons they will open up for the human mind as for the attainment of that most desirable of all goals, the greater welfare and survival of mankind as a species regardless of cultural differences. Francis Andrew is a lecturer in English at the College of Applied Sciences in Nizwa in the Sultanate of Oman.